# THE KILL

EVIE HUNTER

B
Boldwood

First published in Great Britain in 2023 by Boldwood Books Ltd.



Cover Photography Depositphotos and iStock



A CIP catalogue record for this book is available from the British Library.

Paperback ISBN 978-1-80280-291-7

Large Print ISBN 978-1-80280-292-4

Hardback ISBN 978-1-80280-290-0

Ebook ISBN 978-1-80280-293-1

Kindle ISBN 978-1-80280-294-8

Audio CD ISBN 978-1-80280-285-6

MP3 CD ISBN 978-1-80280-286-3

Digital audio download ISBN 978-1-80280-289-4

Boldwood Books Ltd
23 Bowerdean Street
London SW6 3TN
www.boldwoodbooks.com

# 1

Sebastian Carter fixed Henshaw, a screw who'd had a hard-on for Seb throughout the final phase of his incarceration, with a cutting look. Dismissing the man from his mind as an irrelevance, he stepped through the unlocked gate and embraced the sweet, fresh taste of real freedom for the first time in six years. The majority of the prison officers had treated him with respect. Money talked, even behind bars.

Especially there.

Henshaw had made it clear that he bore Seb a grudge. He had probably been paid to make his life difficult by one of Seb's father's rivals. Seb's reputation had preceded him throughout the prison system, inflated no doubt through his father's influence, despite that interference being unasked for and unappreciated.

Henshaw had it in for Seb, no question about it. Probably had a death wish too, given Seb's father's long reach and hard reputation. Henshaw was definitely on the take, Seb knew, but then who wasn't? Every man for himself in this dog-eat-dog world. Henshaw had made sure that Seb was alone in the shower block when his father's rivals had wanted a quiet word. But the prison guard's jaw had dropped open when Seb walked away from the confrontation whistling and unscathed, which was more than could be said for the two men who'd launched a clumsy attack. Seb winked at the bent screw and Henshaw knew his card had been marked.

Seb had kept his head down and avoided confrontation whenever possible, unless it came looking for him, and had done his time quietly. Henshaw was the only thorn in his side in this open prison, his last accommodation at His Majesty's pleasure before they were obliged to release him. There had been others in the Cat Two jails he'd occupied though; inmates who wanted to prove how hard they were. Screws who enjoyed their little bit of power and liked to enforce it.

There were always others.

Seb could have walked free three years previously, had he admitted to the crime he'd been found guilty of committing and shown suitable remorse.

But Seb hadn't done it and was buggered if he'd take the credit.

'Be lucky, Carter,' Henshaw said in what was for him a conciliatory tone as he pulled the gate wide for Seb to walk through.

Seb didn't even look in his direction as he straightened the collar of the leather jacket that had festered in the prison store for the duration of his incarceration. It was loose around his waist; he'd lost weight but had toned up in the prison gym. His shoulders were as broad as ever, filling out the worn leather, and his mind was still a steel trap. Six years was a long time to contemplate the form his revenge would take for being fitted up for murder and eventually going down for manslaughter. Seb had every intention of exacting that revenge but without landing himself back inside.

Outside the gates, Seb paused to throw back his head and breathe deeply the crisp autumnal air that kissed his face and brought his dormant body slowly back to life. A sleek black car with tinted windows glided up to his side. The back door swung open and Seb slid onto the soft leather.

'Okay, boss?' Seb's right-hand man, Patrick Risdon, asked from his seat beside the driver.

'Never better, Pat,' Seb replied, his voice a low, gravelly rumble. A man of few words as a general rule, he had exercised his vocal chords even less frequently over the past six years, speaking only when he had something worth saying. The constant noise inside didn't need any contribution from him. The place was never quiet: arguments, shouting, fights, men jerking off in the middle of the night. Others crying for their mothers.

Seb had survived by allowing it all to wash over him and for his reputation as a man to be reckoned with to do the talking for him. He was afforded respect, for the most part, and left to his own devices.

To a degree.

'Good to see you, boss,' said Mark from behind the wheel. A bull of a man who could intimidate even when smiling – especially then – Mark was as loyal and dependable as they came. Seb's time inside was made that little bit easier by the knowledge that Mark was looking after what mattered the most to Seb.

Mark would kill any man with his bare hands if he came within spitting distance of Seb's sister Lily, or even looked at her the wrong way.

'Mark,' Seb replied. The two men exchanged a nod and a significant look. That was all it took. Normal business was resumed, and the first item on the agenda was for Seb to discover who'd fitted him up.

Given that he'd had little else to think about for six years, he already had a pretty good idea where to start looking for answers. Pat did too but Seb had made him hold off. This was Seb's mess, and he would deal with it. He didn't need anyone else to fight his battles for him and land inside themselves. This was personal.

Besides, Seb had held onto an idealistic hope of not only uncovering the guilty party but of clearing his own name too.

That dream had helped him to get through.

'Welcome back to the land of the living,' Pat said. 'Straight home? Got a surprise waiting for you.'

'Better not be a fucking party.'

Pat chuckled. 'Do I look like I've got a death wish?'

Seb settled back and watched the passing scenery as he was driven in smooth comfort towards his palatial home outside of Chichester. A home that had been polluted by the police when they tore it apart looking for material evidence of his guilt in the murder of that slimy scrote, Paul Blythe. Evidence that wasn't there to be found, hence the reduction in the charges to manslaughter, given the circumstantial nature of the CPS's case. The jury had clearly thought the case flimsy too since he'd been convicted by a split majority. Seb reckoned the judge had shared their doubts, hence a relatively lenient sentence for a capital crime.

A career criminal, Blythe was no loss to society; the judge would have known that too. Seb's only regret was that he hadn't sent the man to the hereafter himself. Had he done so, he would have managed the job with more finesse and certainly not left an obvious trail that had led directly to his door.

One of the reasons why Seb hadn't appealed his sentence was that Blythe was now fish food. Couldn't have happened to a more deserving scumbag. Even so, he reasoned, appreciating the simple pleasure of watching the trees shedding their leaves in a kaleidoscope of colours as the car sped along a country road bordered by woodland, he hadn't been responsible for the bastard's demise. It had been clumsily done; a deliberate attempt to get at Seb's father through his estranged son. A father who was a career criminal; Jason Carter, a name that was feared and respected in equal measure on the streets of South London and beyond. A father with a criminal empire that Seb wanted no part of.

But by using Lily to get to Jason Carter, the perpetrators had crossed a line.

A line that Seb now fully intended to redefine.

He thought of Lily and firmed his jaw. The time had come to get to the truth and if that meant cracking a few heads, then so be it.

Seb and Lily would enjoy walking over the leaves, he thought, as he continued to watch them fluttering down. Hearing them crunch beneath her boots would make her smile and that thought brought a rare smile to Seb's lips too.

His half-sister was everything to him. The only female in his life who mattered.

And thanks to Blythe, she was now damaged goods. Even more so than she had been before the brutal rape. A beautiful woman with the body of an adult trapped inside the mind of a child. If he'd had any doubts about rooting out those responsible – and Blythe, he knew, had been acting on orders – then thoughts of the damage done to sweet, innocent Lily drove them away.

Seb caught sight of his image in the tinted window. Now thirty-five, he knew he'd changed; he was harder, uncompromisingly tough and obviously older, as evidenced by the lines etched into his features. His hair was still thick but the blond was now threaded with the odd strand of grey. He pushed it away from expressionless blue eyes, uninterested in what he absently knew to be a handsome face that before his incarceration had attracted all the female attention he'd ever wanted, and then some.

Keeping emotions locked up tighter than the prison's population had become the new norm, the only way to survive in that hellhole and to remain relatively sane. Having a reputation as a hard man, well able to handle himself, had been helpful. His bland expression gave nothing away but he knew the experience had changed him – would change any man – both inside and out. His father had embraced the criminal world and Seb had grown up surrounded by villains. Despite that, or perhaps because of it, he had been determined to remain on the straight and narrow and make his own way in the world without any help from the financial coffers stoked by his father's illegal activities.

He now knew that life wasn't that simple.

Mark, as always, drove on in silence and Pat had the good sense to leave Seb to his cogitations. Pat had been Seb's only visitor these past six years. He had refused to see anyone else, especially Lily. Whether she would know him now, after six years, was the burning question. Perhaps it would be better if she didn't. He'd received regular reports and knew she was happy in her own private world, cared for twenty-four seven in the fortress that doubled as Seb's home.

How anyone had got to her in the first place, Seb had yet to discover. He suspected inside help but had trusted everyone who worked for him at the time and anyway, a harsh interrogation had failed to turn up the guilty party. Seb had always known that his father's rivals would try to get to the old man through him. That was okay; he could look after himself. The possibility of them targeting Lily instead hadn't once crossed his mind, which was why he felt partially responsible for what had happened to her. He'd let her down in the worst way imaginable and would spend the rest of his life blaming himself for his error in judgement. He had, he knew, been too fucking taken up with making money to properly protect what was his.

That was why he'd deserved to be banged up, even if neglecting the vulnerable wasn't the crime he'd been found guilty of committing.

After the event, he'd made damned sure that his defences wouldn't be breached for a second time. Too little, too late, but his home really was his castle and he wasn't about to suffer an intrusion from uninvited guests ever again. Not that the attack had happened in his grounds, but that was beside the point. He had underestimated the determination of his father's enemies and it had cost his sister what little mind she had once possessed.

Almost her life.

Seb sometimes thought it would have been better if she hadn't pulled through.

'Home sweet home,' Pat muttered as the car swung onto the driveway that would lead to the double gates and boundary walls that guarded his estate, discouraging the curious or those with criminal intent.

Seb had fallen into deep contemplation and only now sat up and took proper notice of his surroundings. The grounds were pristinely maintained, just as they always had been. He could see the roof of the house in the far distance and felt his sombre mood, the near permanent depression that had been his constant companion these past six years, gradually lifting.

'Be it ever so humble,' he muttered, watching as Mark pressed a button inside the car and the gates swung open on silent hinges.

'Is John here?' Seb asked.

'He's on call for tomorrow,' Pat replied, sounding surprised by the question. 'I assumed you'd want to spend your first day home... well, otherwise occupied.'

Seb grunted and let that assumption pass uncontested. Funnily enough, sex had been the thing he'd missed the least.

The car came to a smooth halt on the gravel outside the front door, which was immediately opened by a smiling sight for sore eyes.

'They let you out then,' Sam Greaves said as he opened Seb's car door. 'We were starting to wonder if they'd thrown away the key.'

Seb grinned as he climbed from the car and the two of them shared a man-hug; lots of back slapping that hid a wealth of emotion on Seb's part; the only emotion he'd allowed himself to feel for six long years. He and Sam went way back to the mean streets of South London, where they'd grown up watching one another's backs. They'd gone through their school years together, eschewing membership of the various gangs on offer in favour of getting educated and making something of themselves. Even then, when his father was still establishing himself within the ranks of the criminal fraternity, Seb hadn't wanted to follow in parental footsteps and knew there was only one way to avoid the inevitable.

Through the use of his brains, not brawn.

Sam's efforts had been thwarted in that regard when his mum had taken an accidental overdose and he had been forced to step up and support his younger siblings. But the bond between Sam and Seb had endured and he was the only man Seb had truly trusted to run his home and oversee his business affairs during his incarceration. John fronted the organisation; Sam oiled the wheels from behind the scenes. Neither man could sneeze without word reaching Seb inside.

He trusted them both but had also learned not to trust anyone.

The sound of laughter coming from the side lawn caused

Seb's heart to stutter. The joyous sound of Lily's voice filled his senses and almost broke through the reserve that he had constructed around his heart.

'She's playing in the leaves,' Sam told him.

Seb swallowed and nodded, unsurprised that his thoughts in the car were a reflection of her actual occupation.

'How is she?' he asked.

'Happy,' Sam replied. 'She likes the new woman we've employed to look after her.'

'Ava Harper.'

Seb knew all about the woman. She'd come with impeccable references, which had been thoroughly checked out. Lily had taken an immediate liking to her, which was the most important aspect of the hiring, and thus far there had been no meltdowns on Lily's part, which was nothing short of miraculous. She got upset for no apparent reason that any of the expensive experts Seb employed had been able to explain and her rages were terrifying to witness. The storms tended to abate quickly but Seb always worried that Lily, in her thrashing about and throwing things, would harm herself.

Full-time, residential care had been recommended but Seb was having none of it. Lily was his responsibility and his alone. Seb's father had tried to take her under his wing when Seb had been banged up but Seb's lawyers had put a stop to that and rather than become involved in a legal battle, the old man had backed down, just as Seb had known that he would.

Jason Carter never took on fights that he couldn't win by fair means or foul. Reputation was everything to the old man and he knew that his myriad enemies would seize on any sign of weakness that highlighted the rift between father and son. Lily had already been used and abused. Seb made sure that his father was aware in no uncertain terms that he wouldn't stand for her being removed from the only home she had ever known.

Her security.

Jason has the good sense not to oppose him on such a vital issue, aware that past performance had robbed him of all parental rights insofar as Lily was concerned.

Mark had driven off towards the six-car garage and Pat and Sam stood in the doorway watching Seb, who desperately wanted to round the side of the house and greet his sister, but hesitated. He wanted to ask if she was likely to recognise him but the question stalled on his lips. He wanted to see Lily; the thought of doing so had sustained him through six long years but now that the time had actually come, it felt as though his feet were glued to the ground.

What went on in Lily's damaged mind, he wondered for the millionth time? The question had never seemed so relevant as it did at that moment. Did she remember her ordeal? Did she blame Seb for what had happened to her? If she did then it wouldn't be nearly so fiercely as Seb blamed himself. Would she resent the fact that he had disappeared from her life so abruptly?

He swallowed and forced his feet to move. Sam and Pat remained where they were. This was Seb's moment.

He stood at the side of a lawn edged by trees shedding their leaves. Lily danced amongst them, blonde hair flying out behind her as she laughed joyously, throwing piles of dry leaves into the air and watching them tumble down. Some of them lodged in the hair of her companion, hair as russet as some of the leaves themselves. Hair that tumbled halfway down Ava's back in a riot of unruly curls.

As he watched, something inside of Seb unlocked. Ava was very attractive; more so than the pictures he'd been shown of her. And her laughter was infectious. Seb could gauge at a glance that she cared about Lily, took her disabilities in her stride and lavished upon her all the affection that a simple yet complex woman-child required.

None of Ava's predecessors had stayed the course; Lily was hard work, her moods unpredictable, the security measures that Seb insisted upon restrictive. At first glance, Ava appeared to understand his sister in a way that only someone versed in disabilities of the mind possibly could. Seb suspected then that he didn't know as much about Ava's history as he thought he did, accounting for the fact that she was willing to take this position on when she was qualified to do so much more. Had she held a big part of herself back? The paranoia, survival instinct – call it what you will – that he'd developed inside made him suspicious and yet he didn't feel as though Ava was any sort of threat. What the hell...

Lily threw another handful of leaves high in the air, laughing with the joy of simple pleasures. Her gaze fell upon Seb and her laughter abruptly faded. Lily was wary of strangers, which is what Seb would now be to her. He held his breath, waiting to see what she would do. Ava noticed her charge's preoccupation and turned in his direction, watching Seb through wide, green eyes but saying nothing. She must know who he was; she would have been told that he was expected home today.

But still she remained silent, clearly allowing Lily to make up her own mind.

That was sensible, Seb conceded, even if he wondered how Ava felt about being in the employ of a convicted killer. Presumably she didn't mind too much or she wouldn't have taken the position.

Lily's lips parted as confusion clouded her expression. Now was a defining moment. She would either scream blue murder or... or what? Seb had no way of knowing.

'Hey Pumpkin,' he said softly.

Lily blinked at the sound of Seb's voice and remained stock still. After what seemed like an eternity, the confusion left her eyes and she hurtled herself into Seb's outstretched arms.

'Seb Seb!' she cried. Seb held her close; his heart too full for words, as he breathed in the essence of the woman-child whom he had failed so badly. She hadn't forgotten him. At last, something had gone right for him.

# 2

Ava's heart palpitated as she watched the long-awaited reunion. She kept her distance during this most personal of moments but had no intention of being moved by it. Despite her own reservations about Sebastian Carter, Lily's joy was so unbridled that she was obliged to wipe tears away with the back of her hand.

*Get a grip!*

She had been in her position for almost a year now and was fond of Lily, despite her brother's dangerous reputation. Ava had gambled on Carter not admitting to murder. He had protested his innocence throughout his trial and refused to take the stand in his own defence. Her research had revealed that it wasn't uncommon for the accused to go into denial – juries could be unpredictable in the verdicts they reached. If that gamble didn't pay off, once the reality of prison life sank in, those *innocents* came clean and expressed remorse to parole boards in the expectation of halving their sentences.

Not so Carter.

Ergo, he'd had to serve his full sentence and Ava had seized the providential opportunity to make herself indispensable to his sister – his one weakness – before his release. What she hadn't expected was to come to love Lily so unreservedly. But then again, she reasoned, how could she seriously have supposed that it wouldn't happen that way? Lily was a delight; trusting and vulnerable – an absolute treasure and so very easy to control once one understood what triggered her mood swings. Darkness, loud voices and angry words rated highly in that respect.

Living within this fortified mansion wasn't as restricting as she had thought would be the case. She had become accustomed to the quiet and grown rather fond of the estate, where no expense had been spared on life's comforts. She and Lily had explored the surrounding countryside extensively, taking long rambles and picnicking during some of the long, hot summer days in the South Downs National Park. Ava had resented the fact that they were always accompanied on their rambles by Mark Pearson, a man whom Seb Carter trusted and who Lily appeared to like.

Mark, despite being polite and unobtrusive, made her feel as though she was under constant scrutiny, her every move probably reported back to the man behind bars. In spite of his incarceration, she had come to realise that nothing important happened on the outside without Carter's prior knowledge and approval.

Mark was a bull of a man with a soft underbelly who could make Lily giggle like the child she still was inside her damaged mind. Ava had grown to respect his loyalty to a man who had been in prison for six years. Be that as it may, she hadn't once lost sight of her true purpose and wouldn't let anything stand in her way.

Not even Lily.

Questions had to be answered, and she had recently set the ball rolling by making a few enquiries that had got her nowhere. Within these walls, or more precisely within the head of her admittedly rather formidable employer who now had his sister ensconced in his arms, was the place to find those answers. Ava was convinced of the fact.

The small, devoted band of people who had kept the place going had nothing but good things to say about Seb Carter, especially Jessie, the housekeeper who had known Seb since he'd been a lad. Well, obviously they wouldn't bad-mouth him, she reasoned. They all adamantly believed that he did not kill the man he'd been convicted of bumping off and Ava was inclined to believe them.

Not that she would have blamed him if he had, she thought, watching the reunion through moist eyes, reminded of the ordeal that Lily had suffered at the victim's vile hands. How anyone could force themselves upon such a sensitive, trusting little soul was beyond Ava's understanding and made her seethe with anger whenever her mind dwelt upon the issue, which wasn't often. She couldn't change the past but could – would – shape the future.

Otherwise, what was the point?

It was a testament to Carter's character, she supposed, that he had refused to take responsibility for a crime that he hadn't committed. But that was the only concession she was prepared to make in his favour, at least until she had got the measure of the man himself and decided whether or not he was his father's stooge after all. But already she doubted it because she knew how fiercely he had fought from behind bars to keep Jason Carter well away from his own daughter.

Seb lifted his head and his gaze clashed with hers. His eyes were moist, a testament to his adoration for his poor, damaged little sister, now twenty-five; a love that Ava knew was reciprocated. Lily's eyes shone with happiness as she clung like a limpet to her brother's neck, burying her face in his shoulder and giggling at something he whispered to her. Lily kept a picture of

Seb beside her bed and kissed it every night. Fiercely affectionate, she kissed Ava too, stealing her heart a little more each day in the process and almost distracting her from her true reason for being in this fortress.

Almost.

Lily's excited screams gradually receded. Seb placed her back on her feet but she clung to his hand and dragged him onto the lawns. Clearly, he was expected to join in her games and Ava would be interested to gauge his reaction. Somehow, she wasn't surprised when without hesitation he gathered up a massive handful of leaves and threw them in the air. Lily clapped her hands and screamed. Seb took her hand and led her to a pile of leaves that he started stamping on. Lily giggled and did the same thing.

Leaving his sister to a game that now occupied her complete attention, Seb wiped his hands down his thighs and turned to face her.

Finally, Ava's moment had come.

'Hi, you must be Ava.' He extended a big hand and Ava slipped her own into it. 'Seb Carter. Thank you for taking such good care of my sister. I can see how happy she is and that means a lot to me.'

'It's not difficult, Mr Carter,' Ava replied. 'She is a very easy person to love.'

'Call me Seb.'

Ava swallowed, taken aback by his friendliness, to say nothing of the exacting scrutiny that he subjected her to. 'All right.'

They both turned to watch Lily, still stamping on leaves and laughing. A puppy that Seb knew nothing about – a ragtag creature of indeterminate pedigree – appeared from nowhere and joined in the game, wagging with enthusiasm.

'What is... that?' Seb asked, pointing a finger at the creature and looking highly dubious.

'It's not a *that*, it's a fine example of...' Ava bit her lip to prevent herself from smiling. 'Well, it's a stray, if you must know. Lily and I found him half-starved in the woods. I think he must have been dumped from a car. Honestly, some people can be so heartless and it makes me so angry.' She paused to draw breath, unable to read anything from Seb's stony expression. 'I brought him back here and fed him up. Now he doesn't want to leave. And, as you can see, Lily loves him.'

'Yes, but I'm not convinced...'

'Well, if you don't want him to stay, you'll have to be the one to tell her.'

'That's blackmail.' Seb surprised her by smiling. 'But of course, he can stay. Lily has always liked animals but I wasn't sure if it would be safe to—'

'I'll have you know that Wizard sleeps on Lily's bed.'

'Wizard?' Seb raised both brows, clearly fighting his amusement.

'That was her choice. We've been reading *Harry Potter*.'

Seb held out a hand to the puppy who loped up to him, tail working overtime, and licked Seb's fingers. Lily watched Wizard jumping up and scrambling at Seb's legs and clapped her hands in delight.

With his attention on the puppy, Ava took the opportunity to study the man she'd heard spoken of for so long in almost reverent terms. Rugged features deeply etched with lines defined a strong jaw and sharp cheekbones. He was a handsome man, yet tough and resourceful. Ava knew that he would have to be in order to survive six years locked up. Despite all the complaints about prison being too lenient, Ava knew it was a harsh regime in which the weak were unconditionally exploited.

He was definitely handsome, she conceded, aware of the close physical resemblance between brother and sister. Thick locks of dark blond hair constantly fell across arresting blue eyes that appeared to miss little. He brushed it impatiently aside and Ava was gripped by an irrational desire to do it for him, which was crazy. She hadn't expected to like the man, or to trust him, but was already a fair way to doing both.

'Welcome home,' Ava said when Lily and the puppy ran off, scattering leaves in their wake, and she found herself alone with him again.

'The sweet taste of freedom,' he replied, tilting his head back, breathing deeply and closing his eyes.

She hadn't expected such a direct reference to his incarceration and it threw her. She said nothing.

'How has Lily been?' he asked, opening his eyes again and studying her in a manner that she found disconcerting.

She arched a brow. 'You don't already know?'

'I'm asking you.' His words were crisp, almost impatient, as though he wasn't accustomed to being challenged.

'She gets stressed less frequently. I think the puppy helps. She feels responsible for Wizard, which can only be a good thing.'

'I was obviously too protective, thinking an animal might add to her anxiety issues when it's already clear to me that the opposite is true.'

'I didn't mean to undermine your authority, or think I knew better than you,' Ava said, peeved by the accusation in his tone.

Seb sent her a sharp look. 'I was trying to be complimentary.' The suggestion of a smile flirted with his lips. 'Clearly I have lost touch with the social graces.'

'Well, if you disapprove of the way I handle Lily, I am sure you will let me know.'

'Count on it.' This time he definitely smiled but the gesture looked strained, as though he was unaccustomed to showing emotion of any sort which, Ava supposed, was likely the case. 'But now, if you will excuse me.' He turned away, then swivelled on his heel and faced her again. 'Have a drink with me later once Lily's settled. We need to talk.'

'We do?'

The offer took Ava aback. Everyone in the house was agreed on one thing. Seb Carter was a man of few words who was not socially disposed. Apparently, he liked the ladies but never dated anyone long term. A loner, he preferred to keep everyone except Lily at a distance, including his father.

Especially him.

'Sure.' He shrugged. 'I need more details about Lily's progress.'

'Okay.' Ava thought she could supply that information without the necessity to drink with him but wasn't about to reject the invitation. Besides, he was her boss so she wasn't left with much choice. 'I'll see you later then.'

Lily called to Ava, who returned to her charge, pushing thoughts of her complex employer to one side.

* * *

'He's out.'

Ruby Asquith curled her feet beneath her backside on the soft leather sofa she occupied at one end of her expansive office at the Black Iris, still the premier nightclub in South London, and nodded in response to Bart Fleming, her head of security's words. 'When?' she asked.

'This morning. Early. He's already back at his place.'

'How touching.' Ruby examined her blood-red nails, the exact same colour as the dress she planned to wear that evening, tutting when she noticed a tiny chip. 'Keep a watch on him. He will be out for revenge, which means he'll start digging to see if he can find out who actually killed that waste of space, Blythe, and I don't want him to come gunning for me.'

Bart nodded. 'Can do when he leaves his grounds but that house of his is impossible to infiltrate. All his people are annoyingly loyal.'

'There must be a weak link. Find it. A cleaner, a bloody gardener. Someone must need money and be willing to spy.'

Bart nodded. 'I'll see what I can do but it could be dangerous, drawing the attention to us that you don't want, if it backfires.'

'Do it anyway,' Ruby replied impatiently. 'I have a bad feeling about this. Can we set him up with one of our girls, do you suppose?'

'He seldom sees the same girl twice, or didn't before his stretch. Doesn't like to give the impression of commitment.'

Ruby huffed impatiently, well aware of it. 'If he's coming after me for any reason, I need to know about it before it happens.'

'He won't get anywhere near you,' Bart said with authority in his tone.

'Never underestimate a man who's just come off a six stretch he didn't do anything to deserve. He will want answers.'

'Ruby, you're untouchable.'

She flicked a finger towards the bar in the corner. Without speaking, Bart opened a bottle of Krug, poured a measure into a crystal flute and handed the glass to Ruby. She downed it in one unladylike swallow. She wouldn't allow anyone other than Bart – her rock, the man who had proved his loyalty time and again and would take her secrets to the grave – to know it but she was scared shitless of Seb Carter and his thirst for revenge.

'Jason is due over later. We'll thrash out the terms of our agreement without lawyers muddying the water in an effort to justify their outrageous fees.' She glanced at the screens on one wall showing images of the activity in various rooms. It was still early and there weren't many punters in the club yet. A couple of people were sitting at a blackjack table. One of Ruby's best girls was going down on a fat businessman in a private booth. Another was whacking a skinny backside with a riding crop.

Business as usual.

Bart shrugged his meaty shoulders. 'Okay, I'll let them know downstairs.'

Bart left the room, moving quietly for such a large man. Ruby contemplated refilling her glass but decided against it. She never allowed herself to be out of control. With a sigh, she uncoiled her legs and returned to her desk. There was paperwork. Always paperwork. Ruby didn't commit anything important to the vagaries of computer systems that could easily be hacked.

She picked up her gold Montblanc pen and tapped it against her teeth as she read through the terms of the agreement she had reached with Jason Carter. He was a tough negotiator and wanted everything his way but Ruby hadn't come down in the last shower. Jason wanted out of the club and showing a weakness in that regard could be his Achilles heel.

* * *

Seb returned to the house, unsurprised to find a high-end escort waiting for him. Pat's idea of a welcome home present, presumably. Not such a bad plan really, albeit predictable. Seb, surprised by his lack of enthusiasm and in no mood to drag it out, relieved his frustrations quickly and sent her on her way.

What he really wanted was a heart to heart with John. He'd received regular reports regarding his business; reports that were opened and avidly read by prison officers before reaching him.

That was okay. They wouldn't find anomalies because there were none to be found. Unlike his father, Seb's business was strictly legitimate. That's what the police had been unable to get their heads around and one of the reasons, Seb often thought, that he'd been so clumsily framed for murder. Nothing stuck to Jason Carter, who was an out and out villain, so his enemies targeted his only child who'd gone straight; the one who Jason allowed the world to know he was proud of, thereby showing fallibility.

Seb wondered if that was why he'd been set up. Despite being estranged from his father, the fit-up would have focused Jason's mind, distracting him from his nefarious activities as he screamed for answers. Even as a grown man, Seb was a little intimidated by his father. A hard man, he hadn't survived as a leading player in the murky London underworld by letting his emotions get the better of him. Seb knew the old man had launched full scale war against all those he even suspected of involvement in the frame up. Not that Seb had seen or spoken to him – he'd flat out refused – but word had still got back to him.

Seb ate with Pat but found himself craving solitude once the meal was over. His trusted friend seemed to realise it and made himself scarce. Peace and quiet, to say nothing of alone time in luxurious surroundings, were commodities sadly lacking on the inside and Seb fully intended to make the most of them on this, his first night of freedom.

He sat in front of an open log fire in his lounge, savouring the taste of the ruinously expensive cognac he'd poured for himself, thinking about his next move. Wondering too about Ava Harper. There was something vaguely familiar about her but Seb was pretty sure they'd never met before. She was the same age as Lily and so would have still been a teenager when he went down for Blythe's murder, so even if their paths had crossed, he wouldn't have spared her a second glance. Underage girls definitely didn't feature on his radar.

He'd checked her references again after meeting her today. She'd worked in Switzerland as an au pair for the past three years and for a couple of different UK families prior to that. All her previous employers had supplied glowing references and regretted her decision to leave their employ.

Seb threw back his head and closed his eyes, thinking that she seemed almost too good to be true. And yet Seb had seen for himself the miracles she had worked with Lily, so perhaps she was the real deal and something had finally gone right for him.

For now, he would give her the benefit of the doubt.

As though summoned by the power of his own thoughts, a tap at the door preceded Ava putting her head round it.

'I am disturbing you?' she asked, presumably because Seb stared blankly at her. 'You did say that you wanted to grill me,' she added with an impatient edge to her voice.

Seb's expression relaxed and he beckoned her in. 'I don't think that's quite what I said but come in.'

She did so and closed the door. 'It's what you implied.'

Seb felt wrong-footed by her bluntness. 'Is Lily settled?' he asked.

'No, I left her screaming and tearing up her room.'

Seb sent her the sort of look that had caused the hardest of men inside to back off but it bounced harmlessly off Ava's admittedly rather attractive hide.

'She's usually asleep by nine,' Ava explained, perching on the edge of the chair across from Seb's. 'She has boundless energy during the day, yet tires easily, and the medication she takes makes her drowsy.'

'Right.'

Seb paused. He had never invited one of his female

employees to join him socially before, so this was unchartered territory and he felt maladroit. It had been a while since he'd been in a position to issue any invitations at all, he conceded, but surely he could handle some one-to-one time with his sister's companion without losing his grip?

He told himself that he was triple checking Lily's safety, albeit six years too late. There was something off about Ava and it was bothering him. That same sixth sense that had warned him of potential trouble during his early years inside was on full alert. It was in the way that she stood up to him, he realised. Few people of either sex, inside or out, did so. She was an interesting mix: a challenge, an enigma.

'Would you like a drink?'

She glanced at his brandy glass and wrinkled her nose. 'Not that stuff. It would knock me out for a week.'

Seb offered up a wry smile. 'That's not always a bad thing.'

'Well, no, in your case, I guess you drink to forget. In your situation, I very likely would.'

'What an odd thing to say. You don't know anything about me.'

'True.' She offered him a sunny smile that potentially did more for him than the full-on services of the hooker he'd sent packing. 'I'll have a glass of white wine, if you have anything that mundane.'

'I dare say it can be arranged.'

Seb went across to the bar in the corner of the room, opened the cooler and found a bottle of Chablis Premier Cru. He waved it at her and she nodded absently, probably not even looking at the label. Seb pulled the cork and poured a generous measure into a crystal glass, which he handed to her. She nodded her thanks and took a sip that she appeared to savour.

'Classy,' she said.

Seb found himself smiling. 'Glad you approve.'

'I'm more used to the house plonk in the local pub but that doesn't mean I don't appreciate quality on the rare occasions I get to taste it.'

'I'm glad that you like it.' Seb replied, chuckling.

'I learned to appreciate wine when I worked in Switzerland. The family I was with were experts and took it very seriously.'

'Did you enjoy your time there?'

'Well, I stayed for three years, until the kids no longer had need of me, so I guess that answers your question. Then again, I don't suppose I'm telling you anything you don't already know.'

'I'm not going to apologise for wanting to keep my sister safe. So yeah, I had your references verified before putting you on the payroll.'

'I would be disappointed if you hadn't.'

She spoke offhandedly, leaving it unsaid that perhaps he ought to have taken more care of Lily *before* the attack. Then again, perhaps Seb was seeing shadows on a cloudy day and his conscience was working overtime.

*Again.*

'You don't find it too quiet here?' he asked, filling the long silence that had somehow stretched between them. Ava sipped at her drink, apparently perfectly comfortable with the pregnant pause. Seb found her composure disconcerting. He also felt as though she was the one in control, which was frankly ridiculous. 'A young woman like you probably enjoys the bright lights.'

'That's assuming a lot. We're not all party animals. Besides, I'm not *that* young.'

'Sorry. You'll have to make allowances. Where I've been living there isn't a lot of call for polite conversation.'

'Was it very tough?' she asked, cocking her head to one side and watching through a veil of thick, curling lashes.

'It wasn't the walk in the park that the media will have you believe.' Seb lifted one shoulder. 'There's always someone who wants to prove himself with his fists.' Seb paused. 'Or other parts of his anatomy. Show the slightest sign of fear, of weakness, and your life becomes a living hell.'

'Presumably your father's name was enough to protect you.'

Seb jerked forward in his chair, blinking back his shock. 'I beg your pardon?' he said, his voice a low, threatening growl, the mood spoiled by her throwaway remark. 'What the hell do you know about my father?'

# 3

Ava swallowed, cursing her inability to curb her tongue. She thought she'd been prepared to face Sebastian Carter, that she knew what to expect, but he had already surprised her in so many little ways.

And some not so little.

He was more cultured than she'd expected him to be, and clearly intelligent. He had attended a tough comprehensive in the East End and managed to concentrate on getting an education rather than joining one of the various criminal gangs that created havoc and had no interest in learning. His father had been making a name for himself at the time and had, according to Seb's housekeeper, fully intended to mould his sons in his own image. Seb's younger brothers, Ray and Dennis, had toed the parental line and turned out to be right hard cases. But Seb had made his own way, remaining on the straight and narrow.

Jessie, his housekeeper, was devoted to Seb. She had moved from the father's house to look after him when Jason and Seb had parted ways on bad terms. She also liked to gossip, which is how Ava had learned so much. The loquacious housekeeper had witnessed massive bust ups between father and son when Seb had left school and refused to use his brains to launder his father's ill-gotten gains. By that time, Jason Carter was a force to be reckoned with in London's gangland and saw a son who preferred to keep things legal as a liability. He'd thrown his young son out of the family home, fully expecting him to return with his tail between his legs when he was no longer surrounded by luxury created by the spoils of crime.

According to Jessie, Jason had grossly underestimated his eldest child's determination to remain on the right side of the law. Seb had quickly amassed a fortune through property development but even Jessie didn't know how he accrued his start-up funds. She was adamant though that all Jason's offers of help, once he realised that Seb was never returning to the family fold, were rebuffed.

A fountain of knowledge about the family's affairs, Jessie was also adamant that Seb and his father, who had originally maintained a distantly polite relationship, had fallen out big time.

Jessie didn't know why but Ava had a fair idea.

'I don't know your father to speak to but everyone knows his name.' She paused, aware from the stony set to Seb's features that he would want more from her than that. 'People talk. Look, I grew up in South London and his name was on everyone's lips. He was a legend, but not in a good way. Gangs of kids fought to be in his... well, gang.'

The rigidity left Seb's shoulders. 'I wasn't aware that you hailed from London.'

She shrugged. 'You can't have delved that far into my background then because it's no secret.' She made an effort to curtail her combative tone, making it more conversational. 'My father had a jewellery business in Croydon. It did well so I got sent to private schools, had an aptitude for languages and that's one of the reasons why I landed the job in Switzerland. They wanted a French speaker who could help the kids with their English.'

'Where's your father now?'

'He died from cancer.' Ava looked away from him, unwilling to let him see her eyes welling up. 'Two years ago now.'

'I'm sorry.' His voice was laced with compassion but he remained distant. Emotion, she suspected, was something that he'd learned to keep hidden during his years inside. 'What about your mother?'

'What about her?'

Seb drained his glass and placed it aside. He crossed one foot over his opposite thigh and leaned back in his chair, still studying her closely. 'Do you always answer a question with a question?' he asked.

She lifted one shoulder. 'I'm not sure what it is that you want from me.'

'I like to know who I'm dealing with.'

Ava bridled. She wanted to know a lot more about him, so that she could make up her mind whether or not to trust him, so she figured she'd have to give in order to win *his* trust. Even so, she reasoned that a man of his calibre was used to getting what he wanted, little or no effort required. Ava wasn't about to be that obliging. 'I'm your employee but I'm still entitled to privacy,' she said, looking away from him.

'So you are.' He paused. 'Okay. Ask me anything you like and I'll give you an honest answer.' He wagged a finger at her, clearly a little taken aback by her stubbornness. 'Then it will be your turn.'

'Just one question?'

He nodded, looking faintly amused. 'How many do you need?'

Ava sat a little straighter, thinking she'd never have a better opportunity to get to the truth. To satisfy herself that Seb was trustworthy. But how was she going to do that with just one question? Besides, she would then have to answer his question about her mother. But that would be a good thing, surely?'

'Why did you get custody of Lily?' she asked because even Jessie hadn't been able to tell her the answer to that one. It wasn't what she most wanted to know but it might pave the way for more questions. She had to start somewhere.

'Lily is ten years younger than me. You know that, right?'

Ava nodded. 'Sure.' She leaned forward. 'Go on.'

'My old man doesn't do damaged goods. Oh, Lily was as pretty as a picture but mentally deficient. Well, that isn't how Jason described her, or my brothers either.'

'Your brothers?' Ava realised that she was now perched on the edge of her seat when Seb sent her an odd look. She was showing a little *too* much interest in Seb's brothers and had almost given herself away.

'Anyway,' he added, 'I dare say you get the picture and don't need me to repeat my father's view verbatim.'

Ava ground her teeth. She got it all too well. People could be incredibly cruel. Some of the remarks she'd heard thrown Lily's way since she'd been in charge of her care had made her want to commit a few murders of her own. Fortunately, that was where Mark's presence came into its own. His musculature intimidated to the extent that people kept their opinions to themselves and Lily, who lived in her own world, didn't understand those that she did overhear.

'I gather he tried to get custody of her when you were locked up.'

Seb winced. 'I knew he'd try, so I made sure I had enough ammunition to dissuade him. Anyway, I digress. The old man wanted to institutionalise Lily. Lock her away from public view because she was an embarrassment to him.'

Ava gasped. 'That would have been the death of her. She hates loud noise. And crowded places.'

'Precisely. The old man was trying to keep me in the family fold and wasn't above using my affection for my sister to bend me to his will. But I was having none of it and took her with me.'

'How did you live?'

He waved a hand at her. 'You've had your question. Now it's your turn to answer mine.'

'My mother?'

He nodded.

'Why are you so interested?'

'That's another question and it's your turn to answer one.'

Ava took a deep steadying breath. What to say? How much to reveal? Could she trust this most complex of men? Her instincts told her that she could. She thought back to his touching reunion with Lily, to the way that a young man had found the strength to walk out on a criminal father, taking his sister with him. Perhaps Jason's threat to institutionalise Lily had forced his hand and set his life on a very different path. Perhaps Jason had wrought revenge by setting his own son up for murder. The opinion in this household was that Jason Carter always had to have the last word but would he really go that far?

She glanced at Seb, aware that his steady gaze remained focused on her face and hadn't waivered. He really wasn't going to let her off the hook and the more she prevaricated, the more determined she sensed he would become to get answers.

'My mother disappeared seven years ago,' she said.

'Disappeared?' He raised both brows. 'As in died? Ran off? Had an accident?'

Ava spread her hands. 'No one knows. She simply disappeared off the face of the earth.'

'What was done to find her?'

'You've had more than your quota of questions, so I reserve the right to redress the balance but since we're on the subject of my mother, I don't mind telling you.' Ava inhaled sharply, still feeling unsettled by the subject matter, even after all these years. 'It was a normal day. I was at college, doing A levels, Dad was at work. Mum worked from home, doing the shop's books, ordering stock, stuff like that. She did bookkeeping for private clients too. When I got home, she wasn't there, which wasn't that unusual. She had a hectic social life and went to the gym or spa quite often with her girlfriends. But none of them had seen her that day, or been expecting to. In fact, most of them hadn't seen her for weeks but she'd been going out as usual. I know that because she often wasn't home when I got in, but I didn't think anything of it.'

'Her going missing was reported to the police?'

'Of course it was! But she'd disappeared without trace and... well, they lost interest looking for her. Unbeknown to me, Dad did his own investigating but I only found that out when I was going through his things after he died.'

'Go on,' Seb said when Ava got choked with emotion, his tone soft and sympathetic.

Ava raised her head and looked directly at Seb. 'It turns out she'd been having an affair.' She allowed a significant pause. 'With your father.'

* * *

Seb cursed beneath his breath, wondering if he would ever be free of his father's influence. He'd regretted probing into Ava's private affairs, unable at first to decide why he had. He frowned as he thought it through, betting now that Ava resembled her missing mother. He'd seen his father once or twice in the run up to being imprisoned. His old man had been attempting to develop a legitimate business which had required him to rub shoulders with local dignitaries and Seb had witnessed his father swanning about with a stunning woman on his arm. A woman who, Seb now realised, looked just like Ava. That is why she'd seemed so familiar to him.

'That's why you took this job.' Seb leaned back in his chair, a cynical twist to his lips. 'You assumed I might know something that would help you to find your mother.'

'No!' she cried hotly, her cheeks flooding with colour. 'Well, yes,' she conceded. 'I'm sorry but what would you do in my place? My dad worshipped the ground that Mum walked on, gave her everything her heart desired and then she disappeared without a word of warning. Walked out on us both. He was broken, never the same again. Never laughing or acting the clown like he once had. Perhaps that was because he'd discovered she'd been unfaithful, but I didn't know that at the time. He kept it from me and kept telling me that she'd come back to us. I wasn't to worry. None of it was my fault.'

'That must have been tough.'

'It wasn't the best of times; I won't deny it.'

'What did your father find out?'

She spread her hands. 'I don't know. There's so much I don't know. He didn't write much down and never spoke about it.' She leaned forward. 'It's eating away at me and I have to get some answers. But know this much; I love your sister.' She leaned forward, pinning Seb to his chair with a look of deep intensity. 'I didn't expect to get emotionally involved and will admit that I looked upon her as a means to an end. Initially. I don't suppose you'll believe me but that all changed very quickly and, for the record, I'm very glad that your father didn't get custody of her when you went away.'

She sat back in her chair, looking defiant, puffing out her cheeks. Probably expecting to be fired.

'You think I can help you get some answers?' He shook his head. 'Sorry to disappoint you but I have as little to do with my father as possible.'

'Yes.' She blew air through her lips and let out a deep sigh of defeat. 'I know that now.'

'Don't look so downhearted. I have a feeling that's about to change.'

'Oh.' She blinked at him. 'Why?'

'Because I have questions that need answers too.'

'You want to know who killed the man you were convicted of murdering.'

'Thank you for believing that I didn't do it.'

'No one in this household believes that you did, and they were halfway to convincing me but I decided to reserve judgement until I met you.'

'And now that you have?'

Seb struggled to keep the amusement out of his tone. She was an enigma: intelligent, forthright, unafraid to say what she was thinking. He'd been out of the game for six years, it was true, but still, ordinarily women were predictable and easy for him to read. Not so Ava. His first day home and she already had him guessing. And, unbeknown to her, she'd also challenged him; given him something to think about other than the pressing need to find out who had really killed Blythe.

And why.

Given that he'd thought about precious little else these past six years, the desire for revenge still burnt like acid, keeping him focused.

She shook her head. 'You didn't kill anyone. If you had you would have admitted it and got your sentence reduced. Once found guilty you might have done that even if innocent,' she said thoughtfully. 'Most people would, I'm sure. But I can already tell that you have more integrity than that.'

'Thank you.' He paused, a brief smile flirting with his lips. 'I think.'

'I'm not trying to flatter, if that's what you think. I simply speak as I find.'

'How can you tell if a person has integrity? You barely know me and I could be on my best behaviour.'

That suggestion made her laugh aloud. 'I don't think you put on a pretence for anyone.' She held up a hand to prevent him from interrupting her. 'I have spent my adult life looking after children. Their behaviour mirrors that of the adults immediately surrounding them. Was it Freud who said something about giving him a child for the first few years of its life and he would shape its character? Something like that anyway. Well, if your father had shaped your life then you wouldn't have striven for independence and instead just clung to Jason's coat-tails, much as your brothers have. *That* is how I know you have integrity.'

He nodded, thinking she was right, which made her decision to work for him that much harder to fathom, despite her determination to find out what had happened to her mother. Seb's father and brothers were well known for their criminal activities and Seb was a convicted murderer. She was pinning a hell of a lot of faith on her ability to judge characters.

'You're not afraid to live beneath a possible murderer's roof, integrity notwithstanding?' he chided.

She waved the suggestion aside. 'I have Wizard to protect me.'

Seb laughed, something he seemed to do spontaneously in this woman's presence. 'I am terrified.' His laughter quickly faded.

'But as it happens, I do think my father knows something about Blythe's death. He wouldn't have done it himself but he would have taken grave exception to his daughter being harmed, even though he was ashamed of her disabilities. Anyone attacking a member of his family is attacking him, if you like, perhaps trying to weaken his position and that he would never tolerate.'

Ava frowned. 'But would he set you up to take the fall?'

'No, I don't think he anticipated that happening. I imagine one of his rivals decided upon that little twist.'

Ava threw back her head and let out a long breath. 'I don't understand any of this.'

'Join the club.'

'If he knew what really happened to Blythe why didn't he say… or do something to get you off the hook?'

'And put himself firmly on it?' Seb shook his head. 'You really don't know my father. Besides, having a son that everyone looked upon as a black sheep…'

'Because you went straight?' She shook her head. 'Blimey.'

'Not quite the word I would use but it does the job. The old man took my determination to turn my back on his way of life as a personal affront.'

Ava nodded. 'What will it cost you to get answers from him now that you've served your time?' A worried expression creased her brow.

'Well, there's a question that I've had a lot of time to ponder upon.' Seb stretched his arms above his head, then stood to refill his glass. He nodded towards hers but she covered it with her hand. 'He's attempting to put on a legitimate front, which fools no one, especially not the police. Some of his business is now legit, it's true, but he still has fingers firmly inserted in every dodgy pie in town. He can't help himself. Gets a buzz out of it. He once told me gives him a better high than sex.'

'He wanted you to front his legitimate side?'

Seb nodded. 'And I didn't want to know.'

'That would explain why he didn't try to get you off the murder charge, I suppose. Jessie says that he never forgets a slight, especially from someone who he expects loyalty from.'

'Jessie has a big mouth.' But Seb smiled as he said it.

'Jessie thinks the sun shines out of your backside.'

'She was a kind of surrogate mother to me. It was her who kept on at me when I was a kid to distinguish right from wrong. She tried to do the same with my brothers but there was no hope for them. I was the oldest though and remember the old bill knocking down our door at regular intervals and carting the old man off. Mum crying. Worried that this time the charges would stick. They never did though and he seemed to think he was invincible.' Seb shrugged. 'Perhaps he is, given that he's never had his collar felt. Anyway, it was Jessie who persuaded me to use my brains and I have a lot to be thankful to her for.'

'Where was your own mother?'

Seb shrugged. 'Long gone, way before I finished school. I figure that she couldn't tolerate any more of the old man's womanising. Who's to say? Well, Jessie is, I guess, and that's what she tells me.'

'Your mum didn't take you with her?'

Seb shook his head. 'That wouldn't have been permitted. She could leave, but she couldn't take us boys. That much I know because she wrote to me through Jessie for a while but I have no idea where she is now. I don't even know if she's still alive but if she is then I hope she's remarried and is happy. She deserves to be. I know for a fact that the old man dealt her backhanders on more than one occasion.'

Ava winced. 'Lily isn't her daughter?'

'No, she's my half-sibling. Her mother is long gone too. My

father sheds his women as soon as he gets bored with them. Either that or they leave him when they can't take any more. Suddenly, one day he told us, all casual like, that we had a sister and there was baby Lily.' Seb smiled. 'I have to say it was love at first sight on my part. There was no mother around though and none of us asked questions; we knew better than that. Jason employed a nurse for Lily, Jessie took an avid interest in the baby and life went on as normal.'

Ava nodded and Seb knew he hadn't told her something she didn't already know; at least insofar as Lily's parentage was concerned. She probably wondered now if her own mother was also Lily's. Seb wondered about that too, or would do but for the fact that the dates didn't jibe. Unless, of course, her mother's affair with Jason had been ongoing for longer than any of them realised. There was a resemblance between Lily and Ava but only Jason would know for sure and Seb wasn't about to ask or risk drawing attention to Ava's presence in his household.

'Does her mother, whoever she is, ever try to get in touch with Lily?'

'No. Jessie is the only mother Lily has known and I'm happy for it to stay that way.' He leaned back in his chair, watching her intently, which was no great hardship.

'I wonder why she didn't keep Lily: this mystery woman. I can understand that your old man wouldn't let his sons go, he had plans for you all. But a daughter whom he considered to be damaged...' She spread her hands and let her words trail off.

'Concentrate on trying to find out what happened to your own mother, Ava. I'll help all I can but don't even think of going after my father,' he said, his voice low and firm. 'He might try to seem respectable nowadays but... well, you know what they say about leopards...'

'I know.' She sighed. 'I don't really understand what I hope to achieve now I'm here, talking to you. I hadn't thought beyond this point.' She changed her mind about a refill, stood up and helped herself. Seb watched her, enjoying the elegant way in which she moved. It reminded him of her mother, who, he remembered, had been equally sophisticated and yet natural with it. 'I suppose,' she added, sitting down with her replenished drink and taking a delicate sip, 'that I just wanted to see if I could trust you before making decisions.'

'And since we're having this conversation, I assume you've made up your mind already.' He cocked a brow. 'Sure you wanna put your faith in an ex-con?'

She laughed, an uncontrived sound that lifted Seb's spirits. 'I've seen you with Lily, so if you're intending to put on a hard man act, that ship has already sailed.'

'Damn!' He slapped his thigh, making them both laugh.

'Seriously though, Seb, you want to know who killed Blythe and I need to find out what really happened to my mother. Surely we can help one another. I can go places that you can't and vice versa. I have never believed that my mother walked out on us of her own free will and once I discovered that she might have been having an affair with a criminal… well, I had to know more. I did my research into your family, then this job came up and it seemed like it was supposed to be.'

Seb shook his head. 'My father will take one look at you and recognise your mother.' He allowed a reflective pause. 'In fact, I'm surprised he hasn't already made the connection.'

'We've never met.'

'Perhaps not but he will have eyes on Lily and will already know all about you.' She shuddered and Seb could see that her involuntarily reaction had annoyed her. 'He's probably recognised your name. What is your mother's?'

'Melanie. Melanie Harper.'

Seb shook his head. 'Doesn't ring a bell.'

'In answer to your earlier suggestion, I doubt if Jason would have recognised my name. I dare say a dozen women have passed through his life since my mother's day and he will have forgotten all about her. Anyway, even if he has made the connection between my mother and me, why would he care?'

'That rather depends upon what's happened to your mother.'

Ava looked aghast. 'Surely you don't think he killed her? I never really imagined... I mean, I just supposed that she was... I don't know, too ashamed, I guess, to come home. Or perhaps she tried to but Dad wasn't having it.' She sucked thoughtfully at her index finger. 'But then again, if he'd known what happened to her, he wouldn't have started looking for answers so that won't fly.' She threw up her hands. 'Oh hell, I guess I've been trying to avoid thinking the worst.'

Seb let out a long breath. 'If that possibility hasn't already crossed your mind, then you really are in way over your head.'

'Yeah, I suppose, but anyway...' She put her glass down and leaned forward, elbows planted on knees, a determined expression gracing her features. 'About this partnership of ours...'

'What partnership?' Seb shook his head decisively. 'I don't recall agreeing to anything.'

'No, but you will.' She sent him a confident smile. 'Otherwise, Lily will have to live in this gilded cage for the rest of her natural life.'

'Perhaps that wouldn't be such a bad thing. She's happy here, and secure.'

'But hasn't forgotten what happened to her.'

Seb's body jerked forward in his chair. 'What does she remember?'

'Snippets, usually when she's half asleep and wakes up in

terror. She says random things but doesn't seem to remember them in the cold light of day, which is a blessing.'

Seb slapped his own thigh with the flat of his hand. 'Fuck! Will this never end?'

'That's why we should broaden her horizons, in my opinion. Get her out into the wider world, mixing with people she can relate to.'

'Not until I've found out who killed Blythe.' Seb spoke emphatically. 'Whoever did so will know that I'm out for blood and will be looking to make the first strike.'

'All the more reason for us to team up.'

Seb let out a long breath. 'You don't give up, do you?'

'Nope. You're not the only one who needs answers.'

'Okay.' Seb pushed his hands towards her, palms out, as though fending off an attack. 'What else did your father find out?'

'Who's Ruby Asquith?'

'She worked for my father in his early days. She was a high-class hooker.'

'A bit like the one I saw leaving here earlier?'

Seb smiled but didn't deign to satisfy her curiosity, at least not in that respect. 'She went on to run one of his clubs. She's ambitious, has her head screwed on and finished up running all of Jason's girls. I heard recently that he's getting out of that game and that Ruby's taking over.'

'How did you hear? You were in prison.'

He shook his head and winked at her. 'In prison, not dead. The old man and Ruby had an on-again off-again affair for years.' Seb's mind briefly dwelt upon the elegant woman who'd attempted to get her claws into him when Jason ended their affair. He'd felt nothing but contempt for her then and that situation hadn't altered with the passage of time. 'Anyway, why do you ask?'

'Because her name was in my father's notes, heavily underlined. She was obviously significant but there was nothing else about her.'

'She's a hard bitch.'

'So am I when the need arises.'

'Sweetheart, she is way out of your league in that regard, which is just as well.'

'Stop being so defeatist.' She grinned at Seb. 'Perhaps we should start with her.'

# 4

Ruby watched Jason Carter swagger into her office as though he owned it, which in a way he did, she reluctantly conceded. He was still a handsome man, even if he'd gained a few pounds round the midriff, his thick silver hair was in retreat and his jowls wobbled when he walked. There was a magnetism about him though, an old-world charm that disguised the ruthlessness of a lifelong criminal who'd clawed his way out of the gutter through sheer determination, not caring what he had to do to gain a reputation as a hard man, it would be foolish to cross.

The only person who Ruby knew of who had ever defied him and got away with it was his son Seb. She withheld a shudder when she thought of the beautiful boy who'd rejected her advances none too politely, telling her bluntly that he didn't play with his father's leftovers. That had smarted, Ruby admitted to herself, and still did all these years on. She never forgot a slight but had gotten her revenge, albeit vicariously, taking great satisfaction from the fact that Seb had been banged up for six years for a crime she was pretty sure he hadn't committed.

She was far closer to Seb's age than she was to Jason's and

took good care of herself. What was not to like? Seb ought to have been grateful that she'd given him the time of day, offering to further his amatory education and introduce him to people – legitimate people – who could help him to get ahead. A lot of the movers and shakers who paid a small fortune to enjoy the services on offer from her girls would have jumped at the opportunity to help Seb, and he knew it but had treated her like something he'd scraped from the bottom of his shoe.

How fucking dare he!

She wondered if six years inside had softened him up but somehow doubted it. He was as stubborn as his father and would now be wanting to know who'd stitched him up. Ruby figured she would be high on his hit list, mainly because she'd threatened him, saying stupid things in the heat of the moment because her pride had been hurt.

And Seb would not have forgotten that. Ergo, she would use this opportunity with Jason to get her side of the story across. She'd held stuff back from him until now and although she knew he'd get mad, he would also protect her if it became necessary. He had no choice. They were business partners and the business in question wouldn't bear too close a scrutiny.

'Jason.' Ruby stood, smoothing down the sleek lines of a red dress that clung to her curves as she smiled at her old mentor, lover and partner as he glided across the thick carpet, his ridiculously shiny shoes sinking into the pile. 'It's been too long.'

She reached up to kiss each of his cheeks in turn. He responded by giving her a hefty slap on the rear, as though she was a horse. Ruby tried not to wince.

'Looking good, old girl.'

'Not so much of the old,' she replied, turning to the drinks cabinet and pouring him a healthy measure of single malt without asking him what he'd like. Jason's habits hadn't changed in all the years she'd known him. Nor had those of his younger two sons, she thought, glancing at the screens and noticing them both disappearing into rooms with two of her best girls. She knew that they'd expect freebies. In fairness, it was still their father's operation, at least until the agreement had been signed, so they would get whatever they asked for.

She glanced at the document that lay in the centre of her desk, wondering why Jason hadn't brought his lawyer with him so they could get it out of the way today.

'You didn't bring Barry?' she asked casually, filling her champagne flute and raise her glass to Jason in a salute. 'I thought you might take the opportunity to kill two birds with one stone, so to speak.'

'Why would I need my brief? You were the one who asked for a casual meeting.'

'Sure, but I just thought...' Her words trailed off since there was nothing to say. She'd opened her mouth without thinking; always a mistake when dealing with Jason.

Jason took a chair, crossed his legs and fastidiously adjusted the fall of his well-tailored trousers. He had always been a good dresser, even in the days when he couldn't afford to be. The modern trend for casual had passed him by and he wore a three-piece suit with a crisp white shirt and scarlet tie. He had told Ruby once that you were less likely to be challenged if you dressed the part and walked the walk. It seemed he still lived by that mantra.

'Anyway, you're here now.' Ruby lifted a shoulder, anxious to justify herself when Jason didn't respond. She was supposed to be doing Jason a favour by taking the clubs off his books and showing just how anxious she was could be something he'd use against her in the negotiations if he didn't react well to what she was about to tell him. Not that there was much likelihood of him being anything other than seething, she knew, but she needed to tell him herself before the shit hit the fan. 'I just thought you wanted rid...' She waved a hand in an expansive arc. 'Too many nosey bastards wanting to know what goes on here, you said.'

Hell, why was she chuntering on? Jason had that effect on her. The way he looked at her sometimes made her want to spill her guts. She would hate to get on the wrong side of him; even now when he'd never see sixty again, he was still a dangerous force to be reckoned with.

'So I did.' He took a sip of his drink and glanced at the array of screens. It was getting late and all the girls were busy. 'Christ, that boy of mine has got a fucking flabby arse!'

Ruby followed the direction of Jason's gaze and was confronted by the sight of Ray's buttocks wobbling as he thrust himself into one of Ruby's girls. 'Too much easy living,' she said, grinning and looking away.

'Turn that stuff off. Do you get off on watching it?'

Ruby dutifully pressed a button and the screens went blank. 'I like to make sure that it's business as usual and that none of the girls are being persuaded to give extras on the side.' She shrugged. 'It happens. Especially with the newbies. You taught me never to trust anyone.'

'What's on your mind, Ruby? I hope the old bill ain't been sticking their noses in again. The bastards are still trying to pin something on me and don't much care how they go about it. It ain't enough that they banged my son up on a trumped-up charge. It's me they really want.'

'Haven't you got enough of them in your pocket to get advance warning when they're onto you?'

Jason shrugged. 'That's not the point.'

'Everything is running sweet as a nut here. I make sure of that.' Ruby tried not to take offence at the suggestion of her being anything other than professional. She also resented the fact that Jason was taunting her. Jason had been apoplectic when Seb had been fitted up, convinced that one of Ruby's punters would know who was behind it. He'd told her to offer a generous reward for information but none had been forthcoming. She hadn't known anything definite at the time, and still didn't now but she fully understood the value of self-preservation and it was time to finally tell Jason what she suspected before Seb rooted it out, as he very likely would. She tucked an escaped strand of hair behind her ear and got to the point. 'Seb's out,' she said.

Jason shook his head. 'You think I don't know that?'

'Have you seen him?'

Ruby knew she'd said the wrong thing when a dark frown invaded Jason's brow. Seb was Jason's favourite, always had been. He was also the one person he'd never been able to influence, to control. His failure in that regard had eaten away at him back in the day, and clearly still did.

'What do you really want, Ruby?' Jason asked, a dangerous edge to his voice.

'Seb will want to know who set him up. He'll come looking for answers.'

'Well, it wasn't me and it had fucking well better not have been you.' Ruby tried not to tremble when Jason fixed her with an icy glower. 'I know your pride was hurt when he rejected you.' He gave a mirthless chuckle in response to her astonished look. 'Oh yes, I know you came onto him, heavy like, but even you wouldn't have fitted him up. You don't have that sort of a death wish.'

'It's not that straightforward, Jason. Things in our line of work seldom are.' She reached out a hand and stroked her blood red nails down his thigh. He showed no reaction but didn't slap her hand away either, which she took as an encouraging sign. She had always known how to push Jason's buttons. Still had what it took to get him thinking with his cock.

'Tell me what you know and why I'm only hearing it now,' he said curtly.

'I don't actually *know* anything, but I have unsubstantiated suspicions.' Jason raised a brow and waited her out in silence. 'It was about six months before the attack on poor little Lily.'

Jason did slap her hand away now, just as it had crept towards his hardening cock, and his frown if anything grew more forbidding. 'Go on,' he grunted.

'I was in a restaurant with some would-be investors for the dog racing,' she said, referring to a syndicate that Jason had allowed her to handle. It hadn't been lucrative enough for his taste. Besides, the authorities had tightened up on race fixing, making it even harder to make a dishonest profit. 'Seb came in with Lily and she caught the attention of my clients. One client in particular.'

'Which client?'

Ruby swallowed. 'James Bishop,' she said, sitting back and waiting for an explosion that didn't materialise.

The Bishops were now Jason's rivals in the South London underworld. They co-existed in suspicious disharmony for the most part, keeping clear of one another's operations, but there was friction. Always friction. Jason and Mike Bishop, James's father, had grown up together and had once been firm friends, building up a reputation in Stockwell as men to be reckoned with. But they had fallen out over something and even Ruby didn't know what had made them carve up their enterprises and go their separate ways.

'Did Bishop approach my daughter?' Jason asked in a deceptively mild tone.

'No, but he couldn't take his eyes off her and asked me who

she was.'

'He would have fucking well known.' Jason rubbed the side of his index finger across his lips as he absorbed what Ruby had just told him. He had told Ruby once, in a rare moment of confession, that he regretted abandoning his only daughter. Well, the only daughter that Ruby knew of; there could be more. He probably regretted it partly because his ruthlessness precluded any reconciliation between him and Seb who made no secret of the fact that he adored his half-sister and hated Jason for abandoning his responsibilities.

'We know Blythe was the one who attacked Lily; that's never been in doubt,' Ruby said, hating the fact that she sounded so defensive. 'That's why I never told you about James's reaction to her. He couldn't have got to her. He didn't because, as I say, we know Blythe was the guilty party and that his DNA was already on the database. And as far as I know. Blythe has no connection to the Bishops.'

'You stupid bitch!'

Jason sprang from his chair and slapped Ruby's face so hard that her head snapped back and her neck cracked ominously. She felt dizzy and her vision blurred. But she barely felt the pain. Instead, she was terrified about what Jason might do to her next. She'd seen him burn one of her girls with a lighted cigarette once because she failed to please a high-ranking copper he'd been cultivating.

In all the years she had known Jason though, she had never seen him in such a rage. She had seen him pummel a man half to death with his fists but he had done so without losing control.

Now he was completely out of control and she cowered away from him, worried that this time he wouldn't stop until she... well, stopped breathing.

'Jason, please!' She held up her hands to protect her face. 'I was trying to prevent a war breaking out between you and Bishop. I didn't have any direct evidence of his involvement and convinced myself that he couldn't have had anything to do with it.'

'You know what you've done, don't you? I've often suspected Bishop's hand all over this business. He had an axe to grind. Seb is legit and the only way to pin anything on him would be if anything happened to Lily. Which, in case I need to remind you, it fucking well did!' Jason was roaring now. 'You've made me seem like a cunt who can't look after his own; that's what you've done.'

'But how? Why?' Ruby shook her fuzzy head. 'I don't see how.'

'Of course you don't you silly mare.' Jason raised a hand but dropped it again without slapping her. 'James taking a liking to Lily gave Mike the opportunity he'd been looking for to make me look stupid. And it worked.'

Ruby nodded, finally joining the dots. Seeing what should have been obvious to her before now, had she realised just how deep the antipathy between Jason and Mike Bishop actually ran. But Jason had always been tight-lipped on the subject. There had been no pillow talk between them and he went into a rage as often as not at the mention of Bishop's name, so everyone close to him had learned to... well, not mention it.

Blythe had raped Lily, there was no doubt about that, but he had only done so *after* Lily had caught James's eye at the dog track. Could James have seen a way to set his father and Jason at one another's throats? There was no doubting that Bishop had gained financially when the two men had carved up their joint enterprises, mainly because Jason had been distracted at the time by the allegations subsequently levelled against Seb.

It was just after Lily's attack and Seb's subsequent arrest that he'd started letting his grip on his criminal enterprises loosen and turned mostly legit.

Mostly.

And who had he let his interests go to?

The Bishops.

'Fuck!' Ruby muttered.

'You realise what you've done. You've only gone and started an all-out war,' Jason growled. 'Don't be surprised if you get caught in the crossfire.'

'But, Jason, I had no actual proof,' she bleated, hating the whiny edge to her voice. 'You were so wound up at the time that I didn't want to open my fat gob and make matters worse.'

'You've made me look like a nob who can't tie his shoelaces,' he grunted. 'You'll live to regret that.'

Ruby nodded mutely, realising now it was too late to change things that she'd screwed up. She thought that by telling him what she suspected it would get her back into Jason's, perhaps even Seb's, good graces. Especially Seb's. But she now realised that she'd made matters worse. Or more to the point, hadn't told Jason about the incident with Lily when it occurred. But she hadn't wanted to start a war and knew that by speaking out, she'd make an enemy out of one side or the other. She'd stayed at the top of her game by knowing how to keep her mouth shut. Perhaps on this occasion she should have broken that particular rule, she thought, now that it was too late to turn the clock back.

'Don't mention what we've just talked about to anyone,' he said, walking across to her desk, picking up the agreement she hoped he would eventually sign and dropping it symbolically in the bin. 'The deal's off but you are not off the hook yourself by any manner or means.'

He left her room and slammed the door behind him. She heard his voice, bellowing to his sons, and shuddered, wondering what the hell she'd set in motion.

# 5

Lily had a passion for embroidery, and endless patience that enabled her to produce the most exquisite work. Ava, who couldn't sew to save her life, was in awe of her talent. Lily sat now in the corner of the kitchen, totally engrossed with what she was doing. Wizard lay at her feet, snoring softly.

Ava smiled as she watched her, envying the girl her inner peace. Despite her disabilities, Lily was content, but for the occasional bad dream and the odd tantrum.

She glanced out the window and noticed Seb and John climbing into the back of a car driven by Mark. She knew that Seb had been to see Lily earlier and had spent some time with her, but he'd barely exchanged two words with Ava. He seemed different that morning; a million miles away from the relaxed individual whom she'd spent more than an hour alone with the previous night.

Today it was almost as though he was emphasising the fact that he was her employer by remaining detached, aloof. Perhaps, having had time to digest what she'd told him about her mother, he'd decided she was more trouble than she was worth and wanted rid of her. She couldn't blame him for that; he'd had more than enough grief. Even so, she glanced at Lily and her heart lurched at the prospect of being separated from her. Hopefully Seb would put his sister's interests first and keep her on. Either way, his attitude wouldn't deter Ava from getting answers. If her mother was still alive then somehow Ava would find her and demand those answers in person.

'What do you make of my boy?' Jessie asked her, following the direction of Ava's gaze. 'Handsome, ain't he,' she added, beaming with pride, as though she was in some way responsible for his good looks. Ava had witnessed their reunion; Jessie had wept openly and even tough Seb had seemed moved as he embraced the older woman and swung her off her feet.

'Oh yes, no question. But he's remote too. A man of few words.' She patted Jessie's hand. 'He spoke about you with great affection last night.'

Jessie beamed. 'What he's been through, the injustice of it all, is enough to make anyone resentful. He always was thoughtful though, even as a lad. We all thought he'd serve half his sentence, then get out on licence. But, of course, he would have had to admit to his crime and express remorse in front of the parole board, and that he would never do, simply because he didn't kill Blythe.'

'A man of principle.'

'You would have to be to defy his father.' Jessie settled herself into a more comfortable position. 'Of course, the only evidence against him was planted; taken from this house, or somewhere, and planted.'

Ava gasped. 'Who by?'

'Well, there's the question. I've always suspected your predecessor. A flaky girl called Diane. She didn't take good enough care of Lily but none of us noticed at the time. We have to live with that.'

'It wasn't your fault, Jessie,' Ava said, covering the older woman's hand with her own.

'I should have noticed.' She paused. 'I call her a girl but actually she was a young woman, your age. She'd qualified as a nurse but then took time off to look after her ailing mother until she died. Didn't want to go back into nursing after that and saw this position as a good compromise. Didn't have much of a life of her own... well, not until that waste of space guy came into her life.' Jessie heaved a sigh. 'Anyway, as to Seb, it's good to have him back. I hated the thought of him being locked up in that place with all those criminals. He's always been such a sensitive boy. Unlike his brothers, he'd consider what he wanted to say before saying it and only speak when he has something worthwhile to say. Most people, me included, babble away regardless.' Jessie laughed good-humouredly. 'I began to think they'd never let him out until he confessed. They had to, of course, once he'd served his time.' Jessie rippled her shoulders indignantly. 'I knew he wouldn't admit to the murder though because he didn't do it. Now that he's out, I only hope he doesn't do anything stupid that will land him back inside again.'

Ava nodded. 'You think he will try to find out who really killed Blythe?'

'Well, wouldn't you in his situation?' Jessie asked, folding her arms defiantly, clearly ready to support Seb even if she didn't agree with his actions.

Ava tilted her head, pretending to give consideration to a question that required no real thought. 'Yes, I suppose I would.'

And with a bit of luck, his investigations would turn up something on her own mother too. Ava considered raising the question of her mother with Jessie. She had been tempted to on several occasions but had resisted the urge to unburden herself.

If her mother had been involved with Jason Carter then according to Ava's calculations, they would have got together after Seb had parted company with his father and Jessie had left with him. She probably wouldn't know anything for that reason alone. Besides, it wasn't fair to drag Jessie into her search for answers. She knew that the older lady had little time for Jason Carter though and Ava wasn't averse to encouraging her to talk about him.

'Do you think Jason will try and see Seb?' she asked.

'Oh, I expect so. All his criminal friends will be watching the situation avidly. Of course, it's no secret that father and son were estranged but it will suit Jason's purpose to give the impression of a reconciliation. Jason's going more and more legit, like I told you, and will want his enemies to know that he has Seb's back. Not that Seb will like it seeming as though he needs his old man's protection but there's not a lot he can do about it.' Jessie sighed. 'Seb is as pig-headed as Jason, I'm afraid. There's going to be trouble; I can sense it.'

Ava rather thought that Seb, what little she knew of him, would not tolerate *any* situation that made him uncomfortable and would probably want to emphasise to the world that he and Jason were still estranged. 'Jason will want it to look as though they're reconciled, either to save face or to show his support for his son?'

Jessie nodded. 'Very likely. Seb will have to see him at some point, if only to re-establish boundaries and, I suspect, to pick his brains about Blythe's actual killer.'

Ava gasped. 'Surely, if Jason knew anything about that he would have gotten word to Seb already?'

Jessie smiled. 'That isn't the way it works. Besides, the police would never accept evidence produced by Jason, especially if it wasn't obtained legally, which it almost certainly wouldn't be. Jason uses brawn. Seb has always depended on his brains. And I know which side I would prefer to be on in the event of a confrontation.'

'Let's hope it doesn't come to that,' Ava replied.

'Aye well, we can certainly hope but I've worked for this family for a long time and I can smell trouble in the air.'

All well and good, Ava thought when Lily called her to come and see her work, but that didn't help her much in her own quest for answers. She had been pinning her hopes on Seb somehow waving a magic wand and sorting it all out in a stroke of genius. She realised now how naïve she'd been. Sighing, she got up and went over to Lily's chair.

'Show me,' she said, smiling. 'Goodness, Lily, that's amazing.' And it was truly a work of art; a complicated pattern depicting a dog that looked remarkably like Wizard chasing a ball, and all done without the benefit of a pattern.

'I want to show Seb,' she said.

'And we will, darling, I promise you, as soon as he gets back. Now, come on, let's take Wizard for a walk in the woods.'

* * *

Seb felt his guts slowly uncoiling as he looked at the reassuringly loyal faces of Sam, Patrick, Mark and John. Without their unswerving devotion, he would likely have come out after doing his time with nothing more to his name than debts and a burning desire to find out who'd stitched him up. A desire that *did* burn as fiercely as ever but about which he would have been able to do sod all without the means to kick a few backsides.

'You've all run a tight ship in my absence,' Seb told them. 'I'm grateful.'

'Don't go getting all sentimental on us, boss,' Pat said, clearly speaking for them all. 'I'll tear up if you ain't careful.'

Everyone laughed.

'Tell me what I need to know,' Seb said, all business now.

'A few sharks have circled but I warded them off,' Sam replied. 'Anyway, it's good to have you back boss. All this responsibility has given me a headache. It's been tough; I won't deny it.'

The others nodded their agreement.

Seb smiled as he leaned back in his chair, aware that Sam had thrived on the responsibility and didn't take bullshit from anyone. 'Okay, let's get down to it. How much interference has there been from Jason?' Seb seldom referred to his father by anything other than his Christian name.

'He tried to muscle in at first, but we knew he would.' Mark's expression turned uncompromisingly grim. 'When I wouldn't let him get his grubby hands on your sister, he said he'd find out who set you up and get you out. You only had to give him the go-ahead.'

'Like the Crown Prosecution Service would take any notice of evidence produced by him,' John growled.

Seb nodded, wondering if Jason should have started by looking closer to home. Seb's hot-headed brothers used violence as casually as the majority of men downed a swift pint after a hard day's work. They resented Seb's unwelcome popularity with their father and Seb wouldn't bet against them doing whatever was necessary to wipe him out of the picture. He had no actual proof but Seb did wonder if one or both brothers had 'avenged' their sister's rape by offing the man responsible for the attack. Not that they'd ever wanted anything to do with Lily but to idiots of their limited intelligence, any attack on a family member was an attack upon the Carters' reputation, a personal affront that had to be brutally confronted in order to save face.

'My not running to Jason to bail me out won't have prevented him from doing some delving.'

But if the evidence had pointed towards his brothers, then Jason would have been left between a rock and a hard place. Sacrifice one or both brothers in order to rescue Seb, who wanted nothing to do with Jason, and risk becoming a laughing stock in the process because his family was feuding and out of control. Seb didn't think it was likely that Jason would take that course. Besides, his brothers still appeared to be fully fit and enjoying the fruits of Jason's illegal gains, so presumably there was no evidence to be found against them anyway.

'You still think Blythe's killing was a direct dig at Jason?' Sam asked.

'Don't you? What have you managed to unearth, Mark? I know you couldn't tell me everything when you sent your reports in with Pat's visits – walls have ears and all that. Besides, it was better if I didn't know. Jumping to conclusions when you're banged up and can't do anything about your suspicions can drive a man mental.'

'Well, James Bishop was shouting his mouth off in a pub not long after you went down,' Mark said. 'I heard him with me own lug holes.'

Seb sat forward, alert and very interested in a possibility that hadn't previously occurred to him. Surely Jason's rift with the Bishops didn't run that deep. But he did vaguely recall James Bishop at a dog race meeting ogling Lily. It had made him uncomfortable and the noise at the track had upset Lily anyway, so he'd left. 'About what?' he asked mildly, conscious of his heart hammering against his ribcage. Perhaps it had been wrong to stop Mark getting word to him. Not that he could have done anything about it, but still...

Mark scratched his whiskery chin with a large paw. 'It seemed a bit contrived to me, which is why I didn't say anything before now. You and I both know that the Bishops and your old man used to be joined at the hip but are now deadly rivals.' Mark shrugged. 'Anyway, James was banging on about what happened to Lily and how he could understand a man losing it over her. He'd seen me and was probably looking for a reaction, so I didn't oblige.' Mark sniffed. 'He also said he knew who'd done Blythe.'

'What the fuck!' Seb sat forward in his chair. 'Did you believe him?'

'Nah.' Mark waved the suggestion aside. 'He saw me watching him, grinned and then said it, just loud enough for me to hear. Could be that Bishop hoped Jason would take his eye off the ball; either that or he wanted the last word in their long-standing grudge and James saw an opportunity to use me as a means to stir the pot. Fucked if I know.'

'It would help, of course, if we knew why Bishop and Jason fell out,' Sam reminded them all. 'Can't see the attack on Lily having anything to do with it myself. The timing's all wrong.'

Mark scowled, clearly still feeling responsible when he hadn't even been on duty on the day of the attack. If anyone was to blame, it was Seb, which is one of the reasons why he hadn't taken the easy way out, pride notwithstanding. He didn't deserve to be free when Lily herself would never be able to put the experience from her damaged mind. Ava said she was content but Seb had already noticed the frowns that sometimes invaded her pretty face and sensed that she wasn't the sunny creature she had been before the attack.

'It all came out, that Blythe had raped Lily. I mean, once his body was found,' Seb pointed out, feeling the need to articulate the guilt he'd been living with for so long. 'The police knew Lily had been attacked because that stupid mare, Diane Frobisher, called them in. If you can call what she did caring. Seems to me she spent more time on her phone to her boyfriend, but that's on me.' Seb threw his head back and sucked air through his teeth. 'Took Lily to the park on a day when you were off, Mark, and I was away on business. She had specific instructions not to leave the house without you but used the opportunity to meet up with the scrote she was dating and left Lily alone.' Seb thumped his thigh with his clenched fist. 'I should have vetted the hired help more carefully.'

'Then Blythe got offed, and you got fitted up for it, Seb,' John said, nodding along with everyone else. 'Even though there was no firm evidence. It was a total stitch up.'

'There was evidence,' Seb reminded them. 'That old baseball cap of mine covered in my DNA found at the scene.'

'After the third search,' Mark growled. 'And a witness who conveniently saw you at the time and has disappeared off the face of the earth since your conviction. Never thought a jury would fall for it, but there you have it. Of course, they didn't, not all of them, which is why the judge accepted a majority verdict.'

'Leaving aside the fact that you almost never wear a cap,' Pat said. 'I'd still like to know how it got there.'

'Diane might have set you up,' Sam pointed out. 'She could have taken it from your room at any time. And since she disappeared off the face of the earth too before the trial, it seemed bloody suspicious to me.'

Everyone nodded.

'But you refused to let me try and find her,' Sam said, driving home his point.

'I haven't forgotten about her,' Seb assured them all. 'But there was no point in your harassing her and getting yourselves in trouble with the law. This is my fight. Did you find out anything about the kid she was seeing at the time, Pat?'

Pat shook his head. 'Name of Gary Bennett. That's all I've been able to find out.'

'It seems highly suspicious to me that he scarpered as soon as Diane found out what had happened to Lily, in broad fucking daylight,' John said. 'Behind a few bushes and no one saw or heard a thing. And Diane reckons she didn't know where Bennett lived. Met him in the local but I flashed the cash, as you are aware, and no one could remember seeing him there.' John scratched his chin. 'I've always thought those two were paid to set you up but you wouldn't let me run them down, Seb.' He rubbed the back of his neck aggressively. 'It's fucking frustrating.'

Seb nodded. 'Don't worry about it. We'll get there. Despite the fact that it seems obvious, I'm not convinced Diane was involved; at least not intentionally. You've been concentrating on Bennett, John. Forget him. I have a feeling that isn't his real name. But we know Diane was kosher. If she wasn't, they were the best forged references I've ever seen. She'll still be around somewhere, even if she's married and changed her name. Now's the time for you to see what you can find on her.'

'Finally!'

'There wasn't much point while I was locked up. Besides, she will have stopped looking over her shoulder by now, I would imagine. Thinks she's safe from reprisals.'

'In her dreams,' Sam groused.

'I heard Blythe sometimes worked for Bishop,' Pat said. 'But he got hooked on the old nose candy and became unreliable. He could well have screwed an assignment up, pissed off someone totally unrelated to our situation and wound up dead for that reason.'

'Possibly.' Seb waggled a hand from side to side as he considered the possibility. 'And if Bishop bumped him off, he could have heard somehow about the rape, perhaps even ordered it, although I doubt he would stoop that low, then saw an opportunity to even the score with Jason by setting me up.' Seb paused to reflect. 'Don't see it myself. The Bishop boys aren't the brightest of sparks but they know how to keep their mouths shut. Which makes me wonder why he bragged about Blythe in front of you, Mark.'

'Yeah well, like I said,' Mark replied, 'that set alarm bells ringing but I deliberately didn't react. They wouldn't be that fucking stupid.'

Seb ground his jaw. 'He was using you to goad Jason then.'

'Or would have been if I'd passed on what Mark had overheard, but I didn't,' Pat pointed out. 'I didn't want to start a gang war and I'm pretty sure that word didn't get back to Jason through anyone else; otherwise the warfare I wanted to prevent would have broken out regardless. Wiser heads obviously prevailed. Either that, or self-preservation kicked in.'

'Or,' Sam said quietly, 'going back to Bennett, he could have cultivated Diane on Bishop's orders.'

Seb conceded the point with an abrupt nod. 'Theories are all well and good but we need a few hard facts and finding them six years after the event will be challenging.'

'Challenges are what we do best,' John replied.

'I never did get to the bottom of the falling out between Jason and Bishop,' Seb said into the ensuing silence, 'but there is definitely bad blood between them now.'

'To the extent that they would stitch you up for murder?' Sam looked highly sceptical.

Seb shrugged. 'Hard to say without knowing what it is that came between them.'

'The only way to find that out is to ask Jason, which I suspect you would prefer not to do,' John said. 'There's no saying that he'd tell you the truth even if you did ask. Besides, he'd want to know why you were so interested in ancient history.'

'Perhaps Dameon...' Seb let the suggestion, a suggestion that had been in the forefront of Seb's mind for the duration of his stretch hang in the air.

'It's possible,' Sam conceded.

Seb was referring to Jason's oldest friend. A man who kept out of the dodgy side of his business affairs and acted as advisor, gofer, wise head, calming influence and general keeper of secrets. He had also been Seb's mentor during his formative years, actively encouraging him to listen to Jessie, get a decent education and stay on the straight and narrow. Seb had an enormous amount of time for Dameon.

'They're not so close any more, I hear,' John said. 'Dameon's pushing eighty now and has earned his retirement. Anyway, what will you do about Bishop?'

'Nothing at the moment. I'm being watched by the law and undoubtedly by those responsible for knocking off Blythe. They will be expecting me to retaliate.' Seb yawned as he stretched his arms above his head. 'If nothing else, being locked up has taught me the value of patience. I will perhaps have a chat with Dameon. I'd like to see him anyway. He wrote to me regularly whilst I was inside and, like you just said, he's not getting any younger.'

'Dameon would be a good place to start and won't attract too much interest,' John said, nodding.

'What do you make of Ava?' Seb asked in an abrupt change of subject.

'She's a little ray of sunshine.' Sam smiled and his comment was greeted by confirmatory nods from every man in the room. 'Lily adores her.' His smile faded. 'Why? Do you have doubts about her? I'd be surprised if you've dug up anything to her detriment. Believe me, John checked her reference every which way. Once bitten and all that and she's been perfect.'

'We know how protective you can be,' Pat added.

'Not nearly fucking protective enough,' Seb replied, scowling.

'Don't beat yourself up. You can't change the past,' John said. 'Anyway, I gather the two of you had a long chat last night. What was that all about?'

'Her mother went missing when she was eighteen. Did you know that?'

'Fuck!' Pat shared a bewildered look with the rest of them. 'She kept that quiet.'

Seb scowled. 'Then you won't know either that Jason could have been knocking her old lady off.'

'Hell! She's here looking for answers.' Sam vigorously scratched the outside of his thigh. 'I thought she was too good to be true. She and Jessie are as thick as thieves, you know. They sit with their heads together in the kitchen, chattering away about anything and nothing. I thought it was nice that Ava had found a friend. It can be lonely for a girl of her age, stuck in this mausoleum.' Sam's expression turned aggressive. 'Perhaps now I understand why she's really here.'

'I doubt whether Jessie could have enlightened her about Jason's women,' Seb said. 'He's always been careful about flaunting them in front of the help.'

'Jessie still has eyes in her head,' John said mildly.

Seb shifted his position and nodded. 'I do remember him having a woman who looked a lot like Ava on his arm, and for far longer than they usually lasted.'

'If Ava's ma disappeared and Jason had something to do with that disappearance then it's not something he would have shouted about.' Sam frowned. 'But why would he have needed to take such extreme measures? We all know that he wouldn't balk at knocking off a rival but women and children are off limits. He's old-fashioned that way. He'd be more likely to just pay her off and send her packing.'

'True.' Seb tapped his fingers against the surface of his desk. 'Makes you wonder though. I mean, if she was as inquisitive as her daughter appears to be, and as tenacious, there's a possibility that she might have heard something she shouldn't. Then again, perhaps Ava didn't know the true state of her parents' marriage. She reckoned they were a match made in heaven but she was a teenager when her mum disappeared so what did she really know?'

Sam sighed. 'I take it you've offered to help her find answers.'

'I said I'd see what I can do. I can understand what drives her. Besides, as you say, Lily likes her so I would prefer it if she stays.'

John chuckled. 'I'm sure you would. She certainly brightens the place up.'

Seb grunted but refrained from comment.

'Do you have plans to see Jason, or your brothers?' Pat asked.

'I rather think they'll come to me and yes, I will see them, but only after I've sounded Daemon out.' Seb paused. 'Are you sure no other word has reached you regarding possible suspects? I find it hard to imagine that nothing was said.' He paused. 'Ruby Asquith for example.'

'Ruby?' Sam's eyebrows shot up. 'Why would she...'

'Blythe was one of her regulars when she was still on the game. He'd have done anything she asked him to, for a price, including attacking Lily.'

Pat nodded slowly. 'And Ruby had a hard-on for you but you didn't reciprocate. I seem to recall that you didn't exactly let her down gently either.'

'That's because she wouldn't take no for an answer, but here's the thing: Ava found some notes her father had made regarding his wife's disappearance after he died.' Seb paused. 'Ruby's name was heavily underlined.'

'Holy fuck!' Sam stared at the others as he shook his head. 'Ruby was infatuated with Jason. If he was seeing Ava's mum on the side and not being especially discreet about it, it might explain why she transferred her affection to you, or tried to. Assuaging her hurt pride with a younger man, and all that. What's the mother's name?'

'Melanie Harper.'

'Well, if he was flaunting Melanie and it looked like something more than a temporary fling, there's nothing I wouldn't put past that bitch Ruby. You wouldn't fall in with her plans but she would have known all about your attachment to Lily, so...'

'I hear you,' Seb replied sombrely. 'But I don't buy it. Even Ruby isn't that ruthless.'

'Don't count her out,' Mark advised. 'Remember she's in the sex trade and would likely use sex as her go-to weapon of choice. Even so, it does seem unlikely. Just don't dismiss her, that's all I'm saying.'

'Yeah right, well, we'll have to see.' Seb stood. 'Come on, John. Take me to the new site. I wanna see the layout for the new apartments in situ.'

John grinned as he also stood. 'My pleasure. It will be like old times.'

No, Seb thought but didn't say, it wouldn't. He'd changed. Prison had changed him. Being convicted of a crime he hadn't committed had changed him beyond recognition and nothing would ever be the same again.

# 6

Seb was conscious of far more workers than had reason to be on that part of the site swarming around the gateway, finding excuses to linger as they gawped at him. All were new faces to Seb and obviously keen to get a sight of their notorious boss whose reputation preceded him. Notorious for all the reasons Seb had struggled his entire life to avoid, he thought, gritting his teeth.

He had learned inside to accept what couldn't be changed and so merely nodded at the men without breaking stride. He shook hands with his foreman, Dave Wright, a man who'd been with him since the early days, grateful that his loyalty had endured.

'Good to have you back, Seb,' Dave said. 'It ain't been the same without your ugly mug around the place.'

'It hasn't exactly been a picnic where I've been residing.'

Dave laughed. 'The bastards who fitted you up. Any ideas?'

'A few.'

'Well, I've been keeping my ear to the ground and come up with sod all.' Dave scratched the back of his neck, partially dislodging the hard hat that he wore on the back of his head like a pimple. 'Someone's running scared. Too scared to grass, that's all I know.'

'Don't worry about it, Dave.' Seb slapped his foreman's meaty shoulder. 'I'll get it sorted.'

'Yeah, well I hope you do. What happened to you was a travesty.'

Seb and John, with Mark standing back, alert to the first sign of trouble, spent an hour in the office at the site, going over the plans. Seb found a few areas where changes were needed and Dave promised to implement them.

'We've sold almost all the units off plan,' Dave said, a note of pride entering his voice, and rightly so. 'Our reputation for solid, affordable housing has preceded us.'

'Good to hear,' Seb replied.

It had always been his plan to help those at the bottom of the food chain to get started. Sure, they sold high-end units to the wealthy at inflated prices, but this enabled them to do the start-ups. It was one of the few aspects of his operation that had continued to give Seb satisfaction during his time inside and had only been possible because he'd surrounded himself with loyal people whom he paid well and trusted implicitly.

Satisfied that all was as it should be, Seb had Mark drive them to a restaurant where he had once been a regular and which was still in business. He was greeted effusively by the lady owner who found them a table at once, despite the fact that there was a line of people waiting to be seated ahead of them.

It felt good to be treated with respect again rather than being told what to do and when to do it, right down to when to eat and when to go to bed.

Normal service resumed.

Or would be, once he'd cleared his name.

'The sweet taste of freedom,' he said, raising his glass to John's and feeling as though a small burden had been lifted from his shoulders. But the balance of the weight he carried would, he knew, continue to wear him down until such time as he found out who had killed Blythe.

And why he'd been fitted up for the crime.

Returning home after a superb lunch, he sat in his Aston Martin and the engine purred into life on the first turn of the key. His private vehicles had been meticulously maintained by Mark during his absence and Seb patted the dashboard affectionately, thinking the car was getting dangerously close to earning classic status. That was okay. Old wasn't necessarily a bad thing.

'We all have to get old,' he told the car as he backed it out the garage and set out for Dameon's abode ten miles away, wondering if by talking to a car he might actually be cracking up. Possibly, but who gave a shit, he wondered. He'd had to spend every second of every hour of every day for the past six years watching his back, never showing the slightest sign of weakness. It would have been pounced upon by Jason's rivals inside and Seb would have paid for the sins of the father through a beating, or worse.

Now he could do what the fuck he liked and if he liked talking to his car, he damned well would.

He had the roof down, even though the day wasn't particularly warm. The wind whistled through his hair, reminding him that he was finally free. Reinforcing his determination never to see the inside of a jail cell again. Not that he'd done anything to end up in one in the first place. He had simply been a means to an end. Someone had used him to undermine Jason. Seb ground his jaw as the anger bubbled just below the surface; an anger that had kept him focused for six years. He had an aversion to being used by anyone, especially anyone connected to Jason and his car-wreck of a family and fully intended to redress the balance.

He slowed his car as he turned it between weathered

gateposts and the tyres crunched across weedy gravel. He halted next to a front door protected by pillars in need of a coat of paint. The rest of the façade of the old manor house looked neglected too, Seb thought, as he left his car and climbed crumbling front steps. He jangled the old-fashioned bell and waited, hearing it echoing inside the house like something out of a spooky movie. There was no responding movement from within so he rang for a second time, wondering if he'd had a wasted journey, thinking he should have phoned ahead.

Then there was shuffling.

'Okay, okay, keep your wig on,' grumbled a voice that Seb would recognise anywhere, causing a genuine smile to break out across his face. 'Wadda you want... Seb!'

Seb was taken aback to see Dameon the way he was now: a shadow of his former, robust self. He was aware that he himself had aged and still wore that tell-tale prison pallor, but Dameon was barely recognisable.

Stooped over, shabbily dressed, half his lunch spilled down his shirt, Dameon walked with the aid of a frame. The years had not been kind to the once dapper, energised man he remembered. Seb hoped that it was nothing more than the passage of time that ailed him but given the hacking cough that accompanied his words, it seemed unsafe to make that assumption.

'I thought you must be dead,' Seb replied, attempting to hide his shock with humour. 'Seems the rumours were greatly exaggerated.'

'Well, you know what they say, son. Only the good die young. Mind you, my days are numbered anyway.' He grasped Seb's hand, his grip cold and weak, then shuffled backwards, coughing again. 'Come on, come in. I heard they were letting you out and hoped you'd remember where I live.'

'Not a chance of me forgetting.'

Seb followed Dameon down a chequered hallway that was very familiar to him. The inside of the house was equally shabby, and in need of a good clean, not to mention redecoration. Either Dameon had hit upon hard times or no longer noticed or cared about his living conditions. Why hadn't Jason looked after him, he wondered. For all his faults, his father was ordinarily loyal to his friends. Then again, perhaps Dameon's pride had forced him to rebuff all offers of help.

'Too early for a tipple?' Dameon asked, walking into the sitting room and indicating a decanter on the sideboard.

'Best not. I'm driving and the old bill would just love an excuse to pull me over. I don't intend to oblige. Besides, I just had lunch so I'm good.'

'Pour me one, will you.'

Dameon sank heavily into a chair, the cushions of which had been moulded into the shape of his backside. Seb obliged and placed the glass on the table at Dameon's side.

'Cheers! Welcome to the land of freedom, if you can call it that.' Dameon raised his glass in a salute, then took a healthy swig of his scotch, which brought on another bout of coughing. Seb wanted to question the wisdom of Dameon stubbornly drinking something that clearly exacerbated his condition. He knew his concern would be frowned upon though, so kept his mouth shut. 'Sodding big brother is everywhere nowadays.'

'I hear you.'

'So, I guess you're wanting answers.' Dameon sniffed as he got straight down to the reason for Seb's visit. 'In which case, it seems to me that you need to swallow your pride and talk to Jason.'

'I will, all in good time, but I wanted to talk to you first. You might be ancient but you're still as sharp as a tack, I'm betting, and generally respected. You'll have made your own enquiries after I got banged up, I assume, and kept your ear to the ground in the meantime.'

'Never thought that would happen: that they'd make the charges stick, I mean.' Dameon scowled into his drink, as though he bore it a grudge. 'Criminal, so it was.'

'Old history, my friend.'

'And you've had a lot of time to think about it.' Dameon fixed Seb with a surprisingly astute look through faded, grey and bloodshot eyes. He clearly still had all his marbles, even if his hygiene standards and general state of health had taken a tumble. A bottle of pills sat on the table beside him, enforcing Seb's conviction that his old mentor had medical issues. But he knew better than to probe. Dameon would tell him if he wanted him to know what the problem was. 'What have you come up with?'

Seb answered the question with one of his own. 'What happened between Jason and Mike Bishop?' he asked. 'They used to be solid.'

Dameon raised both bushy brows as he regarded Seb over the rim of the glass he held in a hand that wasn't quite steady. The question had clearly taken him by surprise.

'Ask him.'

Seb shook his head, recognising procrastination when confronted by it. 'Not a chance! But I have my reasons for needing to know, which is why I'm asking you.'

'You think the Bishops might have seized on an opportunity to stitch you up?'

'I didn't, not seriously, until Mark mentioned that James Bishop had been shouting his mouth off, implying that he'd either done Blythe in himself or knew who had.' Seb frowned. 'Can't figure out why he'd do that, even if he was plastered. The boy isn't *that* stupid.'

'If word got back to Jason...'

'Quite. Mark overheard him and Mark must have been noticed in that boozer. He doesn't exactly blend in, not with his bulk.'

'Perhaps Bishop was attempting to provoke Jason into retaliating. I'm guessing that Mark and Bishop don't usually drink in the same place.'

'No, they don't, which means Bishop was on Mark's stomping ground and there for a specific purpose.'

Dameon put his glass aside and spread his hands. 'Sorry, Seb. I've been asking, you can be sure about that, but I don't have the connections that I once had and those I do have are keeping schtum. They either genuinely don't know or are too scared to open their traps. Let me delve into the Bishops now that you've put the idea into my head. They'll be on the lookout for you, but I'm an old man... no one takes me seriously any more.'

Seb nodded, even though he fully intended to carry out his own investigation. Two heads approaching from different angles was never a bad thing. And if word got back to Bishop, that might not be so bad either. Spook him into making a mistake. The upside of having served his entire sentence, if there was such a thing, meant he wasn't out on licence and the watch being kept upon him was covert as opposed to intrusive. Not that he'd actually noticed anyone watching him, but it paid to be cautious. If he put so much as one foot out of line, he wouldn't be treated so leniently a second time. And his sentence *had* been lenient; he knew that. He figured that was perhaps because Blythe's actions and unsavoury background had come out at trial and clearly disgusted the judge. 'You didn't explain why Jason and Bishop parted company. You know now that I had a valid reason for asking so come on, let's have it.'

Dameon picked his glass up again and twirled it in his hand but didn't drink. It was almost as though he was using the gesture to buy time. Perhaps Seb was asking him to be disloyal; he couldn't be sure about that and didn't much care. If Dameon decided not to tell him then he would find out by other means. All he knew was that the more Dameon prevaricated, the more convinced he became that it mattered.

That he'd hit on the crux of… well, something.

Dameon leaned forward in his chair, the exertion seeming to exhaust him, causing him to wheeze. 'Believe me when I tell you that I'm almost as much in the dark as you are but for what it's worth, I think there was a woman involved.'

Seb frowned, wondering if the woman in question could have been Ava's mother. It seemed like too much of a stretch though so Seb consigned the thought to the back of his mind. 'There always is with Jason but he wouldn't let any female come between him and lucrative business contacts.'

'That's what you'd think but…' This time Dameon did take a long swig of his scotch. 'Jason changed after that. Became even harder and less compromising and just the mention of Bishop's name sent him into a rage.'

'Yes, but you must know more than—'

'I don't.' Dameon's voice turned harsh and Seb saw a brief glimpse of the tough character he'd once been. Tough and respected. If he said he didn't know then he almost certainly didn't.

'Okay, I hear you.' Seb paused. 'So, what's Jason's take on it? Who does he think did for Blythe, much as it grieves me to ask?'

'He hasn't got anywhere either and, trust me, he's been scattering money around like confetti, looking for solid intel. As far as I know, he's got nothing but we don't talk as often as we once did. I'm out of the loop nowadays.'

'Either of my hot-headed brothers responsible, do you think?'

Dameon shrugged. 'If they were then Jason would know

about it. They can't keep their traps shut, as well you know, and would likely have bragged about it. They hate the fact that Jason prefers you, even though you've turned your back on him, and would love an opportunity to get one over on you.' Dameon flapped a hand, as though dismissing the possibility. 'Can't see it myself though. They're too heavy-handed to carry out a murder without leaving a trace, not to mention a complex fit-up.'

Dameon paused but whether to emphasise what he was about to say or because he was beset by another coughing fit, it was hard for Seb to know. He reached for the near full glass of water beside Dameon's bottle of pills and offered it to the old man, but he shook his head.

'Fish do things in water. Keep trying to tell that silly nurse what comes in but she won't have it.'

Seb smiled, his suspicions confirmed about Dameon's state of health. He would only tolerate the interference of a nurse if he had absolutely no choice in the matter. 'You're a stubborn old coot, is what you are.'

'Wait until you get to my age. Stubbornness is about the only pleasure you get. Well, that and Scotland's finest.' He lifted up his near-empty glass to emphasise his point. 'The doctors keep telling me this'll be the end of me. Better that than dying of boredom, is what I tell them.'

Seb chuckled. 'I don't doubt it. Anyway, you were about to say something important about the art of murder, I think.'

'Yeah, about those brothers of yours. If they did bump Blythe off, how did they get their hands on that hat of yours that was found at the scene?'

Seb sighed. 'I've been asking myself the same question. I vaguely recognised it as being mine. I remember the logo for Aston Martin. The car that I still have. The dealer gave me the hat when I bought the vehicle.'

Dameon tried to chuckle, but it turned into another bout of coughing. 'Good return for your dosh,' he said, when he recovered. 'You pay through the nose for a gas-guzzling penis extension and get a free hat by way of reward.'

Seb spread his hands. 'Well, when you put it like that... and no, I have no idea how either of my brothers could have got the hat. They sure as hell wouldn't have gained access to my house.'

'You didn't leave it in your car?'

'That's just the point.' Seb sighed. 'I can't remember. I hadn't seen it for years. It might have been stuffed in the glovebox. Probably was, but...'

'Okay, okay.' Dameon held up the hand not clutching his glass. 'You've had six years to remember but perhaps now you're out, something might occur to you.'

'Talking of potential murderers, or the setters-up thereof, what about Ruby?'

Dameon struggled to sit forward in his chair again. 'Now her,' he said. 'I wouldn't put anything past that vicious bitch.'

'Me neither but proving it will be even more of a bitch than you consider her to be.'

'You've heard, I suppose, that Jason's selling off all the clubs to her.'

'I did hear something.'

'Fancies himself as a big-time legit businessman nowadays and keeps threatening to retire so he can enjoy the fruits of his criminal labours. Not that he ever will, mind.' Dameon sniffed, then reached in his pocket for a handkerchief and loudly blew his nose. 'He's got all the contacts to make it happen, an' all; going legit, I mean. All the police, councillors and important people that he's bought over the years will help to pave the way or risk having their own grubby secrets revealed.'

'I thought the girls were his most lucrative asset,' Seb

remarked, leaning back and crossing one foot over the opposite thigh.

'Well, I dare say he has his reasons. It's a younger man's game anyway, keeping control of that lot.'

Seb could see that the old man was tiring, so stood up to take his leave.

'Stay where you are,' he said, when Dameon attempted to struggle to his feet. 'You'll let me know if there's anything I can do to help you?'

Dameon gave a curt nod. 'I'm doing okay, and I ain't dead yet. I'll see what I can turn up for you regarding Jason's dispute with the Bishops. It'll give me something to keep the old cogs twirling for a while longer,' he said, whirling a finger beside his temple to emphasise his point.

'Appreciate it,' Seb replied, shaking Dameon's hand and then letting himself out of the house, back into the fresh air with something akin to relief. It had been depressing in there. Depressing and claustrophobic, but not nearly as depressing as prison.

# 7

Ava's conversation with Jessie had been revealing and given her a lot to think about. The subject of the woman who'd been taking care of Lily at the time of her rape had never been fully explored before, she now knew. Jessie said that Diane had been so bereft, so full of remorse for not taking better care of Lily, that no one had considered her guilty of anything more serious than neglect. Ava knew that everyone in the house felt a sense of collective guilt because they hadn't been able to protect Lily and so Ava had avoided raking over the events that led up to the assault before now, thinking that they couldn't have anything to do with her reason for being at the house, which was to find out what had happened to her mother.

Several other women had looked after Lily since Diane but none had lasted for long. Ava understood why. Seb's house was a prison in a gilded cage and could get lonely. Tempted by the high salary, Ava could see that the sacrifice of a social life would still be too high a price for the majority of young women to pay.

But Ava had never been one to follow the crowd.

She now wanted to know if Lily's brutal attack had been

planned in order to frame Seb for murder, a possibility that hadn't previously troubled her. Not until she'd met the man himself and sensed an integrity about him. If it had been a set-up, she reasoned, then not only was the operation meticulously planned by a conniving individual but, judging by what Jessie had just told her, no one had considered Diane as the link that could have pulled it all together either. Jessie described her as a meek little thing, interested only in her boyfriend, Gary Bennett.

Jessie had seen him a few times and described him as a flash git, albeit good looking, with an equally flash car and high opinion of himself. Jessie had taken an instant dislike to him. He was young – in Jessie's words, 'barely old enough to shave' – which made Ava wonder where the car and fancy clothes had come from.

Ava wondered too why Diane had continued to care for Lily, a job that placed restrictions upon her freedom, when she had supposedly been out to impress Bennett. She wouldn't have been free at a moment's notice to dance to Bennett's tune and there were plenty of other jobs around that would have left Diane with more spare time.

Tellingly, Jessie also mentioned that Diane had scarpered without giving notice soon after Lily's attack and just before Blythe's murder. Jessie thought she had been overcome with remorse for having neglected her duties. Shortly after she left, Blythe had been killed, the police had descended upon Seb's house in numbers and, presumably, Diane's possible involvement in setting up the attack on Lily, or her potential involvement in Blythe's murder, hadn't been considered.

Sloppy, Ava thought. Either that or someone high up in the investigation had been bribed to look the other way. If Seb himself had considered the possibility of her involvement, it seemed inconceivable that he'd gone to prison for six years and not asked anyone he trusted to search for the woman and extract some answers from her.

After their walk in the woods, Lily was ready for a rest. So Ava helped her into bed for an afternoon nap and knew she would have several hours on her hands before she would be needed again. Plenty of time to do a little sleuthing of her own. If, she reasoned, she could shed light on the events surrounding Lily's attack, then Seb would be grateful and would help her with her quest to trace her mother. He had said that he would do so anyway but as things stood, her problems wouldn't be his priority. Besides, she was unsure if he would keep his word. Jessie thought he walked on water but even so, Ava knew that it wouldn't be wise to expect him to find the answers she sought.

Ava had her own, very luxurious, room with an en-suite and separate sitting room. All of Lily's previous live-in carers had occupied those same rooms and left evidence of their presence in them. The odd letter, books with inscriptions in the flyleaves, papers on courses they were taking whilst caring for Lily – things like that. The only problem was, Ava didn't recall seeing anything with Diane's name on it. Well, she reasoned, if she was here under false pretences, intent upon disappearing when she'd done what needed to be done, she would hardly leave a trail.

Be that as it may, Ava started a methodical search, pulling out the contents of a drawer into which she'd consigned all the odds and ends to do with her predecessors, preferring a blank canvas upon which to imprint her own personality. But a half-hour search turned up nothing – no smoking gun, no signed confession, no clues as to Diane's background. She flopped down in a chair, wondering what she had been expecting, conceding that she had a ton of suspicions but not one iota of evidence to back them up.

The sound of a vehicle arriving, followed by voices drifting up through her open window, caused Ava to glance down into the courtyard that led to the extensive garaging at the back of the house. Seb had returned home and was deep in conversation with Mark. His thick, blond hair blew in the breeze and he constantly pushed it away from his eyes, a gesture that seemed both instinctive and impatient.

She wondered how such a good-looking man had survived the harsh regime of prison life. The son of Jason Carter would make a prime target for his father's enemies, she assumed. But then again, Seb looked as though he could handle himself. He projected a tough image, kept in shape, and would know better than to show the slightest sign of weakness. It must have been exhausting though, she thought, her soft heart quailing, to constantly be looking over his shoulder and worrying about possible attacks.

There were deep lines etched into his face; a product of that concern, she supposed. Lines that added to his attractiveness, which seemed a bit unfair when women spent a small fortune on products that supposedly held back all signs of the ageing process. And yet, on men, the passage of time could enhance their appearance.

She wondered where Seb had been, what he and Mark were in conversation about and whether she should share her suspicions with him. She dismissed the idea before it could take hold. He was probably way ahead of her, at least insofar as Diane was concerned. Upon reflection, he would have to be a complete idiot not to have investigated Diane's involvement or otherwise. She didn't yet know her employer very well but was already aware that he was nobody's fool and would likely not appreciate her interference.

Seb was a complex character who bore the weight of both guilt and a massive grudge on his admittedly broad shoulders.

*And* this was still just his first full day of freedom. She'd let the dust settle and wait for him to come to her with regard to her mother. If, in the meantime, she unearthed something, anything, to back up her suspicions about Diane, then that would be the time to go to him.

One thing she could do though was to research the woman's background. Everyone had a presence online nowadays, even if it was just on seemingly harmless social media accounts, that intentionally or otherwise could be highly revealing.

Ava pulled up her laptop and typed Diane's name into the search engine. Not surprisingly, there were dozens of Diane Forbishers. She quickly narrowed the field by restricting the search to the UK and dismissing those who looked too old. She knew that Diane had been in her early twenties when she'd worked for Seb, with red hair and freckles. Problem was that everyone photoshopped their images and the chances were that she'd got rid of the freckles on anything she'd posted online.

Ava persevered.

Lily had liked Diane and occasionally mentioned her name. For that reason, she'd kept a couple of shots of herself and Diane in her room so Ava had a vague idea of who to look for and eventually her patience was rewarded.

'Bingo!' she cried, throwing her arms above her head.

The woman she'd settled upon looked far more glamourous than the photos Ava had seen of her, backing up Ava's theory about photoshopping. Even so, she was pretty sure she'd found who she was looking for. How to access her posts though? Ava slumped in her chair, momentarily defeated. Then inspiration struck. Lily had limited internet access and Ava knew her login details. It was part of her duties to monitor Lily's online activities, just in case she was targeted again or if Jason tried to get in touch with his daughter by that means.

So Ava logged out of her own account and on again with Lily's details and her patience was rewarded. Lily and Diane were friends on Facebook and Instagram. Diane appeared just once on both platforms on the arm of a good-looking man whom she referred to simply as G. Ava enlarged the best picture, concentrating on G's face, and conceded that she could see the attraction, at least aesthetically. He was half turned away from the camera, as though not wanting his image to be captured, but his appearance was still arresting.

They were at a birthday party for someone called Gaynor and a further scroll through Diane's posts confirmed that she and Gaynor were close friends.

'A possible avenue to explore,' Ava muttered, making a note of Gaynor's details.

What little Ava could see of G's or Gary's features was enough to confirm that he was exceptionally good looking. He carried himself with an air of arrogance, as though the world owed him a living. He wasn't the first handsome person of either sex who appeared to assume that their looks were all it would take to conquer the universe and who was to say that they weren't right about that? Certainly not Diane, it seemed. She was looking at him with blind adoration but Gary seemed impervious to her devotion. Ava tapped his image with her finger, having taken an instant dislike to him, although she had nothing concrete upon which to base her reaction.

The post had been added just a few weeks before Lily's assault and, significantly, there were no posts at all on either Facebook or Instagram after that date. But nor had the accounts been closed down. An oversight, or had something bad happened to Diane? Ava shuddered. Despite what Diane might have been coerced into doing, she hoped that the girl hadn't paid the ultimate price for her involvement.

'Right, let's see what we can find out about you, Gary Bennett, or whatever your name really is,' she said aloud, typing the only name she had for him into her search engine. She was unsurprised when she got no hits that could remotely be connected to the Gary Bennett who interested her. His lack of a media presence only served to fuel her suspicions though and she was far from ready to admit defeat. 'There's more than one way to skin a scumbag,' she muttered, scrolling through the comments on Diane's various posts.

After fifteen minutes, during the course of which she'd found no responses from anyone connected to Gary, her lack of progress intensified her suspicions. A narcissist of his ilk would surely want to put himself out there, if he had nothing to hide, wouldn't he? Perhaps she was doing him a disservice and had only her prejudices to convince her that he was in love with himself, courting Diane's affections for reasons that had nothing to do with romantic entanglements.

Having hit a dead end with Gary, she turned her attention to Gaynor Philpott. She couldn't access her posts but she'd put a lot of personal stuff on her public page, enough for Ava to learn that she lived in the Chichester area. There was a picture of her with a guy wearing a wedding ring, his arm draped around her shoulders. The caption helpfully told Ava that the man was her husband, Gordon. More pictures showed them proudly posing outside what was obviously a tiny start-up home, the number blazoned on the blue front door. Number twenty-six.

'Number twenty-six where?' Ava mused, tapping a pencil absently against her teeth.

Another picture showed a building site, the houses under construction with a famous builder's billboards lining a new road. A little more sleuthing turned up the only new site within the environs of Chichester. Ava pulled up a map of the development and found just three roads with numbers that went up to twenty-six. She dismissed one because it was at the end of the road and the Philpott's was mid-terrace.

Her second enquiry with the land registry hit pay dirt.

Ava sat back, feeling satisfied with her afternoon's work. She now knew that Gaynor lived at twenty-six Acorn Drive. There was no mention of Gordon. What to do with that information? She'd come too far now to back off and was convinced she was onto something, if only because Diane's posts had so abruptly stopped.

Before she could decide whether or not to take what she'd found to Seb, someone knocked at her door. Assuming it was Jessie, the only person who visited her room, she called out for her to enter but closed her laptop lid, not ready to share what she'd learned with her friend.

But it wasn't Jessie who put her head round the door but Seb.

'Am I disturbing you?' he asked.

* * *

Ava was sitting in front of a laptop that she hastily shut down, looking a little flummoxed.

'Not at all,' she said, turning to face him, her smile strained. 'Come in; Lily's sleeping, in case you were wondering. She tires easily and we've had an active day.'

'I wasn't checking up on you. You are allowed to have time to yourself, you know.'

She relaxed and moved away from her small desk to sit in one of the easy chairs arranged round an empty fireplace. She indicated its twin with a flip of her wrist and Seb took occupation of it.

She spread her hands. 'Is there something to do with Lily that you need to talk to me about? I've kinda made my own way with her, with Jessie's help, working out what makes her happy, but if you have advice then I'm ready to listen.'

'You've done an amazing job.' He splayed his legs and leaned his forearms on his thighs, concentrating his gaze on the floor beneath his legs. 'I'm just finding my feet again, feeling overprotective, I guess. I've only been out for twenty-four hours and I'm easing my way back into the land of the free. It will take some adjusting.' He gave a mirthless chuckle. 'I still half expect to hear clanging and banging, shouting and fights.'

'That must have been intrusive.'

He shrugged. 'You get used to anything, given time.'

She cocked her head to one side, as though trying to decide why he was going into so much detail about his incarceration. Seb wondered about his need to talk in circles too. Ordinarily, he never answered to anyone, not even when banged up. His father's notoriety afforded him some respect in that regard and Seb knew better than to turn his back on any advantages that came his way, no matter how unwelcome their source. But perversely, his name alone meant there were just as many people anxious to have a pop at him.

It had been exhausting.

'I can't begin to imagine,' she said softly.

'Well anyway, I came to give you an update on my sleuthing.'

She raised both brows and he could see that he'd surprised her, but whether that was because he was willing to share his findings or because he'd started digging already, he was at a loss to know. 'Okay.' She leaned forward. 'Something to do with my mother?'

'Possibly.' He lifted one hand and waggled it from side to side in a considering gesture. 'Don't get your hopes up, but I've been to see Dameon Read.'

'I've heard Jessie mention his name.' She closed her eyes,

clearly struggling to remember in what respect. 'He was a big influence in your life, I think she said.'

'He was. Not exactly whiter than white. A bit of a rascal in a lot of respects. He knew how to cut corners and flirt with the letter of the law but he was never an out-and-out villain, in my father's league.'

'You are clearly fond of him and don't have to justify that fondness to me.'

'He's getting on a bit now and not too healthy, but his mind is still as sharp as ever.'

'You went to ask him about Lily's attack, I suppose, and possible candidates for Blythe's murder. I'm surprised you waited this long.'

'I needed to do it myself. And I wanted to get in before... well, I'd heard Dameon wasn't in the best of health but had a feeling that he might have theories about the attack.'

Ava wrinkled her brow. 'Surely, if he did, he would have got word to you inside?'

Seb shook his head. 'I can be a patient man.'

'But, if he had something that could clear your name...'

'It wouldn't have helped. His reputation is tainted by association with my father. Any decent prosecution brief at an appeal hearing would have been able to cast doubt on his evidence on that basis alone. He would actually need to know who *did* carry out the murder and have irrefutable proof for an appeal to stand any chance. And even then, appeals are seldom successful. Besides, I didn't want anyone muddying the waters. I knew that if I wanted to get to the truth, I would have to do the digging myself.'

'Which is why you were prepared to wait for six whole years.'

Ava's lips parted, shiny and moist, her surprise evident, distracting Seb in ways that he'd almost forgotten were possible.

He *had* forgotten, he privately conceded, because he couldn't recall a time before being banged up when a woman hadn't used the moist lips routine as a deliberate ploy to flirt and hold his attention.

Ava, he knew, was not flirting. In fact, he had no idea what she thought of him. Did she approve of his determination to get to the truth or was she having second thoughts about working for a convicted criminal now that she'd met him in the flesh, despite the fact that she so obviously cared about Lily? More to the point, did she believe in his innocence? Seb had learned not to give a toss what people thought of him, which made his determination to impress Ava with his innocence that much harder to fathom.

She'd had a beneficial effect upon Lily, that much was already obvious, but if she decided to leave then at least Seb was now around to fill the void.

'Yeah,' Seb said, answering her question. 'I guess I had no choice. Prisons are a hot bed of gossip; nothing remains confidential and so I had to tread carefully. Always supposing that someone connected to a criminal gang carried out the killing and set me up for it, if word got through to the wrong people that I was on to them, well...' He spread his hands and left the words hanging.

'I understand.' She paused, looked up and smiled at him. 'What did Dameon have to say for himself?' she asked. 'Presumably something of interest to me, which is what brought you to my door.'

'Well, it's a long shot but the timing fits so I figured you should know about it. It doesn't relate directly to information about Lily's attack, but it does throw light on the dispute between Jason Carter and his old partner, Mike Bishop.'

'Bishop.' She threw her head back and closed her eyes. 'I've heard that name mentioned in derogatory terms.'

Seb nodded. 'He and Jason were partners in crime, quite literally, but something happened some years ago, before I was banged up, to come between them. I never knew what and so I asked Dameon. You see, it occurred to me that if there was so much bad blood between them, then Bishop might have arranged for Blythe's murder and set me up for it to get back at the old man.'

Ava tilted her head to one side as she considered his words. 'He would do that?' she asked dubiously. 'I thought there was a sort of code; an honour amongst thieves if you like.'

'I agree it seems far-fetched. I guess it rather depends on what came between them. It has to have been something pretty serious.' Seb paused. 'Even Dameon doesn't know what caused the fallout, not for sure. But he thinks a woman was involved.'

Seb sat back and waited for her to join the dots. He watched a kaleidoscope of emotions pass across her face: confusion, doubt, and finally that lightbulb moment.

'You think that woman might have been my mother,' she gasped.

# 8

Ava felt giddy; the revelation, the mere possibility was too much for her to handle. In coming here, she didn't know what she'd hoped to turn up about her mother's past, if anything. Her plan had been nebulous, but she'd had to start somewhere. She had not, in her wildest dreams, imagined that her mother could somehow have been connected to warfare between two criminals that had resulted in someone's murder. Perhaps even her own demise. Even so, the possibility answered so many of the questions that had been bugging Ava for years; not least of which, the reason why her mother had never been in touch again.

Her body shook and she must have paled because Seb was at her side in seconds, crouching to take her hand and give it a squeeze.

'I'm sorry,' he said. 'That was insensitive. I should have prepared you better. It's not much of an excuse, but where I've been residing you tend to forget about the social graces. Even so, I shouldn't have said anything until I was surer of my facts. Let me get you something. You're in shock. Water? A glass of wine?'

She made an almighty attempt to pull herself together and

waved aside the offer with her free hand. 'I'm okay,' she said, straightening her shoulders and snatching her hand from his grasp. Seb sent her a probing look as he returned to his chair.

Now wasn't the time to lean on him; on anyone, she reminded herself. She felt drawn to Seb but was also emotionally overwrought and didn't trust her own judgement.

'I'm glad you told me. It gives me a starting point,' she said. 'We're working on the premise that my mother was involved with your father, of course. We have no actual proof of that, but his name was mentioned in Dad's notes. But even supposing they did have a fling, I find it hard to reconcile the mother I remember with a woman who would abandon her family in order to consort with criminals? It never for one moment crossed my mind that she'd gone off of her own volition. I thought... well, I assumed that she'd been prevented from returning to us somehow. I don't know...' She threw up her hands. 'Illness, an accident, but nothing like this.'

'It was stupid of me to repeat what Dameon told me. Forget that I spoke.'

She gave a laugh that sounded a bit manic. 'Not possible, but don't worry, I won't fall apart on you.' Ava inhaled slowly as she waited for her nerves to settle. 'Like I say, I've always suspected that something catastrophic had to have occurred, otherwise she would have found a way to keep in touch. Her marriage might have become dull, perhaps she and Dad had grown apart, had different agendas, but she wouldn't have abandoned him or me; at least not without telling him why. She wasn't perfect but she was no coward either.'

'I have vague recollections of the woman who Dameon must have been referring to. I remember her because she lasted longer than most. I was living alone by that time but my path did sometimes still cross with Jason's.'

'What did she look like?' Ava fixed Seb with an intense gaze. 'Anything like me?'

Seb shrugged. 'She was a looker so yeah, she resembled you in that respect, but I can't remember much else about her. All of Jason's women were attractive, so that doesn't narrow it down much. All I know is that she was around a lot, and then she was suddenly no longer there. I never bothered to ask what had happened to her. There would have been no point. Jason would only have told me his version of events, or as much as he wanted me to know. Anyway, not long after the lady took her leave of Jason's company, he and Bishop had their major falling out.'

'How was that possible, if they were partners in crime? Surely their activities were intrinsically entwined.'

Seb shrugged one broad shoulder. 'I guess they carved up the operation between them. I didn't bother to ask about that either since it was of no interest to me. I had already distanced myself from my family so I wasn't there that much.'

'When was this?'

Seb fixed her with a probing look. 'Around the time your mother disappeared,' he said slowly.

'I see.' Ava swallowed as she absorbed further indications of an affair between Jason and her mother. 'Well, unless you can bring yourself to ask your father about her, I don't suppose we shall ever know. Particularly if something bad happened to her.' Ava lifted her hair from her nape and rubbed the back of her neck, wishing she could erase the tension building up inside of her as easily as she could scratch an itch. 'Unless there's someone on your father's payroll who'd be willing to dish the dirt.'

Seb shook his head. 'Not a chance. Anyone who was around at the time and is still loyal won't say a word. Anyone who's left Jason's employ will put self-preservation first and keep schtum.'

'It doesn't matter.' Ava tapped her forefinger against her teeth.

'If your father and Bishop fell out over her then it can't have been my mum. I have trouble seeing her going with one man outside of her marriage, much less playing two of them against one another to the extent that she caused a rift.'

'You might think so, and I have no desire to denigrate your mother's memory in your eyes, but you were still a teenager when she went missing. You were probably full of your own affairs, taking exams, getting interested in boys. You wouldn't have noticed changes in your mother's behaviour; especially if she hid them from you.'

'She wouldn't have abandoned me through choice.' Ava spoke with firm conviction. 'She took an avid interest in my education, in everything I did. She wouldn't have just left me.'

'But you can't possibly have known what was going on in her marriage.'

She reluctantly conceded the point with a cant of her head. 'I talked to Dad about it in later years and he was adamant that everything had been good between them.'

'And yet the police found no trace of her. No withdrawals from her bank account?'

Ava shook her head. 'She had a joint account with Dad and he said nothing was withdrawn. Nor was her credit card used.'

'You've tried tracing her through her national insurance number, I assume.'

'Duh, well of course! Sorry,' she added hastily. 'I know you're trying to help and sarcasm won't get us anywhere.'

'Just covering all the bases,' he replied easily. 'Returning to your parents' marriage, how much do any of us really know about the capabilities of the people closest to us? Especially when we're only adolescents. The mind tends to play tricks and you recall things being the way you wanted them to be.'

'True.' Ava nodded slowly. 'But I still can't...'

'Let's come at this from another angle.' Seb leaned an elbow on the arm of his chair and shifted the majority of his weight to the right so that he had a clear view of her. 'What did your mother do for a living? Did she have a career outside of the home or was raising you her focus?'

'She worked from home as a bookkeeper and as a croupier in the evenings.' Ava widened her eyes as a possibility slowly occurred to her. 'She wanted to be there for me during the day and Dad took over at night, even though I was beyond requiring a babysitter. But that could be it, couldn't it?' She threw back her head, closed her eyes and growled with frustration. 'God, but I'm so stupid! I've spent years thinking about what might have happened. I knew she quite enjoyed the buzz of the casino but have never been able to convince myself that her work might have tempted her away from family life.'

'Then that will be how she met Jason.' Seb ground his jaw. 'He has an interest in a couple of casinos, or used to have.'

'Ah, I see.' She plucked at the sleeve of her sweater. 'I don't suppose there's any further room for doubt then. They must have known one another and she was swept away by the glamour, got involved with stuff she didn't understand. But... well, I mean where does that leave us?'

'Don't believe all the hype, sweetheart. There's nothing especially glamorous about desperate people gambling with money they don't have to recover loses that they couldn't afford to incur in the first place.'

'All that aside, there's no saying who she might have met during the course of her work. What she might have overheard.' Ava spoke over Seb's attempt to reassure, her mind whirling with possibilities. 'She was so very lovely and men flocked to her like bees to the proverbial, but Dad said he never worried about that because he trusted her.'

Seb reached forward and touched her hand. 'I'm sorry if I've stirred up doubts about your mother's loyalties.'

Ava waved both the apology and his touch impatiently aside. 'I really need to know. The woman, Ruby Asquith, she's involved with clubs, you said?' Ava leaned forward, so close that she could feel Seb's breath peppering the side of her face. 'Could that be why Dad had her name written down?'

'Do you know if he spoke to her?'

Ava shook her head. 'If he did then he didn't make a note of it. He passed on what he discovered to the police, even though they hadn't done much investigating. People go missing all the time according to them and unless the person is a vulnerable adult or there's an indication of foul play, they don't get involved.'

'You do know that the clubs Ruby runs are on the dodgy side of legal: more like high-end brothels.' Seb glanced at her and shook his head. 'Sorry,' he added, 'but if that's what your dad discovered, and it wouldn't have been hard for him to find out, then it would explain why he didn't write anything down about that part of his investigation or pass it on to the police. He was in denial.'

Ava glumly stared at her feet. 'A bit like me.'

Seb's soft and compassionate smile caused Ava's insides to lurch, which was just the sort of distraction she didn't need, despite the fact that she found herself offering him a responding smile. He was, after all, showing a great deal of empathy.

'Not like you at all,' he said. 'I think you're ready to deal with whatever you discover. You've spent all of your adult life without a mother in it. You've had time to form your own views and to discover that not everything in this world is black or white. Most stuff falls in the grey area.'

'Thanks. Let's hope you're right but, for the record, I will *never* believe that Mum willingly stooped low enough to... well, to get involved with your father.' Ava set her jaw in a stubborn line of denial. 'She had no reason to that I'm aware of and was so law abiding that she never even had a parking ticket.'

'You only know what your dad told you after she left, and what you remember as a teenager. Perceptions change with maturity but whatever you find out, even if you don't like it, it won't have the power to hurt you in the way that it once could have. Take it from one who knows.'

'You no longer feel quite so hell bent on revenge after what happened to you is, I suppose, what you're saying.'

Seb nodded and a veil descended over his eyes, making it impossible for Ava to interpret his thoughts. 'Anger can destroy a man, if he lets it. It took me a while to figure that one out, but I got there in the end. Of course, I still want to get to the truth, but I'll come at it from a rational standpoint.' He looked up, held her gaze and smiled. 'But thanks for believing that I didn't do it.'

She nodded. 'I don't think you're anything like your father. Whether you killed Blythe or not I have no way of truly knowing but, for what it's worth, having known you for a whole day, I definitely don't think you did.'

'Thanks.' He paused and grinned at her. 'A bit of a back-handed compliment but I'll take what I can get.' He yawned and stretched his arms above his head. 'I will see what I can find out about the lady in question. I should have done that before broaching the subject with you.'

'By talking to Jason?'

Seb shrugged. 'It will have to be done sooner or later.'

'If, for the sake of argument, he knows what happened to her, or had anything to do with her disappearance, would it be wise to bring it up without evidence?'

'Like you yourself said, we have to start somewhere.'

'We?' Ava flexed a brow.

'Sure. I said I'd help and I'm a man of my word.' He grinned at her. 'Besides, I have a vested interest; you're good for Lily and I don't want you to leave.'

'I don't intend to leave.' She smiled at him. 'Anyway, I haven't been idle and have news of my own to impart.'

'Tell me.'

Seb listened without interrupting as she told him how she'd delved into Diane's background. His expression became more forbidding as the words tumbled from her lips but she saw no reason to spare him, or to hold back on her own theories.

'I am surprised that the police didn't talk to her,' she finished by saying.

'She left without giving notice before Blythe's murder took place. Several weeks before if memory serves. Jessie said we were better off without her. Lily had taken a liking to her though and it was downright cruel just to leave her like that, which showed her true colours. As you know, routine is important to Lily and she gets upset with alterations to it. Jessie also said that Diane spent most of her time keeping tabs on her boyfriend but I didn't read anything into that. She'd come directly to us after nursing her mother so hadn't had much of a social life. I guess meeting the guy turned her head.

Anyway, I assumed at the time that she'd gone off with him. Live-in jobs in a place like this seem glamorous but once the reality sets in...' Seb ground his jaw. 'I have to say, I never once suspected her guy of involvement. Or Diane either, for that matter. I looked upon her as... well, just an unworldly woman who'd fallen hard for a good-looking guy, causing her to neglect her duties at a vital moment. That could have been wrong. I can quite see that now but hindsight can make things seem blindingly obvious, to say nothing of being fucking annoying.'

'Well, I've found Diane's friend; the one who was at the party where the one picture I could find of Gary, or whatever his name is, was taken.'

'You have?' He looked impressed. 'Show me please.'

* * *

Ava moved to her laptop and pulled up the image in question. Seb leaned over her shoulder, inhaling a light floral fragrance of either perfume or shampoo, finding it hard to concentrate on the first solid lead he'd actually had in an investigation that now seemed to be sprouting wings. All those hours spent pondering upon possibilities, of asking himself *what if*, his judgement skewed by a combination of anger and regret. He had been convinced that his father knew more about Blythe's death than he'd let on at the time of the trial, using the carrot and stick approach when Seb was at his most vulnerable in order to entice him back into the family fold. *I can get you out of this if you agree to toe the line*, had been the implication.

A case of ignoring the blindingly obvious because Diane hadn't seemed capable of orchestrating something so wicked, Seb now accepted. He had failed to take into account the feelings of a woman who'd fallen in love for the first time. Jesus, what a basic error! He wasn't safe to be let out on his own.

Ava enlarged the picture and Seb peered at it closely. He couldn't see much of the guy's face but nothing about him rang bells. He didn't recall ever meeting Diane's boyfriend, wasn't even sure he'd known that she had one before the guys had mentioned it after the rape. Another case of gross neglect when it came to the care of his damaged sister, he concluded glumly.

'It could be anyone,' he said, feeling and sounding frustrated. 'I take it you've Googled his name.'

Ava spread her hands, making him feel stupid for asking such a basic question. 'There are thousands of Gary Bennetts,' she said, 'and if he was involved then he would have groomed Diane and that won't be his real name. If he wasn't a part of it then I don't suppose he can help us. But Diane's Facebook friend, Gaynor Philpott, still lives in the same house. I know because I checked with the land registry *and* she lives there alone. The husband appears to be history.'

'You have been busy,' he said, meaning it as a compliment.

'Seven years too late,' she muttered. 'Anyway, I intend to pay a visit to Gaynor tomorrow. I figure she works so the best time to catch her will probably be early evening.'

'We'll go together,' he replied.

'Best not. If she knows where Diane is, always assuming she's changed her name and doesn't want to be found because of what she got involved with, intentionally or otherwise, then Gaynor will probably know why. I know from Diane's Facebook posts that they grew up in the same street and that their friendship was solid. Probably still is. Anyway, whatever, Gaynor will recognise you. Diane will have told her you're out of prison and she might be reluctant to speak in front of you.'

'What it is to be infamous.' Seb sighed but couldn't fault her logic, aware that his picture had been plastered across the papers and online at the time of his arrest and again now that he'd been released. Speculation was rife as to his reasons for not putting his hand up, thereby drastically reducing his sentence. He was surprised that Ava hadn't raised the question herself; most people he spoke to did, including the few cons he associated with inside. He never bothered to explain because they had no concept of integrity. Freedom with a stain on his character would have been a worse sentence for Seb but, he suspected, few people would understand. 'Even so, I'll drive you there.' He held up a hand to halt her interruption. 'That's non-negotiable.'

'Yes, boss,' she replied, giving him a mock salute that made them both smile. 'And then perhaps we should have a word with Ruby Asquith.'

Seb shook his head emphatically. 'She and Jason are joined at the hip, or were. Even if they no longer are, they will never rat one another out. If something unpleasant happened to your mother and Ruby knows about it, she won't say a word.'

Ava looked as frustrated as she obviously felt. 'Then how the hell are we supposed to get anywhere?'

'I've been thinking about that. Ruby had a second in command back in the day. A lady who dealt with the admin, kept the books that were shown to their accountant, hid those that weren't and acted as an agony aunt for the girls. Her name was Nancy...' Seb screwed up his eyes as he struggled to recall. 'Nancy Dupree. She was a bit of a mother figure. Soft on the inside but hard as nails if you crossed her. And heaven help any of the punters who got rough with *her* girls. Now she and Ruby didn't always see eye to eye, but Nancy is still involved with the club. She and Ruby kinda need one another. Anyway, if she remembers your mum then she'll be the best and safest source of information since she won't run to Ruby or Jason, saying we've been asking questions.'

'How can you be so sure?'

'I just can.' Ava sent him a *what-the-hell* look. 'I did her a favour once: a big favour. Let's leave it at that.'

'Good. Well then...' Ava glanced at the clock. 'I'd best go and rouse Lily and Wizard. It's almost dinner time.'

'Okay.' Seb was tempted to invite her to have a drink with him again once Lily was in bed but decided against it. Besides, he had plans for the evening. A visit he wasn't looking forward to making but one he couldn't afford to put off any longer.

# 9

Jason looked at the woman sitting across from him: glamorous, clued up and a fixture in his life since just after Seb had gone down. She'd lasted because she knew how to keep her trap shut, had a brain and had kept him one step in front of the law ever since they'd seriously come gunning for him. It was partly thanks to Farah Jessop that he'd seen the wisdom of going straight. Ducking and diving was a young man's game. Besides, he was minted now and didn't need the aggro. Truth to tell though, he missed the buzz, the respect.

He glanced at his two sons, both handsome replicas of himself, seated at the other end of the room, drinks beside them, engrossed with their phones. Followers, never leaders. His own fault, he figured. He'd been too soft with them. Farah had been right to suggest that he had no one reliable to hand it all down to. Ray and Dennis were good in a brawl but light in the cerebral department.

The crime world had changed beyond recognition over the past couple of decades and even Jason had struggled to keep up. Now, if Seb had wanted in on the family firm, things would have been very different. Jason had taken his defection as a personal slight at the time but in retrospect perhaps the kid had done the right thing, using his brains to get ahead legitimately. Not that it had done him much good, he conceded, taking a healthy swig of his own drink. Six years banged up for a crime he hadn't committed. Six years of taking the wrap for a crime that any man in this room would have been proud to commit considering what Blythe had done to his Lily. Jason was old school. He still had respect for women and had never abused a single one of them.

Not really.

A backhander was one thing but rape. He shook his head. Nah! That was well out of order.

His gaze remained focused on his sons, still unable to decide if either of them actually was responsible for knocking off Blythe. He figured that they had good reason to keep schtum if they had done it. They had benefited the most insofar as it had gotten Seb out of their hair for a good long time. Jason knew that they were jealous of their eldest brother's intellect, and the fact that he remained Jason's favourite, even after he had turned his back on the family. Jason still couldn't figure out how they'd turned out so differently given that they all had the same mother. Of course, it had helped that Seb had *wanted* to learn, whereas the other two seldom bothered to show their faces in a classroom. He sighed; there was no cure for stupid.

'You fancy going to a club tonight?' Farah asked, smiling at Jason.

Jason shook his head. 'Nah, I'm knackered.'

'Fair enough.' She yawned behind her hand. 'I could do with a quiet one myself.'

'We might wander over to Ruby's, if that's okay?' Ray said.

Jason shrugged, wondering why his son felt the need to ask

for permission. At their age, Jason hadn't answered to any man. Kids nowadays didn't know they were born.

Jason felt a surge of guilt, as he always did, when his thoughts dwelt upon his own offspring. If he could turn back the clock then he would have handled poor, damaged Lily very differently. Just because she wasn't all there mentally didn't mean there was anything to be ashamed about. He thought about her mother and knew why the kid had turned out to have mental deficiencies. His blood boiled when he recalled how he'd been tricked into fatherhood again but there had been sod all he could do about it.

Lily, he belatedly realised, had needed protecting and love and routine in her life, not shunting out of sight. But Jason had been younger then, worried about his public image and what advantage his competitors would take over what they could perceive as a weak link.

A weak link that had been the breaking point in his delicate relationship with Seb, which had already been fragile even before Lily's arrival. Jason regretted that almost as much as he hated the thought of what had happened to Lily. He'd kept tabs on his daughter and knew she was safe now and happy in her own little world. He also knew thanks to his contacts inside that Seb had been beating himself up for the duration of his sentence because he thought he'd let her down. Jason would never lose face by admitting that if anyone had let the girl down then it had been him.

That was his cross to bear in private, and he did so.

Continuously.

'Hello.' Ray got up and peered through the window when the doorbell sounded. 'The prodigal returns.'

He spoke casually but Jason could sense the tension in him and knew that he wasn't happy. Jason himself was surprised. He hadn't expected Seb to come to him and had been wondering how long to leave it before he made the first move himself.

His housekeeper would answer the door so he remained in his chair, taking a moment to compose himself, annoyed because he was so anxious. Farah glanced at him, her expression concerned, but Jason pretended not to notice. Even in front of her, he sometimes felt the need to put on an act.

The door opened and Seb stood in the aperture, looking muscled, lean and fit, his expression impossible to read.

'Welcome home, son.' Jason stood, hand outstretched and Seb took it in a firm grasp. 'Your brothers are here,' he added unnecessarily, waving an arm in their direction, 'and this is Farah.'

Seb nodded at Ray and Dennis, then turned to Farah, whose hand he also shook. He assessed her with a swift sweep of his eyes but made no effort to instigate a conversation with her – with anyone.

'Thought you two were going out,' Jason said to his younger sons.

'No rush,' Dennis replied, resuming his seat. The fact that they hadn't exchanged anything more significant than a nod with Seb was not lost on Jason.

'Leave!' Jason made shooing motions with his hands. 'I need to talk to your brother. You too, Farah.'

The three of them obediently left the room and silence prevailed. Seb had always been good at silences, making them work for him. Jason less so. Not many men had the balls to give him the silent treatment and those who did made him nervous.

'It's good to have you back,' he said, indicating the drinks cabinet. Seb declined with a shake of his head. Jason refilled his own glass and resumed his seat. 'You look well, all things considered.'

'Who's Farah?'

'Ah, she's been a fixture for a long time now. Got her head screwed on. I'm getting too old for constantly changing women.'

Seb nodded. 'I did hear something.'

'Yeah well, you didn't want me to visit, so...'

'I didn't need the aggro. Having some of the scrotes in there thinking I needed you to fight my battles would have made things even worse than they were.'

'Yeah, I know that, son, and I'm sorry.'

'Why?' Seb blinked at him. 'You didn't off Blythe, did you? I mean, you said stuff when I was in the frame.'

'Nah. Wish I had. I'd have put me hand up. Least I could have done for a daughter I turned me back on. As to the things I said... well, that was dumb. Emotions were running high and I wanted to help you. To make the charges go away.'

'You wanted me back where you could control me.' Seb sighed. 'Anyway, that's water under the bridge now. I know you've been turning a few rocks over, trying to find out who did it.' Seb's tone remained remote, measured. 'I need to know what you found out.'

'Fuck all.' Jason spread the hand not holding his glass, allowing his frustration full rein. 'And that just ain't right. Someone, somewhere knows something and I put a lot of pressure on, believe you me. I threw big rewards out there but nothing popped. Nothing solid that I could use to get you out anyway.'

'What about Bishop?'

Jason blinked. 'What about him?'

'Don't do that.' Seb didn't raise his voice but it had developed a threatening rumble that Jason didn't like. He might be getting on a bit, and getting out of the game, but he was still a man to be reckoned with and respected. No one threatened him. No one dared to, other than his own flesh and blood, it seemed. Seb, even if he wasn't ready to acknowledge the fact, was more a chip off the old block than either of his brothers would ever be. 'You two had a falling out. From close partners you became sworn enemies. Could Mike Bishop have set Blythe up to attack Lily and then killed him to fit me up? I heard something about James Bishop shooting his mouth off.'

'I did too, only recently. I had a word with Mike today and it came as news to him.' Jason shook his head decisively. 'We'd come to a parting of the ways a bit before Lily's attack. Our partnership had run its course but we had no reason to stitch one another up. We were happy with the settlement we'd reached and didn't want to show outward signs of being at odds, otherwise the predators would have pounced. Anyway, what reason would Mike have to shaft my family?'

'I shan't know that until you tell me why you fell out.'

Jason hardened his expression. 'None of your fucking business,' he said, finality in his tone. 'You want no part of the family firm so don't come sticking your nose in now.'

Jason expected a barrage of questions, objections, reasoned argument. Instead, Seb abruptly stood. 'Fair enough. I wanted to give you an opportunity to set the record straight but if you feel I haven't earned the right to know then I'll do my own digging.' His expression turned to granite and Jason, who feared no man, was a little afraid of his own son at that moment. 'But know this: I intend to find out who set me up and I have no intention of worrying about whose apple carts I overturn in the process.'

Jason opened his mouth to speak but closed it again with no sound emerging. There was so much he *wanted* to say but nothing he actually *could* say. Not without setting his son off on a course that would be much better left alone. After all, he had made a promise and was a man of his word.

'Be careful,' Jason said, standing too. 'There are some dangerous people out there, especially Bishop. He and I get along, after a fashion, but he's turned into a right hard bastard since we parted ways and won't take kindly to you digging into his affairs. Take it from me, son: there's nothing to be gained from upsetting the man.'

'You think I survived six years inside without learning how to watch my back?' Seb shook his head, looking disappointed but far from defeated. 'See you around.'

Jason raised a hand, aware that it would be pointless calling him back. Seb wanted answers, not platitudes and bullshit. He heard Seb exchange a few words with Dennis in the hallway, then the front door opened and closed. A few seconds later, a car engine started up.

'What did he want?' Dennis asked, putting his head round the door.

Jason didn't bother to answer such an inane question. Instead, he picked up his mobile and called Ruby's private number.

'He's just been here,' he said the moment Ruby answered.

'What did you tell him?'

'Fuck all.' Jason rolled his eyes, thinking he was surrounded my morons. 'You'd be better advised to think what you're gonna tell him when he gets round to you.'

'Is he coming here?' There was fear in Ruby's voice.

'Dunno, but don't rule out the possibility.'

Dennis listened to Jason's side of the conversation but had the sense not to ask questions. What he didn't know couldn't hurt him.

Farah returned to the room, smiling. 'Everything okay?' she asked. 'I liked Seb, by the way.'

'Doesn't everyone?' Ray's question was rhetorical and didn't get an answer. 'Come on, bro. Let's get out of here.'

He and Dennis took themselves off and Farah used the opportunity to plant herself on Jason's knee. She was well into her fifties but took care of herself and Jason knew he was lucky to have a woman with looks and brains; one who didn't bore him rigid because she lacked conversation. One who could see the broader picture and steered him away from trouble before it erupted.

He was too old for all the ducking and diving nowadays, just as he'd said to Seb. Even so, the straight and narrow was fucking boring. He missed being the main man who could walk the streets of South London, secure in the knowledge that he'd be treated with respect.

But the Albanians... well, they used violence and intimidation in the extreme as casually as most men discussed the weather.

'You all right?' Farah asked, concern in her tone. 'Not the warm and fuzzy reunion you'd hoped for?'

'He wants answers and I can't give 'em to him.' Jason shrugged. 'Wish I could but I'd rather have him alive and hating me than knowing stuff that could end up causing him grief.'

'Course you would.' Farah placed a kiss on his cheek. 'At least he came to you. That counts for something. Don't worry, you're not responsible for what happened to Lily, or to Blythe for that matter.'

'Tell that to Seb.'

'Darlin', if he even thought you'd arranged it, he wouldn't have called round for tea and a polite chat.'

Jason snorted. 'Whoever did this covered their tracks well and has gotten away with it for over six years. If Seb pokes around and gets too close, I don't hold out much hope for his survival. You can bet the farm that he's being watched. Those responsible will be aware that he's out for revenge and will want to know what he plans to do before he does it.'

'Have him watched and steer him clear of trouble then.'

Jason shook his head. 'Good idea, darling, but he'd notice a tail in about five minutes and it would lead him back to me, making matters ten times worse. Besides, like I say, others will be on him and it'll get crowded.'

'Come on.' She slid off his knee, took his hand and pulled him to his feet. 'We're going out whether you like it or not. You need a distraction.'

* * *

Seb drove away from the confrontation with Jason, convinced he knew a lot more than he'd let on. That wouldn't be difficult, he decided, given that he'd told him fuck all. But Jason had seemed scared and that... well, scared Seb. Jason was a hard bastard and not much got to him. But he'd seen the fear in his eyes when he'd mentioned his dispute with Bishop and wasn't convinced that had anything to do with Seb's problems. It was more to do with their history and the uneasy truce that now existed between them. Seb might have to visit Bishop at some point.

But not yet.

There would be absolutely no point going in blind. Any sign of weakness would threaten the uneasy truce between Seb's family and Bishop's, possibly starting a turf war. Seb had made sure that he'd had nothing to do with that particular issue, but that was before his incarceration. If he discovered that the parting of ways between Jason and Bishop was connected, directly or otherwise, to his problems then he would not only become involved but would crack heads until he got answers. If he could find the identity of the woman who had supposedly come between two of the hardest men in London, and Ava's mother's name was top of a list of one, only then would he stand a prayer of making progress.

Dameon had told him about her, quite deliberately, for that reason. He would be aware that Seb needed a direction in which to focus his enquiries but had waited for his release before setting him on the trail, no doubt conscious of the fact that this was something that couldn't be delegated. Had Dameon told him everything he knew though, or just enough to whet his appetite? Seb managed a wry chuckle. Even in the twilight of his years, Dameon still enjoyed his little games and seldom gave away everything that he knew.

Time would tell.

What to do in the meantime? he wondered. Like it or not, Ava had come up with the most hopeful lead. Truth to tell, after all this time, Seb barely remembered Diane: a painful reminder of the neglectful care he had afforded his sister. If Ava was right and she was involved, then the plot had been more carefully laid and taken far longer to enact than he'd realised or even potentially considered. It meant, of course, that the attack on Lily had been a meticulously planned means to an end, engineered by someone with endless patience and an obscure point to prove.

Deciding what that point could possibly be would be a good place to start, Seb thought, as he negotiated his car along narrow country lanes, enjoying the feel of the powerful engine responding with a throaty roar to his slightest touch. Jason had only become serious about turning legit after Blythe's murder, Seb reasoned. Perhaps someone had been attempting to force his hand. In which case, they'd succeeded, up to a point.

He also knew that Jason was still a force to be reckoned with, albeit in a slimmed-down, murky world of clubs and gaming institutions that flirted with the letter of the law and the expectations of the taxman.

Seb arrived home, garaged his car and was greeted by Patrick the moment he walked through the door.

'How was the family reunion?' his friend asked.

'Decidedly lacking on the warm and fuzzy front.' Seb threw

himself into a chair. 'Jason told me fuck all about the reasons for his split from Bishop.'

Pat flexed a brow. 'You thought that he would?'

'Naïve or what?' Seb gave a self-deprecating shrug. 'I thought, stupidly it seems, that he owed me at least that much.'

'Word on the street was that they disagreed over drugs. Jason was adamantly against getting involved; Bishop saw the growing demand as too good to miss out on.'

Seb nodded and pursed his lips. 'For all my differences with Jason, I do believe that he's opposed to drugs. It's one area where we're in total agreement.'

'Which is more than can be said for your brothers,' Pat remarked into the ensuing silence.

Seb's body jerked forward. 'They wouldn't have the balls, or the brains, to go against Jason and get away with it for all this time even if they did.'

Pat shrugged. 'Don't underestimate them, Seb, is all I'm saying. I've heard whispers about them wanting to branch out alone. Nothing concrete but I've given it a lot of thought while you've been away. Jason doesn't keep them on a tight leash any more. He lost his edge once Lily was attacked and you were banged up.'

'Yeah, but—'

'If, for the sake of argument, they did go into silent partnership with Bishop and his drugs business, how do you think they managed it without Jason cottoning on?'

Seb rubbed the side of his index finger against his lips. 'If it happened at the time when Lily was attacked and we were all diverted, especially Jason and me...'

'Exactly. Then you got fitted up for murder and Jason took his eye completely off the ball.'

Seb nodded slowly. 'Perhaps, but how could they have been

silent partners with Jason's business rival without Jason catching on for more than six years? Apart from anything else, they'd be flush with cash, but they still live at home with the old man.'

'Actually, they do have a gaff in town. One of those fancy glass and steel apartments at Canary Wharf, but Jason knows all about that. Probably financed it to get them out of his hair. If they have additional income, it would be smart to keep their spending within limits.'

'But they're not smart, that's just the point.' Seb shook his head. 'It's an interesting theory but I can't see it myself. Besides, if that's what they've done, why not just ditch Jason and establish themselves independently? It's not as though he has any actual authority over them now. They are grown men.'

'The same thought had occurred to me, which is why I didn't push the issue while you were banged up. I'm just playing devil's advocate here. You know what they say: when you've eliminated the obvious, or some such crap.'

'Yeah, it's a theory. Jason hates the drug epidemic and if they did go in with Bishop that would have been rubbing salt into an open wound.' Seb stretched his arms above his head and yawned. 'What do you make of Farah?'

'She's had a beneficial effect on Jason, that much I do know. A sensible woman who understands that life changes. She's persuaded Jason that he didn't need to carry on with his questionable activities. The competition from the Albanians, who are heavily into drugs and just about everything else, saw his clubs being undercut, his girls poached, and a turf war would have been inevitable. One that Jason wouldn't have won.' Pat ran a hand through his hair. 'I tell you, Seb, you don't know the half of what those vicious bastards get up to. No ethics whatsoever and Jason was no match for them but, of course, he'd never back down. That would have shown weakness. It took

Farah to convince him to voluntarily give up some of his interests – those not already taken on by Bishop – and save face in the process.'

'Did Bishop let his empire be carved up?'

Pat shrugged. 'Hard to say. He still walks the walk and coexists with the Albanians on his patch so it's reasonable to suppose that they've reached some sort of compromise.'

Seb snorted. 'Ruby still operates,' he said, getting up to pour drinks for them both.

'Thanks.' Pat took the glass that Seb handed to him. 'She's reached an accommodation with the Albanians too, is my guess.'

'Jason still has a share in the clubs?'

'Word is he's selling out to Ruby.'

'Why? The clubs are legal... ish.' Seb waggled a hand from side to side.

'Yeah, but he's left the day to day running to Ruby for... well, ever since you went away, come to think of it.'

Seb took a moment to mull that snippet over, wondering if there was a connection to Jason taking a back seat and whoever had set him up. All he knew was that he'd come away from the confrontation with Jason, convinced that the older man was holding something vital back.

'Ava's been doing some sleuthing,' he said, after a moment's reflection, going on to explain what she'd found.

'It jibes with what Dameon told me about a woman coming between Jason and Bishop, which I still find astonishing. She must have been some woman. As you know, feminine company was never short on the ground as far as those two were concerned.'

'I hear you,' Pat replied, nodding. 'It does seem unlikely. There are a lot of good-looking women in the club world. It attracts them. They think it's glamorous; the place to meet high flyers. But what are the chances of it being Ava's mum who came between two hardened criminals?'

Seb shrugged. 'Dunno, but Ava's dad seemed to think so. She's picked up where he left off and won't let it go until she gets some answers. Problem is, she doesn't seem to appreciate how dangerous that could be. These people are not boy scouts.'

Pat chuckled. 'You'll see it as your duty to take care of her then.'

Seb grunted and didn't deign to respond.

'So, what will you do?'

'Take her to see the friend she's unearthed tomorrow. The one she found on Lily's mug-book, or whatever the hell you call it.'

'Facebook?' Pat laughed. 'Yeah, that about covers it when it comes to social media, but take care. Whoever killed Blythe went to a hell of a lot of trouble to cover their tracks, so you poking your nose in will not be appreciated.'

'Being banged up for a six-stretch didn't go down too well either, Pat.' Seb fixed his oldest friend with a dour look. 'The time has come to get some answers, to say nothing of revenge.'

'Yeah, but...'

'Look, I let Lily down once. Ava tells me she still has flashbacks. Bad dreams. How do you think that makes me feel?'

'Seb, it isn't—'

'If you tell me it wasn't my fault one more time then I swear to God...' Seb paused, breathing deeply. 'The thing is, I can't change the past but I can make the present a safer place for my sister. As it is, she can't go anywhere without the equivalent of an armed guard.'

'She's used to Mark and doesn't know why he's there.'

'But I do know and I don't like it.'

'She won't be attacked again.'

'No, she won't.' Seb ground his jaw. 'I'll make sure of that but won't feel comfortable until I'm absolutely sure there's no further threat to her freedom and there's only one way to make sure of that.' Before Pat could respond, the door flew open and Ava stood there clutching her phone, her hair as wild as her expression. Seb half-rose from his chair. 'What is it?' he asked.

'You need to see this,' she replied, thrusting her phone at him.

Seb glanced at an email and read it quickly.

Stop delving if you don't want Lily to be hurt again.

He looked up into Ava's scared eyes. 'What the fuck?' he muttered slowly. 'What have you done, Ava? Who have you provoked?' His voice rose several octaves.

'Don't yell at me,' she replied hotly. 'I made a few phone calls, that's all, to the casino where Mum worked, but the person I spoke to had no idea who she was. Before her time, she said. She refused to delve into employment records that she claimed were confidential.'

'Well,' Seb replied, his tone icy. 'You've made someone nervous, that much is obvious. Can you trace the IP address, Pat?'

'Sure, but I'm betting it won't get us anywhere.'

'I assume you gave the person you spoke to your contact details, Ava,' Seb said.

Ava bit her lower lip as she nodded. 'Yeah. I didn't see any reason not to. But I don't get it: why would anyone at the casino have reason to harm Mum? I just wanted to… well, hoped to speak to someone who'd worked with her before she left us. It might have told me something.'

'Presumably your father did that when she went missing?'

Ava shrugged. 'Probably, but I don't think anyone threatened him.'

'Whoever sent this is aware of Ava's connection to you, Seb,' Pat said thoughtfully. 'And it's spooked them.'

Seb nodded, frowning as though he bore the world a grudge.

'Someone connected to that casino must be hiding something,' Ava said stubbornly.

'I know one thing,' Seb replied, staring off into the distance.

'What?' Ava asked.

'This has now become personal. Someone connected to me was harmed once and I won't have anyone else threatened.'

Ava nodded mutely, wondering what she had set in motion.

# 10

Ava returned to her room, surprised at the extent of Seb's anger regarding the email she'd received. Perhaps she'd behaved rashly but she was damned if she'd sit calmly by and let him do all the digging. This was her fight but she knew that to Seb, it had now become personal. He hadn't been able to prevent the attack on his sister and now seemed dead set on making amends by protecting her.

Lily called to her and Ava returned her attention to drying Lily's hair and then brushing it until it shone, rippling down her back in a shimmer of natural curls. Lily was childlike in that respect – in so many respects – and adored having her hair brushed. She found it soothing and often drifted off to sleep while Ava did the honours. Wizard was already asleep, half on Lily's knee, and the child-woman tugged gently at his ears, content in her own little world.

Ava wondered how she could ever leave the girl when she found the answers about her mother; answers that might require her to move away and pursue other leads. She had never intended to remain in this post for long but the thought of abandoning Lily filled her with guilt.

There had been so many changes already in Lily's life. Instability made her nervous, inevitably heralding the onset of more bad dreams, or a tantrum. Memories of her ordeal at the hands of Blythe came to the fore whenever she felt insecure, Ava knew from the few words that she screamed out. Then again, her brother was home now and Lily clearly remembered him with affection, despite their long separation. Ava tried to harden her heart and remind herself that this was a job, a means to an end, and that Lily was not her responsibility.

Unfortunately, it wasn't working. Lily sang to herself as she smoothed Wizard's silky head and then turned her own head to smile up at Ava: an uncontrived gesture of trust and dependency that caused Ava's heart to skip a beat.

'More,' Lily said.

'Oh, sorry.' Ava hadn't realised that she'd stopped brushing and dutifully continued, sliding the silky strands through the hand not holding the brush to compensate for her inattention.

'What shall we do tomorrow?' Ava asked.

Before Lily could answer, a tap at the door preceded Seb putting his head round it.

'Am I disturbing you?' he asked, smiling at them both.

Lily responded by jumping from her chair and throwing herself into Seb's arms, Wizard yapping at her heels.

'Hair wash,' Lily said, extricating herself from Seb's arms and twirling in a circle, the hair in question billowing out behind her in a soft cloud.

'So I see.'

Seb stayed with them for half an hour, making up stories that Lily absorbed like osmosis. Ava watched them together, so alike physically, and marvelled at the manner in which this tough individual, who had weathered so much in a harsh prison regime, could adapt so quickly. If ever she had doubted his innocence, as she sometimes did, then those doubts would have evaporated at that moment. She didn't question his determination to exact revenge on behalf of a sister whom he clearly loved profoundly, but he was too intelligent to make a hash of it, leaving clues that led directly back to him.

When Lily's eyelids drooped, Ava took her through to her bedroom and settled her in for the night. When she returned to the sitting room, she expected to be alone and so was surprised to find Seb still there.

'Was there something specific that you wanted?' she asked.

'Is she asleep?' he asked at the same time.

'Yes, just about.'

'Come and have a drink with me then. We need to talk.'

'All right.' Ava checked on Lily one last time, dimmed the lights and left her with Wizard snoring over her feet before following Seb from the room. She noticed his shoulders were broad as she walked behind him, but there wasn't an ounce of fat on him. He had clearly kept himself in shape during his time inside and was a mass of solid muscle. She liked what she saw.

A little too much.

She adjured herself not to become attached to him. They needed one another for different reasons but when... *if* they found the answers that they sought, then there was no reason to suppose that their relationship – friendship – call it what you will, would have any reason to endure.

'Wine?' Seb asked, bottle in hand when she joined him in his lounge.

'Please.' Ava sank into a chair and took the glass from his hand with a nod of thanks. She took a swig even before raising her glass to his and sighed with contentment.

'Tough day?' he asked, watching her. 'You look as though you need that.'

'I have a lot on my mind. Wine helps. A little too much.'

'I just wanted to make sure that you've recovered from the shock of the email,' he said.

Ava shrugged. 'It show's we're making progress.'

'Perhaps.' He allowed a pause. 'You're great with Lily.'

'It's what you pay me to do.'

'I don't pay you to care as much as you do. That has to come from the heart.' Seb sat across from her and raised his glass to hers in a belated toast.

'It would have to be a pretty cold heart not to be affected by Lily's *joie de vivre.*'

Seb acknowledged the point with an inclination of his head, watching her with unnerving intensity over the rim of his glass as he did so. 'I guess, what you're saying is that there's something to be said for the comfort of an uncomplicated mind. Lily will never want for more than she already has, whereas the rest of us are never content.'

'I wouldn't go quite that far. Your sister, as well you know, will never live a full life in the way that you and I interpret that phrase but that said, for the most part she's content with her simple existence. But she's still very fragile. A child's mind in an adult body. It's very sad.'

'I almost buckled and confessed to murdering the scumbag who attacked her whenever I thought of her here without me. That way, I would have got out a lot sooner. Only the reports I received of her being well cared for and protected prevented me from doing so.'

'I'm glad you didn't. It would have eaten away at you.'

Seb sent her a surprised look. 'Whatever makes you say that? You barely know me.'

'I know enough to realise that freedom a few years earlier would have been an unacceptable price to pay if you'd had to sacrifice your principles in order to obtain it.' He sent her a surprised look. 'I am a very astute judge of character.' Ava laughed. 'And Jessie talks a lot.'

'Ah, Jessie. I probably would have done something I'd later regret if it weren't for her advice and sound common sense.'

'She holds this household together.'

'Well, anyway, I'm glad Lily remembers who I am. I was afraid that she wouldn't.'

'Jessie kept you alive for her.'

'I know.' Seb dipped his head. 'Anyway, I suggest we go and visit Gaynor Philpott tomorrow. Or more to the point, you visit; I'll act as chauffeur. After that email, you are not going anywhere alone so get used to having a bodyguard.'

'All right.' She nodded, aware that Seb wouldn't back down in that respect, and took a sip of her drink. 'Did you discover anything today to help me, or you?'

Seb shook his head. 'Jason knows more than he's willing to tell me, so I shall have to do this the hard way.'

Ava gasped. 'Surely if he's aware who killed Blythe, or encouraged him to attack Lily in the first place, he'd tell you? Or have done something about it himself while you were locked up? He doesn't strike me as the sort to let an assault on a family member go unavenged.'

'I think there's a lot that Jason suspects but he no longer has his finger on the pulse and if he couldn't get answers at the time, then he won't admit that to me, especially if it has to do with his murky world.'

'He wouldn't even admit to falling out with Bishop over a woman?' She leaned forward. 'Did you ask him about my mother.'

'No.'

'Why not?' she demanded hotly.

'Because the timing wasn't right. And because if she was involved and it was something serious that created the rift between him and Bishop, he wouldn't have told me.' Seb shook his head when Ava gave a disgruntled huff. 'You need to learn some patience. If I go in all guns blazing, it will achieve nothing.'

'Just because you've had to wait six years in uncomfortable circumstances, it doesn't take away from the fact that I've had to wait even longer, albeit without my freedom being curtailed, and am still no nearer to getting answers.' She pursed her lips. 'It's... frustrating.'

Seb laughed, a gesture that emphasised his rugged features and softened his eyes. 'Tell me about it. Even so, you haven't been looking all that time, but only since you found your father's notes. There's a difference.'

'Fine.' Ava returned his smile. 'We'll visit Gaynor and see what light she can cast on Diane's activities. She might even know where she is, but somehow I doubt it. If she was involved with what happened to Lily then the girl would be sensible enough to keep a low profile, especially if word has reached her of your release.' Ava drained her glass and stood. 'Well, if there's nothing else, I'll turn in myself.'

Seb stood as well. 'Have Jessie look after Lily tomorrow afternoon and we'll go in search of Gaynor then.'

'Will do.' Ava turned with her hand on the door knob. 'Good night.'

'Night,' he replied.

* * *

Seb stayed where he was for some time after Ava left him, her light perfume lingering in the air. He figured that her mother *had* to be dead and that Ava was intelligent enough to have reached that conclusion for herself. She was chasing a ghost in her search for answers that she hoped would enable her to put the past behind her. In her situation, Seb wondered if he would have bothered. What would be the point?

She wanted to know if her mother had abandoned her of her own free will, he supposed, answering his own question. That was understandable but, in helping her to get those answers, would he be depriving Lily of a companion who she clearly adored? Seb chased the selfish thought away. One step at a time, he reminded himself as he drained his glass and took himself off to bed.

He kept busy the following morning, catching up on a ton of paperwork on his various building projects that required his personal attention. It was important to Seb that he was seen to be hands on again. But his concentration wavered and his gaze was drawn to the window far too often. Ava and Lily were on the lawn, with Wizard dancing round them. It was drizzling and Seb burst out laughing when the girls joined hands and twirled in circles, heads thrown back as they danced in the rain.

He could hear Lily's laughter and Wizard's barks and was filled with an irritational desire to join them. Shaking his head, he returned his attention to the plans he was attempting to make sense of, resisting the urge to pay a visit to Nancy Dupree, Ruby's second in command. If Nancy knew anything then Seb was pretty sure she'd be willing to share that knowledge with him. Unlike Ruby, she didn't play games or have any sort of axe to grind with Seb. Quite the reverse, in fact. She owed Seb big time.

Even so, he didn't want to risk showing his hand quite yet. Nancy didn't live in Ruby's pocket and was one of the few people who stood up to the forthright woman, or had six years ago. A lot could have changed in that time but he did know, thanks to Pat, that she still worked in the business, so she'd keep. He'd wait and see what light Gaynor Philpott could throw on Diane's involvement in all this before drawing Nancy into the sordid business.

Mid-afternoon, Ava joined him.

'Ready?' she asked. 'Lily's in the kitchen with Jessie and will be fine for a couple of hours.'

'Sure. Let's go.'

Seb collected keys, wallet and phone and they walked together to his garage. He unlocked his Aston and opened the passenger door for Ava. She slid into the low car with effortless grace. Seb closed her door, trotted round the gleaming bonnet and took up his place behind the wheel. He smiled when he turned the key and the engine sprang into life with a throaty roar.

'Boys and their toys,' Ava muttered, clearly fighting a smile as she watched his reaction.

'Instead of wise cracks, programme our destination into the sat nav, would you?' he replied, easing the car off its parking spot.

She did so with the same economical efficiency with which she appeared to do everything. 'It will take about an hour, according to this,' she said, tapping the screen. 'Probably half that time if you drive as fast as I think you do.'

'Have to stick to the speed limit. As far as the law's concerned, I haven't paid for a crime I didn't commit. They think I got away with... well, murder when the charges were reduced to manslaughter and they'd love to lay something else on me. Even something as petty as a speeding fine. Trust me, I know how their pathetic minds work,' he added, thinking of Henshaw, the screw who'd gone out of his way to make his life difficult and who enjoyed his little bit of power too much.

'The whole world doesn't revolve around you. I dare say they have better things to do.'

'It doesn't?' Seb shot her a surprised sideways look that made her smile. 'I've been misled.'

'Idiot!'

Ava tuned the radio to an oldies station and they made the journey mostly in silence, with her occasionally singing tunelessly along. The roads and the volume of traffic on them had changed drastically since Seb had been away. He wondered where all the people were going. Ava was a soothing presence, cocooned with him inside his small car. She didn't feel the need to fill silences with inane chatter, for which Seb was grateful. One of the worst aspects of prison life was the continuous noise. Even at the dead of night, it was never completely quiet.

The screws, with their heavy tread and unnecessary jangling of keys, were amongst the prime offenders and Henshaw the worst of the lot. Seb thought they did it because they could – a petty act of revenge against all the abuse they had to endure in a dead end career. An auditory reminder of the power they wielded. You had to have a certain mindset to take the job, Seb thought, and many did so because they'd failed at just about everything else.

'We're getting close,' Ava said after forty-five minutes. She concentrated on the screen as a disembodied voice told Seb to take the next left. He did so and was immediately instructed to take the third right.

'It's a rabbit warren,' he complained, slowing the car to walking pace to avoid kids on bikes, gangs of youths skulking about, looking sullen, and impossibly young women pushing prams.

'Starter homes and starter families. I read up on it. Seems some of it had to be given over to local authority housing. That was the only way planning permission would have been granted. I wonder why Gaynor hasn't moved on.' Ava peered through her window, her nose pressed against the glass, as she read the house numbers. 'Here. Pull up here.'

Ava pointed to a house that looked better kept than its neighbours, its small front garden carefully tended, the paintwork fresh and clean. Seb reckoned she was stuck here through financial necessity and figured that she'd probably divorced.

Ava suddenly looked unsure of herself and hesitated on the pavement once she'd left the car. Some of the youths had gravitated towards the Aston that looked as out of place as Seb himself felt. Stealing it would be impossible but there was no saying what damage they might inflict simply because they were bored. He zeroed in on the guy who was obviously the leader, reached for his wallet and extracted a twenty.

'The same again if it remains untouched,' he said. 'If it doesn't then I would recommend making yourselves scarce.'

Something about Seb's mordent tone and icy expression – the one he'd used when facing down hard men who fancied a go at him inside – clearly did the trick. The kid took the note and it disappeared into the pocket of his baggy jeans. Then, at a gesture from him, the rest of his gang followed him across the road, where they perched their backsides on a crumbling wall, attempting but failing to look cool, Seb thought, as he placed a hand on the small of Ava's back and steered her towards Gaynor's door.

She appeared to have forgotten that she wanted to speak with Gaynor alone and Seb saw no reason to remind her. He didn't like the feel of this place and would prefer to stay with her, threats to his mode of transport notwithstanding. He suppressed a chuckle when it occurred to him that he was being protective. He didn't know Ava well but guessed that she would be furious if she was subconsciously counting on his support. Seb didn't care. It felt good to be in control of himself and others again.

He pressed the bell and heard its chime echoing inside the house. The door was pulled open by a girl of no more than eight, who stared up at them from beneath a thick fringe and thicker glasses. She appeared to have a calming effect upon Ava, who crouched down to her height and smiled.

'Hello,' she said. 'We've come to see your mum. Is she home?'

The girl nodded, turned away and trotted down the hall, bellowing, 'Mum!'

A woman, looking harried, larger and older but unquestionably the one they'd come to see, emerged from a tiny kitchen, wiping her hands on a cloth. 'Yes?' she said warily. 'Can I help you?' She glanced at them both. Then her gaze returned to Seb and she did a double take. 'You're him,' she said flatly, no expression in her voice.

'Seb Carter,' he replied, just to be sure there was no misunderstanding.

'I saw your picture in the papers.'

'This is Ava Harper.' Seb indicated Ava, who smiled and told Gaynor she was pleased to meet her. 'Can we have a moment of your time?'

'How did you find me?'

Seb shrugged. 'Does it matter?' He glanced over his shoulder at the lads, the guardians of his car, who had sauntered closer, their curiosity clearly getting the better of them, much as they attempted to pretend otherwise.

She saw the kids too and opened the door wider. 'Come in,' she said. 'Can't guarantee that your car will still have four wheels after we've spoken but that's a risk you'll just have to take.'

Seb gave an easy smile, conscious of the tension radiating

from Gaynor. *She knows something.* He glanced at Ava and could sense that she'd reached the same conclusion.

'Go in the garden for a while, Hayley,' Gaynor said when the little girl trailed into a small, spotlessly clean lounge in their wake.

The child nodded and with none of the complaints that Seb had been expecting, she took herself off without saying a word.

'She's well behaved,' Ava said, smiling at the montage of pictures depicting the child with and without her mother dotted about the room. Significantly, there was no sign of her father.

'Kids who live in this dump don't have manners?' Gaynor posed the question without rancour.

'That isn't what I meant,' Ava said, selecting a chair and perching on the edge of it. 'More likely, kids anywhere nowadays always answer back.'

Gaynor let out a long breath. 'Perhaps but... anyway, what can I do for you?'

'We're trying to find your friend Diane Frobisher,' Ava told her.

Gaynor showed no surprise. 'You haven't wasted much time,' she said, addressing the comment to Seb. 'Except that you have... wasted your time, that is. I haven't seen or heard from Diane since she walked away from your employ.'

'In that case, how do you know she walked out?' Seb asked.

'Because when I didn't hear from her, I was worried. We'd planned to go shopping but she didn't turn up, which wasn't like her. Anyway, I phoned her mobile but it was switched off. She often forgot to charge it so I rang your house. The lady there told me she'd left the day before and not returned, which is pretty much what I'd assumed for myself by that point.'

'Why?' Ava asked. 'She was good with Lily and I got the

impression through talking to people that she wasn't the unreliable type. So why would you assume that she'd legged it?'

'She wasn't unreliable until she met Gary Bennett, or more to the point, until my worthless waste of a space husband brought Gary to our flat where we lived before we bought this place, and Diane was there. She took one look at him and was never the same again. I could have told her that he was a loser but who am I to judge? My taste in men is just as lousy. I thought Gordon walked on water but he scarpered as soon as I got pregnant. Has never seen his daughter or paid a penny towards her keep.'

'But your little girl...' Ava waved a hand towards the garden.

'Ain't his but that's another story. Another example of my lousy judgement when it comes to men. The child I had with Gordon is at a party.' A note of pride entered her voice. 'I've worked my fingers to the bone to make sure that both of my kids have the best of everything, including a good education. That way they're less likely to make the bad choices I did and won't get stuck in a place like this.' Gaynor seemed to enjoy railing against the injustices in her life and Seb saw no reason to curtail her rant.

'You mentioned that Diane disappeared,' Seb remarked when Gaynor finally ran out of words. 'Do you have any idea where she went?' He fixed her with a probing look but she held his gaze, almost defiantly. 'Or why?'

'I know Diane was in a right old state about what happened to Lily. Inconsolable, she was. Said it was all her fault. She'd been distracted.' Gaynor huffed. 'Making out with Gary, more like, when she should have been taking proper care of your sister. He could wind her round his little finger, the bastard. But it wasn't her fault. Someone wanted to get at your family by getting at that poor girl, is what I've always thought, and if not through Diane, they would have found another way.'

'You think Gary was paid to distract Diane?' Ava asked before Seb could.

Gaynor waggled a hand from side to side. 'Seems likely. Besides, he disappeared at the same time as Diane.' She allowed a significant pause. 'As did my Gordon. Scarpered without so much as a goodbye, so he did; the man who was supposed to be the love of my life. Didn't take no clothes, his passport, nothing. And before you ask, I haven't heard from him since. I looked at first but didn't really know where to start. Whoever I did ask claimed not to know and well...' She spread her hands and shrugged.

'You think he was somehow involved in what happened to my sister?' Seb asked.

'I think he's dead, if that's what you're asking. Despite everything, he did love me; no one will ever convince me otherwise. We hadn't fought and he was excited about the baby, about becoming a father and about owning his own home, be it ever so humble. Besides, he loved his mum and she had no idea where he got to either.'

'Is she still alive?' Ava asked.

'Nah, she passed on several years ago, hoping right up until the last that her only son would show his face. Heartbreaking, so it was.'

'Let me see if I've got this straight,' Seb said, his mind whirling with possibilities. 'Your husband was a mate of Gary Bennett, who took up with your friend Diane. Now all three of them are missing and you have no idea what happened to them.'

'That about sums it up.'

'Did you involve the police?' Ava asked.

'For all the good it did me insofar as Gordon was concerned. They said he was an adult, blah, blah. I couldn't give them any information about Diane or Gary so didn't even mention the fact that they'd gone off the radar as well. There would have been no point.' She gave a mirthless little smile. 'Stinks of a conspiracy if you ask me but then what else can you expect when you get into bed with a bad crowd?'

'A bad crowd?' Ava and Seb said together.

'Dodgy characters. My Gordon was as straight as a die before he got in with Gary, who persuaded him that working nine to five was a mug's game. We were struggling to raise the deposit for this place at the time. Then Gordon got some night work thanks to Gary. Security, he called it, at some club or other.'

The cogs in Seb's brain were now in danger of overheating. A dozen questions clamoured for answers as his mind went into overdrive but he didn't want to stem Gaynor's flow. It was clear that she'd wanted to talk about this stuff for a while and he wasn't about to disappoint her. He also sensed her nervousness and knew it was the first time that she'd aired her suspicions. She seemed on edge, anxious about something, but it would be a stretch to assume that she was being watched. If she was, then Seb's Aston would stand out like... well, like an Aston on a rundown housing estate, and it was unlikely that anyone would come after Gaynor if they thought she had him on her side.

There was an upside to emerging from prison with a reputation as a hard man, Seb decided.

'In the end, he gave up a promising career. A whizz with computers Gordon was and he helped customers, older people mostly, to understand the digital revolution heading their way, preventing them from being left behind or scammed. I told him it was the future, that his services would never be out of demand, but he said he could earn three times as much as a doorman, or whatever.'

'Did his duties extend to acting as muscle for anyone?' Ava asked.

Gaynor shrugged. 'We'd only just moved here when he took

up with Gary's lot. We were happy at first, excited about our first home. But it didn't last. He was at Gary's beck and call. His time was never his own. He got called out at all hours but never told me where he was going. Said it was better if I didn't know.' She sounded angry and yet grateful for an opportunity to vent that anger. 'Sometimes he was out all night and came home stinking of cheap perfume.' She gave a manic little laugh. 'Too stereotypical for words. I accused him of having an affair. His attitude had changed towards me. I was pregnant, feeling fat and unattractive, and he was mixing in the glitzy club world, so there would be temptations. He denied having an affair, but I didn't come down in the last shower and... well, that was the start of the end as far as our marriage went. No way was I going to be the trusting little woman, left at home but standing by her man, as Gordon found out to his cost.'

'Was this before or after Gary met Diane?' Ava asked.

Gaynor tilted her head, clearly trying to remember. 'After, I think. Once those two linked up I had a bad feeling about it. Diane changed, too. Thought Gary walked on water and would do anything he asked her to. I tried to talk to her, warn her against getting in too deep, but she accused me of interfering, of being jealous. So I looked to my own interests and tried to talk to Gordon but he was seduced by the glamorous world he now moved in and wouldn't see reason. He could have walked back into his old job, safe and secure, and we would have managed financially but he was having none of it.' She threw up her hands. 'I couldn't reach him any more.'

'This club where he worked,' Seb said. 'Do you remember what it was called?'

'Oh yes, I'll never forget. It was the establishment that robbed me of my husband.' She met Seb's gaze. 'It was the Black Iris.'

'Holy fuck!' Seb breathed.

# 11

Ava thanked Gaynor for her time, promising to let her know if they discovered what had happened to the man she'd married: the father of her first born.

'That must be so hard for her,' she remarked, sighing.

'What must be?'

'Not knowing what happened to her husband.'

'Ah, right.'

She looked grim, thoughtful, as they left the house. He paid the lads the rest of their protection money and climbed behind the wheel of his miraculously undamaged car. Ah, the power of economic forces, Ava thought with a wry smile.

She sensed that Seb's mind was reeling. Clearly, Gaynor had told him something that he hadn't expected to hear, or had hoped not to, and it had to do with the club that Gordon had worked at.

The Black Iris; the club managed by Ruby. Her name kept cropping up. It couldn't be a coincidence. The revelation had literally knocked the wind out of Seb and so she asked no more questions, leaving him to concentrate on driving as he mulled the situation over and came to terms with it. He would tell her what he knew when he was ready.

He pulled into the car park of a local pub in a slightly better part of town and still without speaking, climbed from behind the wheel. Ava followed him and had to trot to keep pace as his long stride ate up the ground. His expression remained fixed in granite and Ava was very glad that she wasn't on his shit list. This man, she sensed, understood the value of patience and thirsted for revenge. She had also noticed a marked increase in his determination to get answers since the email she'd received. As suspected, he'd told her that morning that its origins were untraceable. It had bounced around several servers in different countries before reaching her inbox. Despite that, she couldn't blame Seb for wanting answers. In his situation, she would *have* to know why she'd been set up and fully intended to help him get to the truth.

*Whoa*! That determination brought her up short. Since when had his problems become her priority?

'Slow down!' she protested. 'Where's the fire?'

'Sorry.' He flashed an apologetic smile and moderated his pace.

Inside the half-full pub, he ordered a non-alcoholic beer for himself and a glass of wine for her.

'You could have driven straight home and had a proper drink,' she pointed out, once they'd found a quiet table close to the log fire where they could chat without much prospect of being overheard by anyone less discreet than the fat Labrador stretched full length in front of that blaze. Ava didn't think Seb was known in this pub but still one or two heads had turned in his direction. It was obvious that he'd been recognised.

'Less distractions here.' He took a sip of his drink and winced.

Ava laughed at his reaction and made a point of savouring her wine.

'Witch!' He laughed and some of the anger left his expression.

'Okay, give,' Ava said, when they'd worked halfway through their drinks and he hadn't spoken another word. 'What's so special about the Black Iris that it's got your knickers in a knot?'

'Firstly, for the record, I don't wear knickers.'

'Too much information.' Ava blocked her ears with her hands, making him smile.

'The Black Iris,' he said, letting out a long sigh, 'was the first club that Jason and Bishop took on. It was their flagship back in the day. Anyone who was anyone showed their face in order to be seen.'

'I've never heard of it,' Ava admitted.

'It's in Stockwell, not the trendy West End, but it was still a massive success. Filled a need south of the river for the good, bad and wealthy to rub shoulders in a display of decadent excess; no social boundaries.'

'A nightclub, in other words.' Ava flexed a brow. 'With, I assume, optional extras.'

'Whatever you wanted.' Seb leaned one elbow on the arm of his chair and gave a casual shrug. 'There was a licenced casino, a thriving disco, and plenty of entertainment for the gentlemen.'

'Prostitution?'

Seb nodded. 'Prostitution. One of the main earners in all the clubs.'

'It's called the oldest profession for a reason. Supply and demand and all that and it's fine by me, just so long as no one is coerced.'

'It was basically a glamorous cover for the exploits of all the villains in the area. Jason's name over the door was like a magnet.

Some of the leading policemen in the area were offered free membership.'

'And took it?' Ava allowed her surprise to show. 'Well, we are going back a bit, I suppose. Things would be different now. Even so, associating with a villain couldn't have done their careers much good.'

'Would times be so very different?' Seb moodily swigged more of his beer, looking as though he could do with a real drink. 'You're talking to a man who's just survived six years inside for a crime I didn't commit. Nothing really changes. Those on the take are still on the take. They've just learned how to cover their tracks better.'

'The policemen whom your father cultivated with freebies turned a blind eye to his nefarious activities?'

'Something like that, I expect. You're asking the wrong person. But yeah, Jason had policemen on speed dial. Probably still does.'

'And once they'd accepted Jason's hospitality they were on the hook, so to speak.'

'Pretty much. But don't ask me if they took more than the occasional drink and odd shag because I have no way of knowing.' Seb paused. 'I deliberately didn't want to know, growing up.'

'Okay, I get that and I understand why you're bitter.' Ava rested her forearms on the table and leaned over it, her head close to Seb's. 'What I don't get is why the name of the club seemed to upset you so much.'

Seb set his jaw in a grim line. 'Because a friend of mine from way back was murdered there.'

'What!' Ava's screeched response had several heads turning in their direction. She impulsively reached out and covered Seb's hand with her own. 'What happened?' she asked, moderating her tone.' She removed her hand from his and spread it wide, shaking her head as she did so. 'I don't understand any of this.'

'Ben Pike and I were at school together. He went into a mundane job and was seduced by contacts of Jason's – much the same way as Gordon Philpott was.' Seb curled his upper lip. 'I told him not to do it. We'd kept away from trouble throughout our school days but Ben was under pressure from his girlfriend. He felt the need to impress her by flashing the cash and showing her the high life.'

'She wasn't worth having if that was all she cared about,' Ava said softly.

'Yeah, well, Ben was in *love* and would do just about anything to make the object of his affections happy. I can't even remember her name now. I never did get to the bottom of who killed Ben, or why, and it's eaten away at me ever since. Perhaps you understand better now why I wanted nothing to do with Jason's world.'

Ava nodded emphatically. 'No wonder you looked so broody when Gaynor started talking. You probably already knew what was coming and I suspect you know what happened to Gordon too. Is that why you didn't ask any more questions?'

'Yeah. She wouldn't have had any answers and I didn't want to get her thinking the... well, probable. She's better off believing that he's alive and cheating on her somewhere.'

'Is it?'

Seb threw back his head, eyes closed. 'Hell if I know. Damned if I do; damned if I don't. She'd likely blame the messenger.'

Ava protruded her lower lip in a considering gesture. 'In her place, I think I'd prefer to know but you're right. You don't actually *know* what happened and more to the point, you don't know Gaynor. She might be involved, although I doubt it.'

'Right, and if word gets back to the wrong people that I've made unfounded suggestions, it'll create a shit storm.'

'I thought that was what you wanted. Shake these guys out of their comfort zone and see what falls loose.'

'On my terms.' He paused, his expression menacing. 'Especially since you've been threatened.'

Ava swallowed. 'Okay.'

'Jason and Bishop enjoy an uneasy truce, but if accusations of murder are levelled at them and taken seriously, you can bet the farm that they'll close ranks and use their influence to make those accusations go away.' He paused. 'Think back to the tame policemen they have on the payroll.'

Ava nodded. 'In other words, you have to outthink them if you want to finally get answers, as well as closure regarding your friend's murder.'

'Something like that. Talking to Gaynor brought it all back, I won't deny it. That club has always been toxic.' Seb rotated his neck, looking tired as he rubbed the back of it with his hand. 'Which is why Ruby makes such a good manager.'

'I wondered when you'd get round to mentioning her. I was tempted to go and ask her about Mum but… well, something held me back.'

'You were right to be cautious. She's bad news and you would have brought attention to yourself for no good reason.' Seb stretched his legs towards the fire, massaging the dog's backside with the tip of his boot. The dog grunted in its sleep but didn't shift. 'I'm not saying that Gordon was bumped off too. There're only so many coppers Jason and Bishop can bribe to cover up something *that* serious but the fact that he's disappeared off the face of the earth does ring alarm bells.'

Something Seb had said caused Ava to widen her eyes. 'There was no investigation into Ben's death?'

Seb shook his head. 'Total whitewash but I knew what had to have happened when his weighted down body actually washed up by Chelsea bridge. Jason denied all knowledge. But he did remark that Ben had been poking his nose in where it didn't belong. He claimed the death had nothing to do with him but I wasn't buying it. No one so much as sneezed in that partnership without Jason authorising it.'

'You think, I suppose,' Ava said, tapping the fingers of one hand thoughtfully on the tabletop, 'that Jason deliberately separated you from your mate, hoping to drive a wedge between you and keep you on side. When that didn't work he... he what?' She looked up at Seb. 'Surely he wouldn't commit murder simply to make a point?'

'Ben was on a mission and making a nuisance of himself, so he was creating waves. Jason got that part right. The silly bastard ought to have exercised a little discretion. I told him...' Seb sighed. 'His sister had been drawn into the flesh side of the operation at the Black Iris and Ben was convinced that she hadn't gone into it voluntarily.' Seb rubbed his chin, clearly struggling with a past that he'd buried once his own problems had taken centre stage. 'Then he discovered that she was hooked on hard drugs, which is when he became convinced that she'd been manipulated by someone working for Bishop.'

'Or Jason?'

Seb waved the suggestion aside. 'Jason, for all his faults, doesn't have anything to do with drugs. I told Ben to leave it to me, that I'd get her out and get her clean. I tried to convince him that he'd get himself in hot water if he went barging in, all guns blazing. But he was full of guilt because he felt he'd let his sister down and trust me, I know how that feels, so he wasn't listening to reason.'

'And your relationship with your father never recovered?'

'Not really. Like I say, I confronted him about Ben's death when the body was found. He said it had been an accident. A run in with troublemakers trying to storm the door and nothing to do with his quest for justice for his sister. We both knew it was bullshit, especially given that the body had been weighed down and wasn't supposed to surface. But Jason wasn't talking and so I was never going to get to the truth.'

'But you think whoever got Ben's sister on the game had a vested interest in protecting themselves?'

Seb sent her a droll look. 'What would you think? I hate drugs. Bishop was the one who started the drug running without Jason's prior knowledge, which is I think what they really fell out about. Well, that and the mystery woman we keep hearing about. Unless that's a red herring to put me off the scent, in which case it won't work. I've had a lot of time to think about things and everything I've learned since getting out leads back to the Black Iris. Jason is getting out of the club business and if he actually does then Bishop will have control of the Black Iris, so John tells me. And the mainstay of that club is of course Ruby Asquith.'

'Who we can now talk to,' Ava suggested, leaning forward expectantly.

Seb shook his head. 'Not yet. That would be putting our heads straight into the lion's jaws.'

'Seb!' Ava put a wealth of frustration into the one word.

'You wouldn't have lasted five minutes where I've been residing if you can't exercise a little more patience.' He grinned at her and waved a placating hand. 'The Black Iris, I happen to know, remained beneath Jason's control after Ben's murder when Bishop and Jason carved up their operation and went their separate ways. According to Pat, it's still Jason's flagship, albeit less influential than it once was, until such time as he sells out to Ruby. If he does. Jason might be under pressure, of course. I'd never imagined he'd retire completely. He enjoys the cut and thrust too much. But old-time lags have been replaced in the pecking order by totally ruthless foreign gangs who peddle drugs and smuggle people across borders as casually as your average stallholder flogs off bent gear in the local market.'

'No honour amongst thieves any more,' Ava said, shaking her head.

'Don't be seduced by that old nonsense. There never was any honour and absolutely nothing glamorous about watching your back every second of every hour, wondering who'd literally put the knife in if you let your guard down. Especially when you weren't part of the racket yourself.'

'Your surname was enough to make you a threat?'

Seb shrugged. 'Something like that.'

'You didn't have much choice, did you?' Ava remarked after a short, reflective pause.

'Choice about what?'

'About being tainted by association. You don't have criminal tendencies but probably had to work twice as hard as most people to prove it, simply because of who your father is.' She leaned forward, forearms on the table. 'Okay, what now? I still think we should speak with Ruby.'

'I have a better plan.'

'You really are incredibly annoying,' Ava protested when he grinned at her but didn't elaborate. 'Do you plan to share or to make me guess?'

Seb chuckled. 'Nancy Dupree, Ruby's second in command. I mentioned her before.' Ava nodded. 'She and I go way back. She was very fond of Lily and was as devastated as me after what happened.' Seb paused. 'She also owes me a favour.'

Ava frowned. 'But if she and Ruby are tight, won't she tell Ruby that we've been asking questions?

'Nope.' Seb spoke with authority in his tone. 'I doubt it very much.'

'Care to tell me why you're so sure?'

'Trust me, I just am.'

Ava drained her glass and stood up. 'Okay, let's go. If you don't want to share then I'll ask the lady myself.'

'Slow down! This needs to be managed carefully. She won't tell us anything if we speak with her publicly.'

Ava resumed her seat and drummed her fingers again. 'Do you have a private number for her?'

Seb extracted his mobile from his pocket and selected a contact.

Ava only heard his end of the conversation, which was brief, but sufficient for her to know that Seb had just arranged to meet the lady in question at a pub in Chichester.

'Now we can go,' he said, standing and smiling at her.

* * *

Seb drove swiftly and without conscious thought towards the meeting with Nancy. A meeting that he'd anticipated with increasing certainty as he neared the end of his incarceration. Pat had remained in contact with her but although she'd been sympathetic to Seb's dilemma, she hadn't given up anything to get him off the hook. She'd hinted that she knew stuff; stuff that she would tell Seb, and only Seb, in person.

'This is it.'

Seb swung his car into the parking area behind a country pub on the road to Goodwood. He'd been watching carefully since leaving Gaynor's and was as convinced as he could be that they hadn't been followed. He was grateful to Ava for her ability to keep quiet when she had nothing worthwhile to say, despite the fact that she must be bursting with questions. She was an easy person to be around and her natural stillness afforded Seb the opportunity to think, and to plan his strategy.

Ava was out of the car before Seb had switched off the engine, glancing around the sparsely populated car park. Seb left his vehicle at a more leisurely pace and placed a hand on the small of Ava's back as he guided her towards the pub. He ducked beneath the low lintel as he entered a bar that hadn't changed much, if at all, since he'd last been in it. It probably hadn't changed for decades before that and as far as Seb was concerned, that was a point in the brewery's favour. The old-world charm was part of the attraction, as was the roaring log fire that gave off an earthy aroma, adding to the welcoming ambience.

'Is she here?' Ava clutched Seb's arm.

Before he could respond, a woman who didn't look as though she'd aged at all rose from a corner table on graceful legs and walked towards them.

'Seb!'

She held out a hand and Seb pulled her into a fierce hug, feeling the years melting away as he did so. Wishing it could be as easy to turn back time and save Lily from her ordeal.

'Nancy! You look amazing.'

'You don't look so bad yourself,' she replied, leaning back to examine Seb's face. 'Clearly, you didn't let the bastards get you down.'

'This is Lily's carer, Ava.' Seb indicated Ava with a wave of one hand. 'Ava, this is Nancy.'

'Pleased to meet you.' Nancy extended a hand, which Ava shook as to the two women sized one another up. 'Are you... er, sure...'

Seb smiled. 'Don't worry. If I hadn't brought her along, she would have stalked me.' He rolled his eyes. 'She has her own reasons for needing answers.'

'Whatever it takes,' Ava replied. A collusive look passed between the ladies. It told Seb that they'd taken to one another and were well on the way to bonding. He wasn't surprised. Nancy had grown up in a tough environment and wouldn't have lasted five minutes in the club world if she wasn't a shrewd cookie who sensed the goodness in others.

Seb ordered a round of drinks and they retreated to the corner table that Nancy had just vacated. She and Seb took a few minutes catching up and then Nancy grilled Ava on Lily's progress.

'Where do you want to start?' Nancy asked when they ran out of small talk, lowering her voice despite the fact that there was no one anywhere near them in the bar to overhear their conversation. A few people were lingering over a late lunch in the formal dining room and a group of horsy people occupied the opposite end of the bar as they loudly discussed the upcoming race meeting down the road. 'I've had so many theories that I wanted to run past you but Pat told me to keep them to myself.' She grinned. 'Now I've forgotten half of them, or else they've run out of steam, so perhaps he was right to keep me grounded. No point in getting your hopes up, only to have them dashed. Going off half-cocked and all that.' She took a long slug of her drink. 'Was it very bad inside?' she asked in one of her abrupt trademark changes of subject.

'Not exactly a picnic,' Seb replied, the master of understatement.

'Have you seen Jason since you got out?'

'I have.' Seb ground his jaw. 'He insists he had nothing to do with Blythe's death. I tend to believe him but can't say I'm equally sure about my dear brothers, or about the people who Jason surrounds himself with and who have an axe to grind.'

'The best way to get him to take his eye off the ball: setting up his favourite son.' Nancy nodded in response to her own theory. 'I've often thought it could have happened that way. Jason lost his edge once you went down, but as to your brothers...' Nancy shook her head. 'They don't have the intelligence to cover their tracks, or to set you up for it.'

'Or so they would like you to think,' Ava added into the ensuing silence.

Seb and Nancy both turned to look at her.

'What do you mean?' Nancy asked.

'Well, I'm no expert on criminal fraternities but I do know something about human nature. I haven't worked with Lily for that long but I have ears and listen to what Jessie says about the family.' She turned to give Seb her full attention. 'It seems that you've always been the blue-eyed boy, unable to do any wrong in your father's eyes despite failing to toe the parental line. Nancy is right to say you were the favourite, and probably still are. Your brothers, by contrast, did as they were told but never won approval. As I say, human nature being what it is, I wouldn't blame them if they saw an opportunity following Lily's attack to remove the competition in order to gain Jason's attention for themselves.'

'It's a nice theory but if Ray and Dennis were out for some sort of petty revenge, that isn't the form it would have taken.' He took a swig of his drink, full strength lager this time, and focused his attention on Nancy. 'A baseball bat to the back of my skull in a dark alleyway is more their style.' He returned his full attention to Nancy. 'Now then, what do you have to tell me?'

'Why did you continue to work at that club?' Ava asked at the same time.

Nancy glanced at Seb. 'You didn't tell her?'

'Not my secret to tell.'

'No biggie.' Nancy exhaled slowly, her reaction making it clear that it was a huge deal still from her perspective that she'd learned to trivialise on the rare occasions when she referred to it.

'I was married to a bent copper. It ended badly. He made all sorts of threats against me when I left him. He was out to get me. No one walked out on Paul Drake. He was the one who did the walking. Anyway, I knew I wouldn't be safe if I severed ties but would be protected all the time I stayed at the club. Besides, why would I want to leave? I had a child to support and needed the security. I wasn't doing anything illegal in helping to the run the club and it kept me safe, protected from bullies like Drake *and* it kept my little girl away from her dad. Even he, with the power of the police behind him, wouldn't go up against Jason and Bishop.' Nancy paused. 'He tried to get at me there once and Seb here persuaded him that it would be a seriously bad idea.'

'Ah, I see.' Ava screwed up her lips. 'A man not above using a child to get what he wants.'

'Right.' Nancy dashed at an errant tear with the back of her hand. 'Bella died when she was hit by a car walking home from school in broad daylight as a twelve-year-old. The driver never stopped and Paul blamed me for neglect.' She let out a slow breath. 'But not as much as I blamed myself.'

'That's awful.' Ava reached across the table and touched Nancy's hand. 'You think she was deliberately targeted?'

'Even Paul wouldn't go that far,' Nancy said with authority. 'For all his faults, he loved his daughter. But I do think that Lily was set up.'

'Someone with a grudge against Jason or Bishop?' Ava suggested. 'I get the impression there's a lot of face saving to be done in that world and that the consequences are brutal if someone takes the piss.' She paused to rub the side of her chin. 'But surely, children… young women…'

'There were full-on turf wars going down at about the same time as Lily's attack and Bella's death,' Seb said.

'And you've hung in there all this time, hoping to find

answers.' Ava smiled at Nancy. 'But I need answers too.' She swallowed. 'Did you know my mother?'

'Your mother?' Nancy stared long and hard at Ava, squinting slightly. 'I knew there was something familiar about you.' She plucked at her lower lip, nodding slowly. 'I can see it now. You're the image of Mel. You must be her daughter.'

* * *

Dennis and Ray Carter watched Seb, Nancy and Lily's carer all cosied up around a table in a pub through binoculars.

'He hasn't wasted any time,' Dennis muttered.

'Let me have a look, bro.' Ray held out his hand for the binoculars and shrugged. 'It's no biggie. He's pissing in the wind.'

Seb, for all his supposed street cred, didn't appear to know that he was being watched. Things had moved on since his day and a person didn't need to have a physical tail in order to be followed. Ray had put a tracking device on his car when he'd called to see Jason. Not that Jason would be too happy if he knew that the favoured son was being watched but what the old man didn't know wouldn't hurt him. He had a blind spot where Seb was concerned. He was also getting on a bit and losing his edge.

It was time for the younger generation to take over and the sooner the better. Preliminary discussions with Bishop were in the offing but had to be handled with kid gloves. It was delicate. Bishop and Jason, for all their animosity, still had a bond that Dennis and Ray found hard to fathom.

And more to the point, Jason still had his claws into some of the prize assets in their former joint venture. If Dennis and Ray could convince Bishop that they were the heirs apparent, and if they could do so before Seb did anything to upset the applecart, then they would be made.

Seb would be out for revenge; Dennis was absolutely convinced that was why he'd kept his head down and served his full term. That had surprised Dennis and he reluctantly afforded Seb the respect he deserved for sticking to his guns. Dennis wasn't sure he'd have done the same thing in Seb's position.

But now the old man wouldn't stop harping on about Seb's principles.

It was infuriating.

'Wish we could hear what was being said,' Ray complained.

'Nancy will be bleating about her kid.'

'Rightly so. Taking kids out just ain't right.'

'Yeah, I hear you. Still if she gives Seb any tips about who might have put Blythe onto our Lily then we'll be there to follow up and give the bastard the thrashing he deserves.'

'Move on! We have to make sure Seb don't stir up a turf war in his quest for revenge, nothing more.'

Dennis sniffed. 'Best make sure Dad don't catch on.'

Ray laughed. 'He thinks that because he's going legit the past won't catch up with him.'

'He's got a point though, about going legit, I mean. Our game ain't what it used to be. Can't trust no one. Those Albanians are right vicious bastards. Cut your throat as soon as look at you.'

'We still make the rules.'

'Yeah right, keep telling yourself that.' Dennis shook his head as he paused to adjust the binoculars. 'Wonder why he's taken Lily's carer with him.'

Ray laughed. 'Wouldn't mind taking her a few places myself. Even so, it's odd that he's got the woman with him.'

'Yeah, he gets out and they're instantly joined at the hip.' Dennis shook his head. 'It's the only out of character thing he's done and it bothers me.'

'Hey up, they're moving.'

The brothers ducked down behind a tree as Seb and Ava left the pub, deep in conversation with Nancy. They loitered for a while beside Seb's Aston as they continued to talk. Then there were hugs all round before Seb opened the passenger door for Ava and she slipped into the seat.

Ray nodded his approval as she elegantly folded her long legs into the space. 'Wouldn't mind a taste of that myself.'

'Forget it! Seb's clearly got her in his sights. Hopefully, she'll distract him.'

'From what?'

'From whatever shitstorm he's planning to create.'

'I thought that was what we want him to do.'

'Yeah, well...' Dennis scratched his arse. 'We need to get our ducks in a row so we're in a good negotiating position with Bishop. If we can be the ones to resolve the niggle between him and Jason, we'll be golden.'

'And get the blue-eyed boy out of our hair once and for all,' Ray said, standing to watch the Aston leaving the car park, bitterness in his tone.

'He survived a six stretch so don't underestimate him,' Dennis reminded his brother. 'He might not want to be part of the family firm but he's no pussy either.'

'Yeah, I hear you,' Ray replied. 'So, what do we do now?'

'We follow,' Dennis replied, getting behind the wheel of his own motor and firing up the engine. 'I have no idea what Nancy told him, or if she even knows anything, but we have to stay on him.' He watched the dot which was Seb's car on his phone's screen as he pulled out into the road. 'Something tells me that Nancy will be the key to the whole fucking business and if we can prove to Bishop that she's not as loyal as he thinks then we'll have it made.'

# 12

'So, there's no further doubt,' Ava said, breathing deeply, her eyes moist with emotion as Seb took her elbow and walked her towards his car at a brisk pace. 'Nancy confirmed that my mother was loved up with your father. Do you want to tell me why you didn't let me ask more questions? You suddenly got all furtive and dragged me out of there like your arse was on fire.'

'We will ask more,' he replied, glancing over his shoulder.

'What's up? What is it?'

'Probably nothing. And to answer your question,' he replied, unlocking his car with the remote and opening the door for her, 'Nancy told you that she didn't know what happened to your mother.'

'And you believe her?' Ava asked, her tone incredulous.

Seb waggled a hand from side to side as he climbed behind the wheel. 'Nancy says your mother was there, a permanent fixture, then she wasn't. Sorry, but that's par for the course for Jason.' Seb frowned as he checked his mirrors. 'Something wasn't right about that pub; I didn't feel comfortable. I couldn't shake the feeling that we were being watched. Whoever sent that email to you will have you in their sights, that's for sure.'

'You're getting paranoid,' she replied, shrugging the suggestion aside.

'Perhaps, but it's a sixth sense I developed inside and learned to trust. When I got that feeling, there was almost always someone out to make trouble.'

'Nancy has a lot more to tell us though.' Ava slipped onto the edge of her seat, restrained from bouncing impatiently by the tug of her seatbelt.

Seb shrugged. 'I don't think she has anything concrete insofar as my situation is concerned, just suspicions. Theories. But that isn't what really interests you.'

'I'm sorry if I—'

'I understand your need for answers.' He turned his head and smiled at her as he spoke to reassure, talking over her interruption. 'Don't worry, we'll link up with her again later if necessary.' He removed one hand from the wheel and covered hers with it. 'You okay? It's been a shock.'

Ava let out a long breath. 'I'm not sure what I feel, to be honest with you. It was one thing supposing that your dad and my mum had linked up but it seemed far-fetched. I came here in hope rather than expectation. Now that I know they did have a fling, I've no idea what to do with that information, other than to take it to your father.'

Seb held up a warning hand. 'We'll think of something. Anything, other than that. And if we do decide to confront him... well, I'll do the confronting. I don't want you exposed to his methods.'

'Oh, for goodness sake!' She huffed indignantly. 'I'm a big girl, Seb.'

'Who has yet to play with the big boys.' His tone hardened.

'That email should have taught you at least that much. Let me make the decisions about Jason. I promise not to do anything without consulting you first.'

'Okay.' She allowed a significant pause. 'I still don't see why we just can't ask though. What are you so afraid of?'

'We can't ask because if something bad happened to your mum and Jason knows about it, or had a hand in it, he's hardly likely to condemn himself and might even decide that he doesn't need nosy daughters asking awkward questions.'

'Now you're just being dramatic,' she replied, folding her arms defensively.

'Welcome to my world.' Seb drove on for a few seconds before speaking again. 'If you want my help, you need to do this my way. I promise we'll get there, but if you go off half-cocked then I can't protect you *and* you could screw up my chances of ever finding out who set me up.'

'You don't fight fair,' she replied stubbornly. 'That's about the only thing you could have said to prevent me from doing things my way.'

He chuckled. 'Whatever it takes.'

Seb drove the rest of the way home in silence and Ava forced herself to be content with his decision, even if she privately thought he was being a tad paranoid about cutting the meeting with Nancy short. And so many other things besides. Surely Jason wouldn't harm his favourite son, who'd already suffered the injustice of a long prison sentence? And what possible reason could he have for hurting Ava? She had questions about her mother's disappearance but no proof that anything bad had happened to her at Jason's hand or anyone else's.

Questions, she most definitely had in abundance. She was burning to know how her mother had behaved with Jason Carter and why she had left the family home to be with him. Had she done so willingly or been coerced? It didn't seem remotely possible but perhaps Ava's childhood memories of her beautiful mother, always laughing, always with a ton of time for Ava, was wide of the mark. Perhaps her mother had put on a good show for her, for her father, for the world in general, but had been unhappy. Dissatisfied.

'We'll meet Nancy later. It's her night off,' he told Ava as he garaged his car. 'Nine o'clock suit you? Lily will be settled by then and Jessie can listen out for her.'

'Sure. I'll be ready. Oh, and Seb. Thanks.'

He looked surprised. 'What for?'

'For going that extra mile for me. I know you have more pressing priorities and I want you to be aware that I appreciate it, despite the fact that I've done nothing but question your decisions.'

He smiled at her. 'My pleasure. Besides, I have a feeling that I'm helping myself as well as you.'

Ava widened her eyes. 'You think it's true what you've been told? That your father and Bishop both had designs upon my mother and fell out over her?' She shook her head. 'I still find it hard to believe that the mother I remember would willingly abandon her family for one other man, much less two. And if she had argued with Dad and told him she was leaving, why did he do all that sleuthing and discover Ruby Asquith's name?'

'Well, that's another thing we—'

'Besides, she would have found a way to let me know she was okay, even if she and Dad had come to a parting of the ways.'

'I'm sure she loved you very much.'

'Platitudes.' Ava smiled up at Seb as they walked towards the house, hoping that smile would take the edge off her sarcasm. She felt unsettled; argumentative and emotional but none of that was Seb's fault. She'd found out more in the less than two days he'd been out of prison than she had in all the months before that when she'd been floundering in the dark. *Hold that thought.* 'Thanks for trying to make me feel better. Not that I did anything that I regret so I don't feel responsible for Mum abandoning me. I just want to know why. That's all I've ever wanted to know.'

'I hear you.'

'Anyway,' Ava added as they walked into the kitchen and Lily hurtled herself into Seb's arms. 'I'll let you get on.'

'Everything all right, love?' Jessie asked as Seb gently untangled Lily's arms from around his neck and took himself off to his office. 'You look preoccupied.'

'The more I find out, Jessie, the more confused I become,' Ava replied as she sat herself at the kitchen table and smiled at Lily, who had returned to her sewing, secure in her own little world.

Jessie placed a mug of tea in front of her and Ava smiled her thanks. Since Seb's return, Ava had opened up to Jessie, telling her everything she and Seb found out or suspected. Jessie knew everything that happened in the family and might have seen Ava's mother and Seb's father together, even if she hadn't made the connection to Ava before now. Sadly, that proved not to be the case. She didn't condemn Ava for having an ulterior motive in taking on the care of Lily, going so far as to say that in Ava's position, she would be looking for answers too.

Ava told her what they'd found out from Nancy.

'Whew!' Jessie plonked herself down on the other side of the table and leaned the side of her face on her cupped hand. 'It's been quite a day then.'

'You could say that,' Ava replied with the suggestion of a smile.

'I'm trying to think back to that time. I really can't recall your mother. Sorry,' she added hastily, 'but Jason had so many women. It was hard to keep track. You mentioned that your mother worked in a casino, which would explain how they met but not why your mother would walk out on her husband and child.' She threw up her hands. 'Oh, the man could be charismatic, and generous, and persuasive but...'

'I know. That's what I keep being told.' Ava plucked absently at her sleeve. 'It's annoying that I couldn't ask Nancy more questions. Seb insisted that we leave just when it started to get interesting. He said he had a *feeling*, whatever that means.'

'But you're going to meet Nancy again, somewhere else?'

Ava nodded. 'Yeah, but...'

'Well, there you are then.' Jessie gazed off into the distance. 'I'll tell you something for nothing. If your mother was the cause of the rift between Bishop and Jason then she must have been quite something.'

'Oh, she was!' Ava's expression softened. 'She lit up every room she entered. I remember wishing I could grow up in her image.'

'You probably did.'

'She's dead, isn't she?' Ava said after a reflective pause. 'I've always thought that must be the reason why she never tried to contact me and explain. But still, all the time I didn't know for sure there was always an element of hope.'

'I understand.'

'Once I came across Dad's papers, I felt this compelling urge to find out. Now part of me wishes I'd left well alone.'

'I wonder if the war between Jason and Bishop resulted in...' Jessie nodded towards Lily, still totally absorbed with her sewing as she hummed to herself.

'That's what Seb wants to know and I'll tell you something, if that proves to be the case then I wouldn't want to be either of them.'

'Nor me. Seb always avoided the violence that his father and brothers used but that doesn't mean it's not in him.'

Ava sighed deeply. 'I know.'

'If we're right then it must have occurred to Jason that Bishop was the guilty party and if there was a shred of evidence then he would have purged the entire Bishop clan.' Jessie shook her head. 'No, sorry love, but I can't see Bishop taking out his spite on a harmless girl, especially not over a woman, no matter how attractive.'

'I keep hearing about how protective the Carter men are of their family image and yet Jason wanted to shut Lily away.' Ava rubbed the side of her temple, sensing a headache coming on. 'I just don't get it.'

'It's a matter of saving face. If someone attacks one of theirs then they have to do something about it or risk being seen as fallible.'

Ava rolled her eyes. 'Men!'

Jessie chuckled. 'You said it, darling.'

Lily put her sewing aside when Wizard woke from his place in front of the Aga and jumped all over her, wagging his entire rear end as he licked her face, making her giggle.

'He wants to go out,' Lily said, clapping her hands.

'Then we shall.' Ava stood up. 'Come on, sweetheart. Let's get our coats and give this dog a run in the woods.'

* * *

Seb was having a tough time concentrating on the plans he was attempting to examine on his computer regarding the changes he'd asked for with the latest development of apartments. He tutted, convinced his architect still hadn't got it right, but then again, it could be him who wasn't seeing the overall picture.

Small wonder given Nancy's revelations. He hadn't actually believed that Ava's mother and Jason had been seriously involved. Jason didn't do serious. Now he knew differently, it changed everything, but he was having a hard time thinking the implications through. Instead, his mind kept reverting to Ava, and the total look of disbelief on her face when Nancy had dropped her bombshell.

Somehow, Ava's mother now held the key to everything that had happened in his family this past eight years, notably the attack on Lily. Seb ground his jaw, convinced that must be the case. Would Bishop really go that far just to settle a score over a woman? To men of his wealth and stature, women were ten a penny. Seb shook his head. It couldn't be that simple. There had to be more to it than that, as evidenced by the email that Ava had received. Seb would not permit history to repeat itself. Whatever else happened, Ava would not be harmed on his watch; on that point he was fiercely determined.

'Got a moment?' Mark stuck his head round the door.

'Sure.' Seb threw aside the pen he'd been twiddling with. 'What do you need?'

'We have a problem.'

'When don't we?' Seb let out a long breath. 'Tell me.'

'We have a lad who helps with the cars and with the garden. His name's Simon MacDonald. A good kid. Eighteen. Been with us for about six months. He's a hard worker and gets on well with everyone. Never given any trouble.' Mark paused. 'Until now.'

'O... kay.' Seb leaned back in his chair, wondering where this was going. Even before he went inside, he hadn't dealt with staff issues in person. That was what he employed Mark and Pat to take care of.

'He's got one of the rooms over the garages.'

Seb nodded, aware that several of the ground workers lived in.

It was a bonus insofar as they didn't have the expense of maintaining their own place, which was tough for single guys to manage and still afford a social life.

'Well anyway, he's been out of sorts today, snapping at everyone and almost getting into a ruck with one of the other lads. I asked him what had got into him and... well, I think you'd best hear it for yourself.'

Without giving Seb an opportunity to respond, Mark opened the door and a lad who Seb had seen in the grounds, a redhead with the obligatory freckles decorating his nose and a muscular body that he didn't look comfortable in, shuffled awkwardly into the room. He didn't make eye contact with Seb and seemed to find something to occupy his attention on the surface of his muddy boots.

'Simon, is it?' Seb asked.

'Yeah.'

'Tell the boss what you just told me,' Mark said, his voice brusque but not unkind.

'I go to the Black Iris once a week,' the kid said, a hint of defiance underlying his tone.

Seb shared a glance with Mark, surprised that he could afford Ruby's prices, to say nothing of making his way up to town for that purpose. Her girls were the best, or used to be, and didn't come cheap.

'I visit my mum on me day off. She lives in Stockwell.'

Seb nodded, thinking that answered his question. 'Go on,' he encouraged.

'There's a weekly no-limit poker game.'

'Ah.' Seb nodded for a second time. Now this was starting to make sense. He knew of the games but they always used to be invitation only. He wondered how the kid had managed to inveigle such a coveted invitation.

'Me dad used to go there. I remember from when I was a kid.'

'Where's your dad now?' Seb asked.

Simon shrugged. 'Dunno. He scarpered when I was still small. Me mum bought us all up in a single family.'

Nothing new there. Mark and Pat liked to try and help the kids who came from disadvantaged backgrounds, most particularly the area where Seb grew up, by offering them work in the hope of keeping them on the straight and narrow.

'You got into debt, I take it.'

Simon nodded. 'Then today, a guy from the club approached me when I went into town on an errand for Pat. Said he'd wipe out my debt if I kept him informed about things here.' He made eye contact with Seb for the first time. 'Specifically about you. Where you go, who comes to see you. Stuff like that.'

'Seems our Simon has a conscience,' Mark said, irony in his tone. 'When I asked him what was wrong, I didn't have to torture the information out of him.' Mark cracked his knuckles. 'I reckon he was glad to get it off his chest.'

'Would you have done it?' Seb asked.

Simon shrugged. 'I wasn't given a lot of choice. I'd never have been able to pay off my debt. At least not as quickly as the guy said I'd have to. *And* he said he'd increase the rate of interest if I wasn't prepared to help.'

'How much are we talking?' Seb asked.

'A couple of thou.' It was Mark who answered.

'Did they know at the Iris where you work?' Seb asked.

'I didn't think so. I never said.' Simon lifted one shoulder. 'I just thought they remembered the old man.'

'They could have found out easily enough if they've been watching the place since you got out, Seb,' Mark said, 'and then made the connection between Simon here and his visits to the club.'

'Right.' Seb nodded at Simon. 'Don't look like you're about to face a firing squad.' He paused. 'Can I trust you?'

'Absolutely, Mr Carter. I don't want to be no grass but that guy... said his name was Bart Fleming. I've seen him about the place. He's Ms Asquith's minder.'

Seb glanced at Mark, who nodded.

'Built like a brick shithouse, he is.' Simon appeared more talkative now; anxious to please. 'Not the sort of guy you mess with.'

'Well then, Simon. I suggest you don't mess with him. Have you given him an answer to his proposition yet?'

'No, but he told me to go to the club tonight. That's what I was wrestling with when Mark asked me what was wrong. I like working here and don't wanna...'

'We'll tell you what to say,' Seb replied. 'Get off back to work now and see Mark before you go to the club tonight.'

'I will.' Simon breathed a huge sigh of relief. 'Thanks, Mr Carter. I won't let you down.'

'Well, well,' Seb said as the door closed behind Simon. 'The plot thickens.'

'Someone's getting worried about you being out and about,' Mark replied.

'With good reason.' Seb picked up his pen again and spun it through his fingers. 'Whoever set me up, Mark, has connections – close connections to the Iris.' He went on to tell Mark what he and Ava had learned from Nancy.

'Christ!' Mark dug his fingers into his scalp and had a good scratch. 'What the fuck...'

'My thoughts precisely.'

'What will you do?'

'See Nancy again later tonight. See what else she can tell us. She's between a rock and a hard place because she still works for Ruby and yet there's no love lost between them.'

'Why don't she leave then?' Mark asked. 'The poor woman no longer has a daughter to worry about.'

'No, but she has an ex who's in a position of power within the police, though. I gather he's now a DCI and if I try to protect her from his fists again, it will be all Drake needs, the excuse he's been looking for, to throw me back inside. He won't have forgiven me for what he sees as my interference in his domestic affairs.'

'How the corrupt have risen,' Mark replied, raising both bushy brows.

'Yeah well, he's on the Iris's payroll but still has a hard-on for Nancy. He knocked her about but never thought she'd find the courage to leave him. All the while she's still working for Ruby, she's safe from his clutches but I get the impression that he knows how to bear a grudge and if she breaks free then he'll consider her to be fair game.'

'Bastard!' Mark growled.

'Yeah, right.' Seb abandoned his pen and tapped the fingers of one hand restlessly against the surface of his desk instead. 'It's funny, all the time I was inside I had tunnel vision and one objective only when I got out.'

'To find out who offed Blythe and set you up for it.'

'Right.' Seb nodded emphatically. 'I haven't been out for forty-eight hours yet but already I find myself wanting to help Ava get answers *and* to free Nancy from Ruby's ubiquitous clutches, as well as those of her scumbag ex.'

Mark laughed. 'A right Sir Galahad.'

'Ha!' Seb threw back his head and groaned. 'That's me.' He sat upright again, his expression now set in stone. 'Seriously though, Mark, this ham-fisted approach to Simon indicates desperation.'

'Perhaps.' Mark seemed unconvinced. 'Simon's obviously a gambler and gamblers can usually be depended upon to do whatever it takes to wipe out their debts. If I hadn't come across him when I did, there's no guarantee that he would have 'fessed up.'

'No, perhaps not, but I think he's glad that he did. We can rely on him now.'

'Yeah, but I'll be watching him like a hawk.'

'Relax! There's nothing goes on here that he can report back that will interest Ruby. We have to assume that Bart was acting on Ruby's orders, as always.' Seb leaned back in his chair. 'She obviously knows more than she's let on and is running scared.'

'Jason hasn't got it out of her in all this time?' Mark looked sceptical.

'Dunno, but clearly someone doesn't want me muck-raking and every turn I've taken so far leads back to the Iris.'

'Which puts Ruby and your father squarely in the frame.'

'I reckon that if I can find out more about Ava's mother then I will also find out who set me up. Don't ask me why I think that way.' Seb shrugged. 'Sometimes you have to go with your instincts.'

# 13

Full of nervous expectancy, Ava felt as though the hands on the clock were turning backwards as she waited for nine o'clock to come round. Never had time moved more slowly. Lily, probably sensing her distraction, was in a stubborn mood and threw a tantrum, refusing to go to bed. Wizard saved the day by jumping onto the bed in question and yapping excitedly, like the therapy dog he hadn't been trained as. Good humour restored, Lily climbed beneath the covers and cuddled the little dog so tightly that he yapped for a very different reason.

Ava pulled the duvet over her charge, brushed the hair away from her face and kissed her cheek.

'Sleep well both of you,' she said, kissing Wizard too.

'You get yourself off, love,' Jessie said, coming up behind Ava on silent feet. 'I'll keep an eye on her until she drops off.'

'Thank you, Jessie. I'm not much good to her in the state I'm in anyway.'

'Get along with you. It stands to reason that you'll be excited.'

'Not sure excited is the right word. Apprehensive would be more appropriate.' She took a deep breath, using the opportunity to assimilate her oscillating thoughts. 'I've been searching for answers for months, simply assuming Mum had been a victim of an accident, her remains never found or identified. It was the only explanation that made any sense.' Ava offered up a wry smile. 'Or perhaps the only one I wanted to consider.'

Jessie's double chin wobbled as she nodded. 'Understandable.'

'Seb's been home for less than two days and already he's thrown up alternative explanations. Explanations that I would prefer not to have to face but must.' She sighed. 'In retrospect, ignorance was bliss. Knowing for sure will probably be better than all the increasingly wild speculations now running through my head, though.' She paused. 'I wonder if Dad found out more, which would explain why his investigations abruptly stopped. I thought he'd given up because he was too ill to continue delving but perhaps he didn't like what he discovered and so stopped looking.'

'Aye well, Seb always was a man to get things done and clearly nothing's changed during the past decade. Stick with him, love. He won't let you fall. And he needs to find answers himself, don't forget.'

Ava impulsively kissed the older lady's cheek and went off to her room to get herself ready to face whatever the evening decided to throw at her. Whatever came to light, she would handle it, she told her reflection as she brushed her hair and dabbed on some lip gloss to give her courage.

She met Seb in the hallway. Like her, he was dressed in jeans and looked unnaturally sombre, which did little to quell Ava's nerves.

'Ready?' he asked brusquely.

'As I ever will be.'

Seb chose to drive a dark Range Rover that evening. Ava

didn't bother to ask why he'd altered his mode of transportation, assuming he had done so simply because he could. He fired up the engine, continuing to look preoccupied, and pulled the car out of the garage.

'Something's happened,' she said after they'd travelled for five minutes in tense silence. 'Come on then, give.'

Expecting to learn something else about her mother, Ava was almost relieved to hear that one of Seb's employees had been bribed to spy on him.

'The Iris again,' she said, tapping her fingers on her knee. 'That place is definitely toxic. It shows that we must be onto something. Perhaps my email is something to do with someone there.'

'I agree. I just wish I knew what.'

'Nancy seems reliable but if she does know anything, why would she have kept quiet for so long?'

'Who would she speak to about your mother?'

Ava shrugged. 'True, I suppose.'

Following instructions issued by the disembodied voice in his sat nav, Seb indicated and turned off the dual carriageway into a modern housing estate on the outskirts of Chichester. He took another turning when told to do so and slowed to walking pace.

'We're looking for number six,' he told Ava.

'Why does she live in Chichester and yet work in Stockwell? It's quite a commute.'

'Our family relocated here the moment Jason started to make money. He thought it lent us an air of respectability and distanced us from his day job. He left it to others to look after his interests south of the river. Anyway, when Nancy wanted to get away from Drake, I suggested that she relocate to Chichester and make a fresh start. It was easier to keep an eye on her here too.

She's obviously moved since I last went to hers though because I've not been here before.'

Ava lowered her window, stuck her head out and pointed when she saw the house in question with a fairly new Peugeot parked in the drive. Seb stopped across the drive and cut the engine.

'Okay,' he said, releasing his seat belt. 'Game on.'

Nancy opened the door before they had a chance to ring the bell. She had changed since they'd seen her earlier and now wore yoga pants and a loose top. Her hair had been released from its up-do and hung to her shoulders in sleek waves that implied a lot of expensive attention was regularly lavished upon it. She wore minimal makeup that Ava guessed had been recently applied, as though attempting to make a good impression. As far as Ava was concerned, she would reserve judgement upon Nancy's character and motivation. Seb might trust her and although Ava had taken an instinctive liking to her, she had also learned to be cautious.

Trust had to be earned.

'Come in,' Nancy said, peering round the open door after Seb followed Ava into the hall, almost as though she wanted to be sure that they hadn't been followed. Clearly, she was nervous about something.

Nancy led them into a neat sitting room with a blazing log fire, in front of which a large marmalade cat was stretched full length, toasting his belly.

'Sit down. Can I get you anything?'

'Not for me, thanks,' Seb replied.

Ava shook her head too as she took the seat beside Seb on the settee. Nancy sat across from them and curled her legs beneath her: a casual pose that looked affected. Definitely nervous, Ava thought, which only served to increase her own anxiety. Whatever she was about to tell them, Ava sensed that she wouldn't like it.

'You look a lot like your mother,' Nancy remarked into the ensuing silence that neither Ava nor Seb felt inclined to break.

'So I've been told. I don't see it myself.'

'You carry yourself in the same way.'

Ava recognised procrastination when confronted by it and so remained silent. The tactic worked. Nancy took a deep breath and started talking.

'What I'm about to tell you is mostly educated guesswork,' she cautioned. 'Stuff that I put together for myself and one of the reasons why Ruby and I disagreed. Well, that and the fact that some of the girls who came to work for us didn't appear to be doing so of their own free will. *That* was my major beef. I knew better than to blow the whistle but did make it clear that unless the girls were with us because they wanted to be then I would walk, vengeful exes notwithstanding.'

'And you had too much knowledge about the operation for Jason and Ruby to let that happen.' Seb screwed up his nose. 'I wasn't aware that Jason had resorted to forced prostitution. In spite of everything, he tends to stick to his principles.'

'To be honest, I'm pretty sure that he had no hand in it.'

Seb looked concerned. 'Then who…'

'I think Ruby went rogue on him and linked up with Bishop.'

'Fucking hell!' Seb breathed. 'Why would she?'

'Well, you know what they say about a woman scorned. Jason dumped her and did so without thought for her finer feelings.' Nancy allowed a significant pause. 'And he replaced her with your mother, Ava.'

'I didn't reject her advances too politely either,' Seb remarked, rubbing the side of his index finger against his lips. 'Although I did nothing to invite them either. She wanted to use me to get back at Jason. I thought so at the time and nothing has happened to change that view.'

'Is that what Bishop and Jason fell out over?' Ava asked. 'Forcing girls into prostitution?'

'That I couldn't say.' Nancy didn't meet Ava's gaze, leading her to suppose that she *did* know more but wasn't prepared to let on. 'There had been niggles in paradise for a while, that much I do know.'

'Okay,' Seb said. 'Back up a little. Tell us more about Ava's mother. How did a respectable wife and mother come into Jason's orbit?'

'She worked at the Golden Hind as a dealer,' Nancy said.

Ava bit her lip and nodded. 'The casino. Yes, I know that much,' she said, her mind on that threatening email.

'Right. Jason had a minority shareholding in the place at the time. Not sure if he still does. Anyway, my understanding is – and bear in mind that I've pieced this together through snippets of information that I picked up along the way – that Jason saw her and was instantly besotted. He was with Ruby at the time but... well, a commitment of that nature would never prevent Jason from moving on to his next victim. Sorry,' Nancy added hastily when Ava winced.

'The mother I recall would never fall for something that obvious,' Ava said with conviction, despite being obliged to concede that she was no longer sure what temptations might have appealed to a mother, who had not been part of her life now for over half of it. 'She had her standards,' she added weakly.

'Are you aware that she took over the bookkeeping at the Iris?' Nancy asked, sharing an enquiring look between Ava and Seb.

'No,' Ava replied without hesitation. 'You think that's how Jason tempted her into an affair?'

'It certainly ruffled a few feathers when she came to the club to check the books over.'

'Mum always did her bookkeeping from home,' Ava said.

'Clearly, not always,' Nancy replied. 'I saw her at the club frequently during the day and rather liked her. She talked about you, Ava.'

Ava blinked. 'She did?'

'At the drop of a hat.' Nancy paused. 'Ruby disliked her on sight and was incensed when Jason brought her in. She claimed that their previous bookkeepers had done a first-rate job and the change had been unnecessary. Needless to say, she also disliked the competition.'

'Did Mum always go to the club to do the books?'

'She was there fairly frequently. Jason ran a tight ship and didn't like the books being done anywhere other than on the premises, despite the fact that it was all digital. He also said that he could trust Mel absolutely, which seemed odd. No one without a death wish would try to pull one over on Jason. Besides, I hadn't heard any complaints about the previous people's performance.'

Seb had remained unusually quiet during the exchange and the deep timbre of his voice as he spoke now jolted Ava out of an uncomfortable reverie.

'Jason needed to launder his ill-gotten gains through his flagship club and expected Mel, whose reputation was impeccable, to do the books for that reason,' he said in a speculative tone. 'He wouldn't trust anyone not personally connected to him with a situation that could ultimately come back to bite him on the arse and land him behind bars. He's far too wily for that.'

'That's my take on it,' Nancy agreed. 'HMRC had been sniffing around and, as you know, Jason hated any interference from officialdom. I heard him arguing with Ruby over the whole business but even the bent coppers on the club's payroll couldn't control the taxman. Anyway, Jason accused the previous bookkeepers of losing their edge and blaming them for the fact that HMRC was all over them like a rash.'

'Mum wouldn't agree to do anything illegal.'

'You underestimate the persuasive charm of Seb's dad,' Nancy replied. 'Your mother adored you but her marriage was far from satisfactory; take my word for it.'

'How can you say that?' Ava demanded hotly, her entire body jolting with indignation. 'Did you ever see my mum and dad together?'

'If a person is happily married then nothing on God's green earth would persuade either party into an affair,' Nancy replied without hesitation. 'Trust me, I know about what I speak. I have spent the majority of my adult life working in clubs like the Iris. A heap of married men partake of the services on offer and a lot of them feel the need to justify themselves afterwards either to the girls or to me. "My wife doesn't understand me" and all that crap. Having said that, I cannot think of a single one who claims to have had a marriage made in heaven.'

Seb nodded. 'The possibility must have occurred to you, Ava,' he said softly.

'I suppose... but still. I remember how broken Dad was when she disappeared. And anyway, even if there were bumps in their marital road, I don't believe Mum would abandon me without a word either.'

'I agree,' Nancy said softly. 'At least insofar as leaving you is concerned.'

'Then what...'

'She had something on her mind; something weighing her down, that much I do recall from a conversation I had with her not long after she took over the books,' Nancy said. 'I asked her why she'd chosen to work at the casino. It takes a certain type and although she had the looks, she didn't strike me as the sort who would enjoy that line of work. She said it was a matter of necessity. In other words, she needed the money.'

'That can't be right!' Ava felt incensed. Making assumptions about her mother with no obvious evidence that Ava had yet heard to back those assumptions up was totally unacceptable. Ava might have developed niggling doubts about her mother's motivation herself over the past day or two but that didn't give a comparative stranger the right to denigrate her memory. 'Dad's business was thriving.'

'Was it?' Nancy fixed Ava with a penetrating look. 'Know that for a fact, do you?'

Ava opened her mouth to speak but closed it again with no sound emerging. Seb briefly touched her hand but refrained from speaking too. The ominous silence in the room afforded Ava the opportunity to think things through. She had always looked upon her mother as a victim of some heinous accident, never the orchestrator of her own disappearance.

And that changed everything.

'No, I don't know as it happens,' she eventually said in response to Nancy's question. 'I simply assumed. I never overheard discussions about a lack of funds. There wasn't any tension and I wasn't denied anything I wanted.'

'Let's come back to that,' Seb said. 'I guess we can find out easily enough. But first, are you absolutely sure that Ava's mother and my father had an affair?'

'No doubt whatsoever,' Nancy said without hesitation. 'He paraded her about on his arm like some prized possession and sorry, Ava, but Mel appeared to enjoy the attention. She certainly didn't give the impression of being coerced into anything.'

'Don't mind me,' Ava replied, her voice sounding sullen. 'I no longer know what to believe.'

'Like I say, Bishop and Jason had come to verbal blows about the girls who were forced into working at the club.'

'I thought Bishop was a silent minority partner in the Iris,' Seb said. 'It was Jason's baby.'

Nancy chuckled. 'And that would stop him moving his girls in? Jason didn't get involved with the hiring and firing and probably wasn't supposed to know.'

Seb tilted his head in agreement. 'Bishop was provoking Jason. Going against his wishes with the connivance of a vindictive Ruby, who was out for revenge because she'd been unceremoniously dumped?'

Nancy nodded. 'Yeah, there was tension between them. Then Bishop saw Mel and he was totally smitten. Never seen the like of it before. He certainly didn't attempt to conceal his feelings.'

'Blimey,' Seb remarked. 'She was a looker, I get that, but attractive women were par for the course for those two. Bishop would never poach on Jason's turf.' He frowned. 'Would he?'

Nancy shrugged. 'None of this is provable, but I do know that the two of them were disagreeing more and more. That *is* a fact. What I *think* is that Bishop was looking at a way to provoke a parting of the ways. There were changes in the London criminal world: ruthless gangs from overseas doing whatever was necessary to gain turf. Gangs without your father's morals, Seb.'

Seb nodded slowly. 'Jason, for all his faults, did have some boundaries that he wouldn't cross. Forcing girls to work for him is one. Hard drugs was another.'

'Right.' Nancy's expression turned grim. 'Bishop had no such qualms though and was spoiling for a fight. I think he was tired of Jason holding him back with his old-fashioned morals.' Seb grunted but refrained from comment. 'Bishop was of the view that they must move with the times or risk being usurped. He noticed that Jason was fixated on Mel and saw an opportunity to create a fight by making a play for her.'

'But why would she fall for that one?' Ava asked, probably looking as perplexed as she felt. 'I'm struggling to imagine the mother I remember doing any such thing...'

'You think Bishop had something on her that forced her hand?' Seb asked into the awkward silence that ensued.

'I'm pretty sure that he must have,' Nancy replied without hesitation. 'Now, this part is all conjecture: an educated guess, if you like.' She paused to take a sip from the glass of water at her side. The cat stirred, rolled over to toast the opposite side of its body and appeared to have fallen asleep again immediately. 'Assuming that Mel was cooking the books in order to make up for your father's losses, Ava, then you can bet that Ruby picked up on it. She was gunning for Mel, looking for a reason to get rid of her, *and* Ruby's not just a pretty, albeit ageing face. She knows her way around a spreadsheet and can smell a scam at twenty paces with the wind in the wrong direction. More than one of the girls who've worked at the club have tried various ruses to feather their own nests but not one of them has succeeded, at least not as far as I know.'

'So you think that Ruby picked up on whatever my mother was doing, always assuming she was doing something out of order, and ran to Bishop telling tales?'

'Sounds highly plausible.' It was a grim-faced Seb who answered her. 'I know from experience just how ruthless and vindictive Ruby can be.'

All three occupants of the room fell silent, the only sound now being the crackling of logs and the ticking of a clock as they contemplated the situation.

'How sure are you of your facts?' Seb eventually asked.

'Sure enough not to have breathed a word about my suspicions before now,' Nancy replied with asperity. 'I wouldn't have lasted five minutes in that club if I didn't know how to keep my trap shut.'

Seb nodded. 'Fair point.' He shifted his position and stretched his arms above his head. 'Which begs the question: what happened to Mel? Where is she now?'

'And more to the point,' Ava added. 'Is she still alive?'

# 14

Seb could see that Ava was on emotional overload. He knew that she needed to get her head round what she'd just heard. Whether she could be persuaded to believe it was another matter. Seb already knew that there had to be an element of truth in what Nancy had told them and suspected that her speculations as to Mel's motivation weren't far off the mark.

The only question he couldn't answer was why a woman who was supposedly a devoted wife and loving mother would willingly share Jason's bed. And Seb didn't doubt that she had willingly shared it. As far as he was aware, Jason had never forced his attentions where they were unwelcome; he'd never needed to. Women came on to him in droves, attracted by what appeared from the outside to be a glamorous lifestyle. Nancy had said that Mel looked perfectly comfortable being paraded about by Jason and that was good enough for Seb, since Seb vaguely recalled that was the case himself. If Mel had been with him unwillingly then someone with Nancy's experience in the game would have picked up on the signs.

'Thanks, Nancy,' Seb said, standing. 'I know that wasn't easy for you.'

She looked directly at Ava as she spoke. 'I have always wanted to know what happened to Mel but there was no one I could trust to confide in before now.'

'I think it's obvious what happened to her,' Ava replied, gulping. 'She's dead because she broke the rules. Jason killed her for exploiting her position, always assuming she was skimming for reasons I have yet to decide. Either that or she was done away with for taking up with Bishop. He doesn't sound like the type who would stand for disloyalty.'

'Amen!' muttered Nancy, not completely able to suppress a shudder.

'Or perhaps Bishop did it because she *wouldn't* switch allegiances.' Ava lifted her shoulders in a negligent shrug. 'I have no way of knowing and don't suppose I'll ever find out after all this time.' She glanced at Seb, an apology in her expression. 'I'm making all sorts of accusations against your father with nothing to back them up other than speculation. Sorry.'

'Don't be. Jason wouldn't ordinarily harm a woman but there's no way of knowing what he might do if he discovered that one was stealing from him.'

'Even so.'

'Let me know what happens,' Nancy said, impulsively hugging Ava who remained statue-like and unresponsive in the older lady's arms. 'I imagine you will have questions for Jason,' she added, releasing Ava and turning her attention to Seb.

'Not yet. I can't prove what you've just told me and Jason will guess who did the telling if I broach the subject. I don't want to drop you in it.'

'Then what?' Ava's voice sounded thin and distant.

'Come on.' He took Ava's elbow. 'We'll talk in the car. Best

Nancy doesn't know just in case our stirring things gets her in trouble. What she doesn't know she can't repeat.' He turned towards the door. 'Later, Nancy.'

'Stay safe, both of you.'

Seb unlocked his car and opened Ava's door for her. They sat cocooned in their seats but he didn't start the engine right away.

'Fire away. I know you must have dozens of questions,' he said softly.

'Do you trust her?' Ava asked at the same time.

'I do, as much as I trust anyone. I've met her ex and he's a hard case. The passage of time won't have lessened his desire for revenge. No one walks out on Paul Drake and gets away with it indefinitely. And he will have found lots of little ways to remind Nancy of the fact, which makes the risk she took just now all the more commendable.'

'Then why did she do it?'

Seb smiled. He'd been wondering the exact same thing. 'A number of reasons is my guess. She has a conscience, otherwise she wouldn't have found the courage to make a stand on behalf of the girls forced to work at the club against their will. She doesn't share Ruby's questionable morals and probably wants to bring matters to a head so that she can finally get out from under. But she had to wait for the right opportunity, which you provided by asking questions about your mother.'

'But she never will get out all the time her ex is alive and out for revenge.' Ava turned to face him, her eyes widening. 'Unless he's somehow involved with something. Either my mother or your false imprisonment and this is her way of setting you on his tail.'

Seb nodded. 'The same thought had occurred to me.'

'Then again,' Ava mused. 'Nancy could have been told to say what she did. Whoever set you up will know you're out.'

'But not that I would go to Nancy asking about your mother.'

Ava slumped back in her seat. 'I suppose not.'

'Anyway, there's an easy enough way to find out if her suspicions are on the money.'

She looked at him, huge eyes moist with emotion. 'Which is?'

'Your father's business.' Seb fired up the engine and pulled away. 'If we look into it and discover that he was in financial trouble, it would explain why your mother went to such extreme lengths.'

Ava blew air through her lips. 'Including enjoying being on your father's arm.'

'Put emotion to one side and let's come at this objectively.' He paused to gather his thoughts. 'Did your father retire and sell a thriving business?'

'Yes.' Ava shook her head. 'Well, actually no. It was the pawnbroking that made all the money. He was one of the first in the locality to get into it. Then others jumped on the bandwagon, offering better rates and not being too particular about the provenance of the items they took in. Knowingly accepting stolen goods is... well, a crime, and Dad was careful in that regard. Others weren't so choosy, apparently. I remember him complaining about the playing field no longer being level.'

Seb nodded as he overtook a slow-moving car.

'That made things tougher but I have no idea if he finished up in the red,' Ava continued. 'He still did a healthy trade in second hand items: things that were pawned and not collected. After a certain amount of time and issuing warning letters to the owners, he was permitted to sell them in order to recover his initial outlay. Obviously, he made a decent profit because he didn't lend more than the item was worth.

'Anyway, he sold out the jewellery side and remaining pledges to a rival. He didn't own the premises so it was just the value of the stock and the goodwill that he got paid for. I never asked how much but assumed that his life's work had left him well situated. Now, I no longer know what to think.' She sighed. 'I should have asked; taken more interest but he never gave any indication that he was unhappy with the sale. Quite the reverse. He said he was looking forward to retiring.'

'Was this before or after your mother's disappearance?'

'After.' Ava blinked. 'Why?'

'Not sure, but if your mother *was* doing something in her capacity as bookkeeper to help your father's failing business then his selling up after he'd given up hope of her return would make sense.' Seb removed one hand from the wheel and rubbed his chin. 'Did he plan his retirement or did it come out of the blue?'

Ava blinked. 'It did come as a bit of a surprise, I suppose, now you mention it. He hadn't reached retirement age but his light faded when Mum disappeared. Not surprising really, I suppose. Anyway, he said he couldn't compete with the cut-throat opposition that had sprung up; he'd been made an offer and had decided to take it.' Ava ran a hand abstractly through her hair. 'To be honest, I encouraged him to take the deal. I never asked if he was getting as much as he deserved. Told him it would give him an opportunity to travel, to do all the things he'd put on hold. I thought it would help him to get over Mum because he'd been depressed ever since she went missing, much as he tried to disguise the fact. He put on a cheerful face in front of me but I knew he was suffering big time.'

'And did he? Travel and make new friends, I mean.'

'Actually, no. Whenever we spoke, a big trip was always in the pipeline but never materialised for one reason or another. I worried but, of course, I wasn't living at home, he sounded cheerful enough whenever we spoke and... well, I blame myself for not keeping a closer eye on him.'

'You have nothing to blame yourself for. You had no idea what was going on with him.'

'I was so wrapped up with finding the parent I'd lost that I forget to take care of the one I still had.'

'None of this is your fault, Ava.'

'Perhaps not, but that isn't the way it feels.' Ava let out a long breath and dashed impatiently at an errant tear. 'Anyway, then he got ill so the travelling never got off the ground, so to speak.'

'It sounds to me as if he started seriously delving into your mother's disappearance only after he retired.'

Ava nodded. 'Yes, that ties in with the dates on some of the emails he printed out. Dad was very methodical that way.'

'So, the next step.'

'What do you suggest we do?'

'Let's take a peep at your father's business accounts. They would have to have been filed with HMRC.'

'We can do that?'

Seb smiled at her. 'We can do anything. Or more to the point, John can. I'll get him on it straight away.' He checked his mirrors for the tenth time since leaving Nancy's house, worried that the same car had been on their tail for a while. He breathed more easily when it peeled off at the next junction. 'If there are financial anomalies then your mother's willingness to fall in with Jason would make more sense.'

'You think she went *that* far to bail Dad out of trouble?'

'Anything's possible. People do out of character things all the time when their backs are against the wall, their living standards under threat.'

Seb concentrated on the road, leaving Ava with the time she needed to come to terms with his take on what they had learned, or suspected.

'Even if what you say is true,' she remarked as Seb pressed a button that opened the gates to his property and drove through them, 'how would money laundering help?'

Seb gave a one-shouldered shrug. 'Either she was paid well to break the law or she used her skill as a bookkeeper to skim off some of Jason's profits, which she could have ploughed back into your father's business.'

'She wouldn't!'

'The mother you remember wouldn't, but did you really know her?'

Ava nodded with apparent reluctance. 'Clearly not.' Seb glanced at her profile and could see that she was deeply disturbed. 'If she stole from your father that would be enough to get her killed, wouldn't it?' she asked, her features frozen in horror.

* * *

'Whoa! Don't shoot the messenger.' Bart pushed his palms towards Ruby in a conciliatory gesture. 'You asked me to recruit someone inside Seb's place and that's what I did, even though I think you're overreacting and it's not necessary. Not my fault if you don't like what you find out.'

'Can you trust him, though?' Ruby took a hefty sip of her champagne, sneezing when the bubbles went up her nose.

'The kid's into us for several thou. He wouldn't dare to feed us duff info. Besides, I scared the shit out of him.' Bart sounded pleased about that, and Ruby knew he got off on intimidation and threatening behaviour.

'But what he's told us don't help much.'

'You're losing your edge.'

'Watch your mouth!' Ruby glowered at her minder. Anyone else who spoke to her so disrespectfully would be out on their ear but Bart had proved his loyalty time and again over the years and had earned the right to speak his mind. Besides, he knew too much about Ruby's nefarious activities for her to risk letting him off the leash. She needed him where she could keep him under control, dancing to her tune. Pandering to her every need. Giving her, for the most part, sound advice.

'What he's told us is golden.' He placed his meaty fists on his hips and sighed. 'Okay, I'll spell it out for you. The girl taking care of Seb's sister is none other than Mel Harper's daughter.'

Ruby's frown intensified at the mention of Mel's name and she took another long swig of her drink, draining the glass and holding it out to Bart for a refill. 'Why did he make a point of telling you that particular snippet?' she asked, scared of obvious implications that she hadn't needed Bart to spell out for her. Mel had been trouble with a capital T, swanning in and wrecking all Ruby's carefully laid plans. The daughter was probably cut from the same cloth and Ruby wasn't about to put up with it for a second time. 'How did he even know that it would interest me?'

'He didn't. When he came in tonight and agreed to work for us, I asked him for specifics about who's employed there, just to test him. When he mentioned the girl's name it rang a bell, so I delved a bit and had it confirmed.'

'It can't be a coincidence, her going to work for Seb not long before he was released.' Ruby tapped red talons restlessly against the stem of her glass. 'What does she think she knows? Why would she...'

'Calm down and think it through. There's nothing for her to know. If she found out that Mel worked here and wanted to know more, she'd have come knocking at your door. No need for subterfuge. You didn't get rid of her mother, did you?' He waved a hand to prevent Ruby from answering him. 'Forget I asked. If you'd wanted her silenced, you'd have given the job to me, and you didn't, so why are you getting your knickers in such a twist?' Bart narrowed his eyes at Ruby. 'Come on, give! I can't have your back if I don't know what I'm protecting it from.'

Ruby sent Bart a long, speculative look, took another fortifying sip of her replenished drink and sent him a malevolent smile.

'I might have expressed my concerns about Mel to someone not directly connected to me,' she said sweetly.

* * *

Ray and Dennis sat across from their father, absorbing the full force of his hostile glare without backing down.

'What the fuck do you think you're playing at, spying on yer own brother?' he demanded to know.

'We're looking out for the family's interests.' It was Dennis who responded. Out of the two of them, Jason was aware that he had slightly more nous, which wasn't saying a lot. Ray was definitely a follower who trailed behind his brother like an oversized puppy dog, using his fists to resolve problems. 'Seb ain't been out for forty-eight hours but already he's muck-raking. Don't want him stirring things up and queering our pitch.'

'Well, of course he's fucking well asking questions! What else did you expect?' Jason closed his eyes, threw back his head and roared. 'God give me strength! If you'd been banged up for a six stretch, wouldn't you want to know who put you behind bars, and why?'

'The point is, he met with Nancy in a country pub, all out of the way like,' Dennis said, a stubborn edge to his tone. 'Why would he do that?'

'Nancy don't know nothing,' Jason replied, breathing slightly more easily.

'Then why meet in secret?' Dennis demanded to know.

'Because, you moron, Seb most likely wanted it that way. Until he unearths something, he'd prefer to keep a low profile. The filth will still be watching him and he won't want them sticking their oar in.'

'Is that right?' Dennis flashed a smug smile that made Jason feel uneasy. His sons might privately think he was past it but they never openly challenged his authority. Dennis had chosen the wrong time to grow a pair and Jason would soon chop him off at the knees. 'Then how come he took Lily's little minder with him?'

Jason shrugged. 'I dare say you're going to tell me before I die of old age.'

'Because she's Mel Harper's daughter is why,' Dennis replied after a prolonged pause that irritated the hell out of Jason, looking proud of himself.

Jason, who'd been leaning back in his chair with one foot crossed over his opposite thigh, abruptly sat forward. His feet hit the floor with a resounding thud.

'What the fuck! Why am I only hearing this now?' Dennis's triumphant expression gave way to a furtive look and he was unable to meet Jason's eye. The fool had, of course, got above himself. In his desire to undermine Seb, he'd forgotten what relatively harmless yet vital responsibilities Jason had entrusted to him. It seemed like the right time to remind him, and to reassert his authority.

'It... I dunno.' Dennis continued to avert his gaze. Ray picked at a hangnail and looked as though he would much prefer to be elsewhere. 'Didn't seem...'

'You didn't know who she was, did you?' Jason didn't raise his voice but knew that the low, threatening rumble he employed instead was ten times more intimidating. 'I specifically tasked you with looking out for your sister. You were supposed to know the shoe size of her various carers and alert me if anything seemed off. How hard can that be?'

'Yeah, I know but...'

'You didn't know, did you?' Jason said for a second time. As the truth slowly dawned on him, Jason slammed the flat of his hand against a table top so violently that the items on it wobbled. Dennis jerked upright in his chair as though he'd suffered an electric shock. Ray clenched his fists and looked bewildered. Nothing new there.

'Nothing to say for yourself? Not so cocky now, are you son?'

Neither of them answered him, not that Jason had expected them to. He took a deep breath and a moment to think the situation through. Little Miss Harper turning up at Seb's just before he got out couldn't have been a coincidence. Presumably, she wanted to know what had happened to her mother and hoped that Seb would find the answers for her. If she was even half as good looking as her mother then she wouldn't have too much trouble persuading Seb to help her.

Thinking about the mother gave Jason a hard-on like he hadn't known for years and he shifted his position to hide it from his boys. He had never gotten over Mel, not completely, and still missed her every second of every day.

What the hell was Jason supposed to do now? What could he do? If he tried to warn Seb off then he'd only delve deeper. Jason regretted not telling him something – anything – to send him off on a tangent when he'd called round the day before. He'd always known that they would see one another and he'd had six years to think of something plausible. Not that anything short of telling him who'd set him up would have stopped Seb in his tracks.

And if Jason had known the answer to that question then he would gladly have told Seb long ago.

'Okay, boys,' Jason said, striving for patience. 'Keep a discreet watch on your brother, and on the girl. I want to know every move they make and do not cock it up.'

Jason waved a hand in dismissal and reached for the whisky decanter. Changing his mind at the last moment, he reached for his mobile instead and called Paul Drake. It was beyond time that his tame detective earned his corn.

# 15

Ava found it hard to concentrate on Lily's requirements the following morning. It was drizzling and so the two of them remained in the kitchen. Today Lily was sketching a likeness of Wizard asleep on his back, paws pointing skywards, which was remarkably good. She possessed a natural artistic talent that Ava encouraged Lily to explore, and which kept her absorbed for hours.

Seb joined them just before Lily was about to have her lunch. He spent a few minutes with his sister, praising her efforts, but it was clear that he too was distracted.

Leaving Lily in Jessie's care, Ava followed Seb into his study.

'What's up?' she asked. 'You look angry.'

'More concerned.' He ushered her towards a chair, closed the door and sat across from her. 'I told you about young Simon, who we're planning to use to feed information to Ruby.'

Ava nodded. 'What about him?'

'Bart Fleming, Ruby's minder, grilled him last night about the people employed here. He mentioned your name, which elicited a great deal of interest on Bart's part. He obviously didn't know you were here.' Seb allowed a long pause. 'But now he does.'

Ava shrugged. 'So what? I've never kept it a secret. I didn't realise that I needed to. Why are you so wound up about it?'

'I'm concerned because I worry about your safety and because it will make getting answers that much harder.'

She spread her hands. 'I don't see why.'

'Bart will assume that you're here for a reason and if he knows what happened to your mother, it will give him time to cover his tracks.'

'He's had a ton of time already. I don't suppose there's much left for us to find now, unless someone talks and that's not very likely, is it? Besides, I'm safe enough here in your house and I never get to go out without Mark tagging along.'

'When you go out with Lily. You do get time off for bad behaviour.'

She smiled at his feeble attempt at a joke. 'Why would anyone try to do anything to me if there's nothing for me to find out? That would only create a shit storm.'

'That I couldn't say but still, I don't like it.' He stood with arms folded, his stance projecting a toughness warring with vulnerability. *He cares about me*. Or more to the point, Ava thought, he's worried that something will happen to me on his patch and then the police would be all over him.

*Again.*

And this time they would throw away the key.

She chased that thought away. Seb had done nothing so far other than to go out of his way to help her find answers. He pretended that those answers might help him to resolve his own situation but that was far from certain. Then again, he'd seen how well she and Lily got along. Perhaps he hoped that in helping her, she would feel obliged to remain in his employ after she'd found the answers she sought.

'Anyway.' He turned to smile at her and the demonic look left his eye. 'Suffice it to say that you won't be going anywhere alone until we have a better idea who and what we're dealing with. Hope you don't have any hot dates lined up.'

'Oh, at least a dozen.'

He sent her a droll look. 'I wish I could convince myself that you're joking.'

'No convincing necessary. I am.'

Seb resumed his seat across from her. 'John's come up with some information that might interest you.'

'Do I want to hear it?' she asked, swallowing.

Seb reached behind him and lifted some papers from his desk. 'Your father's business thrived until about a year before your mother went missing. Then it went downhill fast, drowning under a mountain of debt.'

'His returns mentioned debts?' She twitched her nose.

'John can be very resourceful. The business should have gone under but there was an influx of capital from somewhere at the eleventh hour.'

'Doesn't its source have to be declared?' Ava asked, feeling calm and detached as she peeled away the layers of adoration and began to see her father in a different light. Human. Fallible. Unable to compete in an increasingly cut-throat world where a gentleman's agreement no longer meant anything. A handshake had been her father's bond and in retrospect she could see that the speed with which the modern world moved, the underhand tactics that were employed to get ahead, could easily have been the downfall of such a decent and trusting man.

She wondered if her mother, who had always been more

worldly, more cynical than her father, had realised it too and if she had tried to open his eyes to the way things now were. Had she become disillusioned with the man she had married and his inability to adapt to the times? Could that be why she'd been seduced by the glamour and sophistication of Jason's world, or did she agree to Jason's terms in order to save her husband the humiliation of failure?

If she had been seduced, that is.

Ava was yet to be convinced, despite the evidence that was mounting up, because she desperately wanted to hold onto her childhood memories of a woman who was a devoted wife and mother. But the adult Ava also knew that grown women had desires and needs that a disintegrating marriage could easily exacerbate and so she tried to withhold judgement; at least until she was in possession of more facts.

'John did more digging.' Seb's voice snapped Ava out of her reverie and she offered him her full attention, glad for a reason to break off a train of thought that felt both logical and disloyal. 'He found out that your father took some equity from his house, but not enough to account for the subsequent amounts that were drip fed into his business, keeping it afloat.'

'Ah.' Ava sighed. 'I knew about the house. Sorry. I should have said something earlier but it didn't seem relevant. I was obviously Dad's sole beneficiary and the solicitor explained there was less to come than the house was worth because of the equity release. I never thought much about it. I'm not the type of daughter who assumes she has an automatic right to an inheritance. I'm perfectly capable of making my own way.'

'How much was left from the sale of the business?'

Ava told him. 'That doesn't seem like much, does it,' she said pensively. 'Clearly, something was going on and I was too stupid to realise it.'

'Something was going on and you're far from stupid.' Seb reached across and took her hand in his. 'I don't want to upset you but John called in a few favours from contacts he has in useful places and discovered that your father, at about the time of your mother's disappearance, was being investigated for handling gemstones smuggled into this country from India.'

'No!' Ava snatched her hand from his and placed both of hers on the sides of her face. Her mind was reeling. Being old-fashioned, incompetent – call it what you will – was one thing. Resorting to criminal behaviour was entirely another and completely out of character. 'I don't believe it,' she said. 'He wouldn't.'

* * *

Seb handed Ava the printed report that John had got his hands on and watched her as she scanned it, sceptically at first, repeatedly shaking her head before throwing it aside. She picked it up again almost immediately and read it for a second time, more slowly, her lips moving all the time. Her entire demeanour gradually changed, which is when Seb knew that she'd accepted the truth.

'Why would he?' she asked aloud. 'I really didn't know him at all, did I? If he did this then he must have been coerced, or desperate, or... well, something!' She threw up her hands, a wild look in her eye. 'Perhaps he was desperate to regain Mum's respect, or he wanted to make it unnecessary for her to work at the casino. Like I say, he had old-fashioned values and it wouldn't have sat well with him if he had to depend upon his wife to keep his business afloat. As far as he was concerned, the man was the breadwinner. I don't know what made him do it. I just don't know and it's killing me. I should have noticed that he was struggling.'

'The last thing that either of them wanted was for you to know they were in trouble; I'm absolutely sure of it.'

'Which doesn't make me feel any better.'

'Put yourself in your father's position. He was sinking beneath a swathe of debt, fighting against competition he couldn't... well, compete against and needed to reassert himself as head of his family. You said yourself that he prided himself on being the provider, which explains a lot. It also explains why your mother worked at the casino and subsequently agreed to work at the Iris. The extra income might have made all the difference.'

'And driven a wedge between my parents.' Ava sighed. 'Okay, I get that, but why go to bed with Jason?'

'He probably bailed your father out financially and made the investigation into the gem thefts go away. Someone with a lot of clout sure as hell did because the evidence was pretty compelling.'

Ava looked sceptical. 'He has that sort of power?'

'He does.'

Ava nibbled at her lower lip, looking perilously close to tears. Tears that she didn't allow to fall. This girl was tougher than she looked and ready to face distressing, disillusioning news head on. Clearly, knowing the truth was more important to her than constantly wondering, even if that truth cast doubts upon her fondest childhood memories. Seb admired her grit and would do everything he could to help her.

Even if that meant going to Jason and forcing the truth out of him.

Somehow.

'Okay,' she said, squaring her shoulders. 'So Dad was a gem smuggler and Mum used Jason to get him out of trouble. But that still doesn't explain what happened to Mum.' She turned to look at Seb, her expression resolute. 'Do you think she's still alive somewhere and if so, how do we track her down?'

'No, I doubt whether she's still alive,' Seb replied, seeing no reason to prevaricate. Ava wanted the truth and he'd give it to her the way he saw it. 'Sorry, darling, but she was out of her league when she got involved with Jason and Bishop, especially if she played them off against one another. We don't know what she actually did, but the chances are she threatened to expose their money laundering for reasons only she would know about. Or perhaps she realised that girls were being forced to work in that club and, unlike Nancy, wasn't prepared to keep schtum about it. Now *that* would definitely have gotten her killed.'

'It would also have been stupid and she was never that. It already looks as though she had more nous about her than my dad. She was prepared to bend the rules but would never have countenanced forced prostitution. Although, then again, I'm not really qualified to say what she would or wouldn't have done, it seems.' Ava let out a long breath. 'Anyway, what do we do now?'

'That depends on whether you want to carry on digging. Like I say, the chances of your mother still being alive and not having found a way to contact you for all this time are remote. Sorry,' he added, wincing when her face fell. 'But facts have to be faced. Jason's world is brutal and you have to weigh up the likelihood of finding anything out that will help you against the risks of getting involved in shit that Jason will want to keep buried and go to any lengths necessary to ensure that it is. Sorry,' he said for a second time. 'Unfortunate choice of words.'

'I hear you, but—'

'You now know that your father got involved in dodgy dealings and that your mother tried to get him out of trouble, which is more than you knew or even suspected this time yesterday. It almost certainly didn't end well for her. Best let things be.'

'Almost certainly?' She folded her arms and drummed the fingers of one hand against her opposite forearm. 'I know you're right, but I can't let it rest. Until I know for absolutely sure that Mum is dead then I won't know any peace.'

'Fair enough but you need to promise me that you won't do anything rash.' He grinned when she opened her mouth to speak, her expression indignant, and cut off her protest with a slash of his arm. 'This isn't a game, Ava. These are dangerous men who will do whatever it takes to protect their freedom without any qualms.'

'I hear you.' Ava paused, clearly still pondering upon these latest revelations. Everything she thought she knew about her formative years had just been brought into question and she was having a tough time accepting that both of her parents actually had feet of clay. 'Do you think Mum found it exciting being in Jason's orbit, which is why she got in deeper than she intended, and then found there was no way out?'

'Being a wife and mother wasn't enough for her?'

Ava waggled a hand from side to side in a considering fashion. 'I thought so but... well, if Dad had disappointed her and she saw another side to life. I'm pretty sure she must have taken the job at the casino only after Dad's business got into trouble and that it maybe opened up a whole new world to her.'

Seb nodded. 'Very likely,' he said. 'It can seem that way at first.'

'I'm sorry,' she said.

'About what?'

'Well, we seem to be fixated on my problems when all you want to know is who set you up.'

Seb smiled at her. 'Don't worry. I'm a patient man.'

'So, what do we do now?'

'I guess I need to invite Jason to pay us a visit.'

'I thought you didn't want him anywhere near Lily? I won't risk her security just to get answers.'

'I appreciate your thoughtfulness but it won't come to that. I'll invite him to come over in the evening after Lily's in bed.'

'Okay, but do you think he'll tell us anything?'

Seb wondered the same thing. 'We need to shock him out of his complacency, which is why you need to be there when I see him. I suspect you look much like your mother did when he knew her. If he really had feelings for her, that could give us the edge.'

'Of course. You would have had a tough time keeping me out.'

'I'm betting that he didn't know you worked here. If he had, it would have raised a red flag and you would have heard from him. But now, Simon unwittingly told Bart, which means Ruby knows, so Jason probably does by now as well.'

'And he won't think my being here is a coincidence, which of course it isn't. He will want to find out how much I know.'

'Which is why you have to tread carefully. If, and I don't mean to scare you... but if your mother is dead, and if Jason gave the order, then he won't hesitate to do away with annoying daughters who have a talent for asking difficult questions.'

Ava swallowed but her expression remained defiant. 'I understand. When will you...'

Seb's computer pinged with an incoming email. He turned to see who it was from and did a double take. 'Well, well,' he muttered.

Ava looked over his shoulder. 'Gaynor?' She looked as bewildered as Seb himself felt. 'What does she want?'

Without responding, Seb opened the email and they both read it.

Your visit forced me into going through Gordon's things. They are in the loft and I haven't touched them for years. Not sure why I didn't get rid of them. Guess I've always held onto the hope that perhaps, one day… Anyway, I came across this memory stick. Don't recall seeing it before. It was hidden in an envelope amongst some old letters. I opened it and it contains a load of pictures that mean nothing to me. Perhaps, since he hid it, they're important and might help you to find answers.

If they give you any idea of what happened to Gordon, please let me know.

Gaynor

'Whew!' Seb stood upright and glanced at Ava, who was literally hopping from foot to foot with excitement.

'Well, are you going to open the attachment before I die of old age?' she asked impatiently.

Feeling apprehensive himself, Seb clicked on the zip file and a dozen blurry photographs were revealed.

'A back passageway,' Ava said, sniffing. 'What does that tell us?'

'Potentially a lot. Before even looking at the people I can tell you that's the side entrance to the Black Iris. Part of Gordon's duties as doorman would have been to ensure that no one attempted to sneak in through the tradesman's entrance.' Seb paused, unsure why he felt the need to procrastinate. He wanted to discover what Gordon had recorded and why, but a part of him also didn't want to know. 'It's also the entrance that people like Jason used in order to be discreet. Now, who do we have here?'

'And why did Gordon feel the need to take pictures?'

'Probably got in over his head and wanted some bargaining power. That's Bart Fleming. The guy we spoke about earlier.

Nothing happens in that club that he doesn't know about. He's been with Ruby for years and is as devoted as they come.'

'He's in love with her?'

Seb shrugged. 'No idea. Possibly. Probably. But Ruby would never lower herself to consort with the hired help. She always had loftier ambitions. Probably still does.'

'Then either she pays him very well or he can't walk away. Who's Bart with in that first picture?'

'Jason,' Seb replied through gritted teeth. 'His back's to the camera and the picture isn't very good but I'd know him anywhere. I think the guy facing the camera was head of the local planning committee at the time. I had dealings with him back in the day over my legitimate business interests. Anyway, I'll have John check to see if Jason or anyone connected to him had planning applications pending at the time.' Seb checked the date stamp on the picture. 'This was taken at about the time your mother disappeared. And that's Bishop in the background, half turned away.'

Ava screwed up her eyes and peered more closely at the picture. 'Jason and Bishop would have wined and dined the guy, persuaded him to take advantage of the full range of services on offer in the club, and then used the evidence to blackmail him into pushing their application through?'

'Probably. It would likely have been a joint venture because they were still in partnership at the time.' Seb flicked to the next picture. 'No idea who any of the people in that one are.'

Ava mumbled something unintelligible, probably fighting her impatience because her mother hadn't shown up in any of the shots.

'That's her!' Ava bounced on her toes when Seb pulled up the next shot and a woman stood beside Jason, his arm possessively draped around her. Seb glanced at her and saw the disappointment in her expression. Any fading hope that Nancy had got it wrong and that her mother's relationship with Jason had been purely business-related withered and died as she stared at that picture with parted lips.

'And the planning guy is in the shot too,' Seb said, zooming in on Mel's features in the hope of seeing her more clearly. The shot was too fuzzy and he gave up. 'Taken in the same time period as the previous one. And he has one of the girls from the club on his arm.'

Seb scrolled through the rest of the shots, which were a variation on a theme. Jason and Bishop were in them all but Ava's mother only featured once more. Significantly, Bishop was always alone and Jason didn't show up with any other women in tow. That was unusual enough to reinforce Seb's opinion that the two men had fallen out over Mel.

She must, he concluded, have been quite something. Glancing at her daughter, he found that easy to believe.

Returning his attention to the screen, Seb was at a loss to know what use to make of the pictures, other than to see what building projects Jason and Bishop had on the go at the time. He scrolled to the final picture, expecting it to throw up more questions than answers but jerked upright, a frisson shooting through his bloodstream, when it appeared on the screen. His breath hitched in his throat when he enlarged the shot, half-convinced that his mind must be playing tricks on him.

'What is it?' Ava touched his arm, clearly concerned by his reaction.

'That's Paul Drake, now DCI Drake, Nancy's ex.'

'Okay, but why are you so shocked? You already knew that he's bent and in Jason's pocket.'

'It's not him that concerns me.' Seb pointed an unsteady

finger at the other guy, who was looking directly into the camera. 'But him I didn't expect to see.'

'Who is he?'

'His name is Henshaw.' Ice trickled through Seb's veins as he considered all the petty humiliations that Henshaw had enjoyed inflicting upon him. 'He was a screw in the open prison I was moved to before my release and he made my life a living hell.'

# 16

Ava could sense the anger radiating off Seb in waves, perhaps because it so closely reflected her own angst. Seeing her mother openly consorting with people she wouldn't have expected her to give the time of day to had been a total shock. She had held onto the belief that her mother had somehow been coerced. People make mistakes all the time: jump to the wrong conclusions on the basis of flimsy evidence. There was always an alternative explanation. Being in the club with Jason could still have been explained away but in an alleyway, a party to a private conversation between two criminals and their associates, left no further room for doubt.

Ava's heart sank. 'What did you get caught up in, Mum?' she asked aloud.

Her mother's features had been indistinct but Ava had still recognised her immediately, and the red dress she'd been wearing. She recalled getting home early one day and catching her mother in the act of stashing the dress at the back of her wardrobe. Ava had admired it. She recalled still the feel of the flimsy silk beneath her fingers when she touched the skirts with reverent awe. She had never seen anything half so exotic and asked her mother when she intended to wear it. Was there a special occasion that she and Dad were required to attend?

Her mother had become flustered, saying it had been an impulse buy. Ava saw the label and even as a teenager, had known it was a designer brand that had to have cost a fortune. But still it didn't raise red flags. Should it have? She wrinkled her brow, attempting to recall those times, wondering if there had been clues. Something that ought to have told her that her parents' marriage was in trouble. If there had been any way in which she could have prevented the tsunami that had torn apart the two people she'd loved the most in the world.

'There's nothing you could have done.' Seb, clearly attuned to her thoughts, gently touched her arm.

She smiled at him, regretting her selfishness when his feelings ought to be her priority. Clearly, seeing the man Henshaw had blindsided him. He looked furious and Ava was a little afraid of him when he was in such an uncompromising mood. She took her turn to touch his forearm. The muscles were rigid.

'Tell me about Henshaw,' she said softly.

'He was a petty tyrant, proud of his peaked cap and the little bit of authority he wielded over us all. Some of the warders I came into contact with were decent blokes but a lot of them shared Henshaw's characteristics. He was the worst of the lot though. He picked on me constantly, simply because he could, hoping no doubt that I'd lose my cool. I didn't. I think his inability to get a reaction from me irked him more than anything else.'

'Knowing your family connections, wasn't he taking a risk?'

Seb shrugged. 'You'd have thought so but after seeing those pictures, it makes more sense. He used to make cracks about Jason: deliberate provocations.' Seb scratched the back of his neck. 'He used to have this smug way of looking at me, like he knew something I didn't. Now I know why.'

'He was on Jason's payroll.'

'Looks that way. Probably paid to keep Jason in the loop about my situation and abused that privilege. He probably knows who did kill Blythe. Hell, he might even have done it himself. Nothing would surprise me about that scumbag.' Seb took a long breath. 'Either way, he would have got a kick out of knowing that I was serving time for a crime I didn't commit.'

'We don't know that Jason killed Blythe,' Ava pointed out. 'Or had him killed. And if he was behind it, he would never have let you take the fall.'

'Perhaps not but Bishop would.'

'Could that be why the two men fell out? It had nothing to do with my mother and everything to do with Bishop setting you up. Jason wouldn't have been able to do anything about it because he and Bishop had too many illegal activities in common. If Bishop went down, presumably he would take Jason with him.'

Seb nodded. 'Possibly,' he conceded, 'but unlikely. If Jason knew that Bishop had killed Blythe and set me up for it, then his retribution would have been swift and violent. No police would have been involved. Anyway, I did discuss the possibility with Jason when I saw him yesterday. He said he'd already dismissed the possibility but when I told him that his son James had been seen to take an unnatural interest in Lily, he promised to revisit the possibility.' Seb took a moment to reflect. 'Bishop might well have had Blythe killed but if he did then he covered his tracks far too well for Jason to find out, which is saying something.'

'So, what do we do now?'

'I'll have John look into Henshaw. He's obviously more than an annoying screw with grandiose ambitions.'

'I can understand serving policemen being of use to Jason and Bishop, but what use would they have for a prison officer?'

Seb chuckled. 'Half the screws in those places are more

corrupt than the prisoners they're supposed to be guarding. How do you think the flow of drugs and God alone knows what other illegal contraband gets past the prison checks? And why do you suppose that blind eyes are turned when inmates get a beating?'

'Those beatings are ordered by people like Bishop?'

Seb nodded. 'And Jason. I also suspect Jason had something to do with my not getting a hammering, which is annoying.'

'Just be grateful.'

'I didn't need the world thinking that I couldn't take care of myself and needed Daddy dearest to look out for me.' Seb's voice dripped with a combination of sarcasm and resentment. 'But still, it would certainly explain why Henshaw got frustrated. He'd been given orders not to lay a finger on me so he did the next best thing to assuage his wounded pride and kept niggling me.'

'Could you have stopped him if he'd tried to use physical violence?'

'I could have beaten the slimy worm to a pulp but then I would have been up before the governor accused of attacking a warder,' Seb replied, rolling his eyes. 'And Henshaw would have just loved playing the part of the victim. He used to provoke me in all sorts of little ways, probably hoping that I would eventually retaliate. Fortunately, I was able to rise above his pettiness, which must have frustrated the hell out of him.'

'Will you confront him now?'

'Oh yes.' He firmed his jaw. 'We will.'

'Good!'

'Good?' Seb looked down at her in confusion. 'I thought you would advise caution.'

'Oh, I do. I'm simply glad that you spoke in the plural and haven't decided to cut me out of things. If I'm there, then I won't let you do anything stupid. Use your brains, not your fists, Seb.

You can outwit a man of his obvious limited abilities with your eyes closed.'

'Thank you.' He paused. 'I think.'

She planted her fisted hands on her hips and huffed. 'Unlikely as it seems, your being fitted up and my mother's disappearance are somehow connected.' She sent him a look of firm determination. 'We are now definitely in this together.'

* * *

Ava resumed her duties whilst Seb briefed John and Mark on their findings.

'Fucking hell!' John said, scratching his neck.

'My thoughts exactly.' Seb leaned back in his chair, watching his two friends pouring over the pictures on Seb's computer.

'This guy Henshaw really had it in for you?' Mark asked, cracking his knuckles.

'Big time but he never got physical. I did wonder, not about when the attack would come but whether I'd find the strength to resist retaliation. Now I know why it didn't happen. What I don't know is how long he's been in Jason's pocket and how much he knows about Blythe's death.'

'You think he offed him?' John asked. 'Is he capable of murder or is he just a bully who likes to intimidate people not in a position to fight back?'

'That's what I intend to ask him,' Mark said, his expression thunderous.

'Do a bit of digging first. See what you can find out about his personal circumstances. Then we'll pay him a little visit.'

'You'd best keep out of it, Seb,' Mark said. 'If the shit hits the fan, I don't want your collar tugged again.'

'Henshaw is hardly going to tell tales, not with what we have on him. But I hear you. We won't go in, all guns blazing. At least, not straight away.'

'Fair enough. What else do you need?' John asked.

'The councillor in that picture, the guy used to chair the planning committee. We knew him, John. Can't recall his name, can you?' Seb screwed up his eyes in an effort to recollect. 'It began with an A, I think. Armitage? Avery?'

'Arnold,' John said, snapping his fingers. 'Harry Arnold. He didn't stand for re-election after you were sent down and I think I heard that he'd moved to Malaga.'

'The Costa del Crime. How appropriate,' Mark said, rolling his eyes.

'I'm all over it,' John said, gathering up his stuff and standing. Before he could leave the room though, Jessie tapped at the door and put her head round it.

'Jason's here,' she said, referring to Seb's father in the same informal way that everyone else did. 'Says he's not going anywhere until he's spoken to you and that it's important. What do you want me to do?'

'Want me to send him away?' Mark asked, looking as though he would relish the assignment.

'No, I'll see him.'

'Want me to stay?' John asked.

'No. This is a conversation that I need to have with him alone.'

'Wouldn't it be better to wait until I've got more on Arnold and Henshaw?' John asked.

'In an ideal world, perhaps.' Seb firmed his jaw. 'Send him in, Jessie, but make sure Ava stays out of sight. And Lily too. I don't want him to see either of them until I know why he's here.'

Jessie nodded. 'It's stopped drizzling so they've gone down to the woods with that dog and will be there for ages. They always are. It's Lily's favourite place and her favourite time of the year.'

'I'll go down there and keep them company,' Mark said. 'Just in case they decide to come back to the house early for any reason.'

Seb took the minute or two that he was left alone to assimilate his thoughts and prepare himself for a confrontation – a proper confrontation, as opposed to their opening salvo the previous day – that had been six years in the making. And this time, now that he had ammunition, Jason would answer Seb's questions rather than fobbing him off with platitudes.

It felt good to have the upper hand.

He heard Jason's booming voice and heavy tread as Jessie showed him through a house he'd never set foot in before.

'Nice place,' Jason said, walking into Seb's study and taking in the surroundings with a nod of approval. 'Classy.' He held out a hand that Seb ignored.

'Sit,' he replied, pointing to the chairs in front of the fire.

'I ain't a fucking dog.' Jason's congenial expression showed early signs of strain.

'Why are you here?' Seb asked, taking the chair across from Jason only after the older man had seated himself. He knew better than to create a disadvantage by sitting first and having to look up to Jason. This game of cat and mouse was one that Jason had invented the rules to and still played with the hand of a master. But he hadn't spent the past six years nursing a grievance and that, as far as Seb was concerned, gave him the edge.

'Look, I won't beat about the bush. I've only just heard that you've got a woman here looking after our Lily and I have to warn you, there might be more to her reasons for taking the job than you know about.'

'Is that right?' Seb crossed one foot over his opposite thigh and leaned back in his chair, casual. Unconcerned. His stance, he knew, would confuse Jason, who had probably expected some sort of explosion.

'I thought you cared about your sister.' Jason frowned. 'Ain't you even gonna ask why the girl caring for her has an alternative agenda?'

'My half-sister,' Seb corrected. 'And I care a damned sight more than you do. This display of fatherly concern comes far too late to pack a punch.'

'Look, son, I...'

Seb's formidable expression caused Jason's words to stall on his tongue; a situation unusual enough to afford Seb considerable satisfaction. 'Who is Lily's mother?' he asked abruptly, aware that it couldn't have been Ava's mother, for which he was grateful. According to Seb's calculations, based on what Ava had told him, her mother and Jason's paths hadn't crossed until well after Lily had been born.

Seb held Jason's gaze and could sense his growing ire. The man wasn't used to being questioned and was holding on to his temper by a thread. By coming here though he had displayed a weakness and probably already realised it, which implied it was something serious: something to do with Ava, or more likely her mother.

'Jean Arnold,' Jason subsequently said into the heavy ensuing silence.

Seb's head reeled. He knew that name, vaguely remembered a face. Then it all slotted into place in a blinding flash and things began to make sense.

'Christ! You were screwing the wife of the planning committee's chair,' he said, his voice dripping with disgust.

'Oh, grow a pair, Seb. It takes two.'

'Never heard of safe sex? The woman was almost past childbearing age, which would probably account for Lily's disability. Presumably she didn't want to keep the child.'

Jason looked away and didn't say a word.

'You must have had something you really needed pushed through that committee,' Seb remarked, thinking it through. 'The woman wasn't your usual type but I do seem to recall that Arnold idolised her, and probably forgave her indiscretions provided she didn't keep the child. Am I right?'

'Spot on,' Jason replied with obvious reluctance.

'You got your plans approved, then Arnold didn't stand for re-election once you'd got what you needed from him and swanned off to Spain with the handsome pay out you gave him.' When Jason didn't say a word, Seb knew he was on the right path. 'What was so important that you had to break up a marriage over it?' A habit he'd gotten into, Seb thought but didn't say, his mind focusing on Ava's mother.

Jason waved the question aside. 'You don't need to know that.'

'You came to me, Jason,' Seb said, feeling calm and in control of a conversation with his father, perhaps for the first time ever, 'so you're in no position to throw your weight around.'

'Look, I didn't know you had the Harper kid working here.' Jason threw back his head.

'Care to tell me why it matters to you so much that you've come running here like the caring father you've never been?'

'Look, son, the kid has issues and may not have Lily's best interests at heart, is all I'm saying.'

'Bullshit!'

Seb's feet hit the floor with a resounding thud as he sat upright and reached behind him to the photos that he'd printed out and which now rested in the centre of his desk. He flipped through them, found the one of Jason with Ava's mother and

Arnold in the shot and passed it to Jason without saying another word.

'What's this?' Jason removed a pair of glasses from his inside pocket and perched them on the end of his nose. His features blanched when he realised what he was looking at. 'Where the fuck did you get this?'

'Does it matter?'

Jason took another long look at the picture, then cast it aside with an expression that combined regret with anger, and something more fundamental. If Seb hadn't known better, he might have been persuaded to think that Jason was moved by the sight of Mel Carter. But, of course, he knew better. Much better. No woman ever got beneath Jason's staunch defences.

'I don't know what you think you know but—'

Seb slapped his hand against the arm of his chair, the sound of flesh hitting leather louder than a gunshot in the otherwise silent, tension-filled room. He fixed Jason with a look of pure vitriol and didn't say a word.

'Okay, look, it was a deal me and Bishop had going. We needed planning permission to convert a big, old, terraced house in Stockwell into bedsits.'

'Bedsits?' Seb raised a sceptical brow.

'Yeah well, Bishop wanted to turn it into a low-rent knocking shop. I was lukewarm on the idea but went along with it.' He paused. 'At first.'

'I take it the plans hit a bump in the road.'

'Yeah, and we knew we had to get Arnold on side. He'd resisted our previous attempts to bribe him.'

'You can't corrupt an honest man.'

'Nah, but you can hit his weak spot.'

'His wife,' Seb replied, attempting to keep the disgust out of his voice. Just how low could a man stoop? he wondered. He hadn't thought that Jason could feature any lower in his own opinion but had already been proven wrong.

'Yeah, Bishop knew that he idolised her but also found out somehow that she had a wandering eye and a liking for the high life.' Jason paused to remove his glasses and scrub a hand down his face. 'I'm not proud of this next bit.'

'Bishop's idea, I'm guessing,' Seb remarked, making no attempt to keep the sarcasm out of his voice.

'Yeah. He said one of us needed to get to Jean. We tossed a coin and I lost. The idea was for Arnold to find out about it.'

'Surely that would have made him even more determined to block your planning application?'

'Bishop figured that his pride would bring him to heel. He really did adore Jean and would hate for people to think that he couldn't control his own wife. He was a pompous bastard. Besides, we only had to tip his fellow councillors the wink as to Jean and me and... well, they would have drawn their own conclusions.'

'I see.' And Seb did see all too clearly. He didn't much care for the view either. 'And Lily?'

'That was never supposed to happen, so help me God.'

Seb grunted. 'God didn't have much to do with it.'

'Jean told me she was beyond childbearing age and couldn't have them anyway. It was her dearest wish to have a child but it just never happened.' He shrugged. 'Seemed she was wrong about her body clock. Arnold must have been firing blanks.'

'She didn't want a child enough to keep Lily.'

'Oh, she wanted her but Arnold put his foot down. He was willing to take her back and forgive her. Blamed me for everything and agreed to do what we wanted on the strict understanding that Jean never saw the child again. He wasn't about to have my bastard in his nest were his exact words if memory serves. Of course, Jean thought I returned her feelings, would take her in and we'd play happy families.' He snorted. 'Silly bitch.'

'You didn't want Lily either, not once you realised that she had something wrong with her.'

'Yeah well, that was a mistake that I will always regret.'

'You paid Arnold off when he refused to stand for re-election and funded his lifestyle in Spain, I assume.'

'Something like that.'

'So,' Seb said, shifting position in his chair, 'we come to the elephant in the room.' He fixed Jason with a probing look. 'What happened to Ava's mother?'

Jason's entire demeanour changed and his expression turned pensive. 'Now her, I'll be the first to admit; she got to me, big time.' He held up a hand. 'I'm being straight with you, son; no bullshit. I saw her dealing blackjack in one of our clubs and... well, I can't describe it. Something in me changed and I couldn't get her out of my mind.'

'But your usual charm offensive didn't work?'

'Nah, not at first but you know me... when I want something, I can be tenacious. And I wanted her; couldn't seem to think about much else.' Seb nodded, unwilling to accept that Ava had already got under his skin in a similar fashion. 'I made it my business to find out more about her circumstances, discovered that her husband was in financial straits, hence her need to work at the club. I saw an opportunity to help her out and, trust me, for once, my intentions were on the level. I didn't realise quite how clever she was, though. She soon found out we were sanitising a load of dodgy cash through the books. I thought she'd throw a wobbly but she actually suggested better ways to cover our tracks, in return for a larger remuneration.'

Jason's remarks had actually shocked Seb. 'She was willing to be a part of it?'

'Yep, no coercion required. She said that she'd never so much as had a parking ticket in her entire life and was totally law-abiding. But her husband had been tricked into handling stolen gems by a customer who knew he was struggling to keep his head above water. Even so, she swears he didn't know the stones were stolen. He thought he was just helping his mate to avoid import duties and... well, defrauding the taxman is more a national pastime than a crime in a lot of people's opinion.'

Seb made a sceptical face.

'Yeah, that's what I thought too, but you know how people can be when their backs are against the wall. They believe what they want to believe. Anyway, Mel needed as much money as she could muster to pay a decent brief. I told her there was another way.'

'You used Paul Drake to make the charges go away.'

'I did. Damning evidence went missing, the case fell apart and Mel was grateful. She said her main priority was her daughter's future. She adored the kid and didn't want her to grow up with a criminal for a father. Mel's old man would have been banged up, no matter how good a brief Mel managed to get to defend him, make no mistake about that. The guy who got him into it had covered his backside and scarpered, along with the majority of the stones, leaving Harper to take the fall.'

Seb nodded. It sounded plausible. 'Why didn't she go back to her family at that point?' Seb added.

'She was grateful and she liked me. A lot. We had fun. I more than returned her feelings, I don't mind admitting it.'

'What I don't understand is that picture. That would have been after your affair with Arnold's wife, quite a few years after, and yet he was still serving on the council presumably. Why didn't you pay him off and let him quit immediately?'

'We still needed him and by that time we owned him. Besides, even pompous pricks like him enjoy a taste of the good life. He had a passion for the gee-gees and I was able to support his gambling habit.'

'You let him go only when he was of no further use to you?' Seb let out a long breath. 'So, why the furtive meeting in that alleyway?'

Jason looked angry as he rested his elbow on his chair's arm and the side of his face on his splayed hand. 'Bishop shafted me over the use of that house in Stockwell.'

'I heard he had the hots for Mel as well.'

'Nah.' Jason flapped a hand in casual dismissal of the suggestion. 'He liked her, everyone liked Mel. She had class but he wouldn't poach on my territory. Neither of us would have let a woman come between our solid partnership.'

Seb believed him and was relieved to discover that Ava's mother hadn't attempted to play the two men off against one another. Given her circumstances, he couldn't altogether blame her for falling for Jason's charm. A man with looks, charisma and shedloads of money who led what must have seemed like a glamorous and sophisticated life would tempt even the most dedicated of wives, especially one who felt disillusioned because her husband's stupidity had jeopardised her family's stability.

He was glad too that she'd done what she had to do to protect Ava's future. Unfortunately, her subsequent disappearance only made the probability of her death even more likely.

'Mel got wind of the uses the house in Stockwell were being put to.'

'She did. She still had more morals than I've had hot dinners and blamed me. Didn't believe I had nothing to do with it. Bishop and I had branched out separately, as you know, but still had interests in common. That wasn't one of them.'

'So, you pulled Arnold in to prove to Mel that it was Bishop's baby?' Seb frowned. 'You cared about her that much?'

'I did. Arnold wouldn't enter the club so we had to meet out back.'

'Let me guess. Bishop was using the house for forced prostitution, housing imported immigrants, drugs... all of the above?'

Jason nodded. 'Pretty much. Bishop was both feared and respected in all walks of life, believed his own hype and reckoned he could do anything he liked, making it look legal.'

'So, what happened to make you two fall out?'

'I don't have any truck with drugs,' Jason said, pulling himself up to his full height in his chair. 'Never have and never will.'

No, Seb thought, but he didn't seem to care about illegals being forced into the sex trade.

'That's what he used the house for. He ran a few girls from it and used the rest of the accommodation to house the guys who cut and peddled his coke. He had a full-scale factory in the basement, if you can believe it.'

Seb nodded. He could.

'Mel found out?'

'She did. One of the girls who worked there was brought to the Iris because she had potential. Mel got chatting to her and found out what was going on. She went apeshit and wasn't prepared to keep her trap shut.'

'Bishop had her silenced,' Seb replied, feeling anger radiate through his body. Anger at Mel's stupidity, fury at Jason's inability to save the woman he clearly adored. 'That's what the two of you fell out about.'

The door burst open. Both men turned to see Ava standing in the aperture, her face a study in anxiety.

'Mel, is that you?' Jason asked, eyes wide in disbelief as he half-rose from his chair.

# 17

Ava had known something was wrong when Mark joined them in the woods and made excuses not to return to the house when it started to rain again. Wizard had eventually taken that decision out of his hands. He hated getting wet, gave a yelp and headed full pelt in the direction of the house. Lily laughed and ran after him.

'What are you not telling me, Mark?' Ava had asked as she and Mark followed behind Lily at a slightly slower pace.

'Nothing, it's just that...'

Ava laughed. 'You're a terrible liar. Come on, out with it. What doesn't Seb want me to know?'

'Jason's here,' Mark admitted with obvious reluctance. 'Seb didn't want me to tell you or for him to see either of you, that's all. No drama.'

'Who the hell does he...'

'Look, Ava, I know what's going on. Seb and Jason are long overdue a heart to heart. Let them clear the air first. Seb won't cut you out.'

Ava bit her lip, aware that she was testing Mark's loyalties, which were firmly in Seb's corner, and she didn't want to upset the balance. Even so, once she got back to the house, something stronger than her own will drew her to the door of Seb's study. She glanced at Mark, who stood beside her, shuffling his feet with indecision. Ava took advantage of his hesitation, aware that he would probably prevent her from entering the room once he got his act together. She mouthed the word 'sorry' and opened the door.

Ava took several steps backwards, overwhelmed by the strength of Jason Carter's reaction when he turned his head and gaped at her. He had clearly mistaken her for her mother and looked at her with an expression of total adoration. Seb rose from his chair, looking equally bewildered.

'You shouldn't be in here,' he said softly, but nodded to Mark to close the door anyway, probably sensing that he would have to forcibly evict her. She took a seat beside him, observing Jason closely. He was still standing, watching her with unnerving stillness and gently shaking his head.

'The resemblance is uncanny,' he said softly.

'What's going on?' Ava directed the question to Seb. Her gaze fell upon the picture of her mother and Jason which had dropped to the floor at Jason's feet. Clearly, she had interrupted their conversation at a vital point.

'Jason was just explaining to me how matters concerning your mother got out of hand,' Seb replied, an edge to his voice.

'Then perhaps one of you would care to enlighten me.'

Ava cast a considering look at Jason as she spoke. If he could see a resemblance to Mel in her then Ava was able to reciprocate. Jason was definitely an older version of Seb. His rugged features were lined and yet somehow his attractiveness had been enhanced by the passage of time. He still sported a full head of hair, albeit heavily threaded with grey, and his hazel eyes were faded yet still astute. There was no mistaking their relationship and Ava could see why her mother had been tempted by such a charismatic man. If he turned on the charm, she suspected that few women would be able to resist.

Seb gave her a concise run-down of their conversation, as far as Ava could tell, not leaving anything out.

'Mel really did adore you,' Jason assured her when Seb ran out of words. 'Everything she did was to protect you.'

'Including jumping into bed with you?' Ava asked aggressively.

'Ah, well...' Jason smiled and spread his hands. 'Have you ever tried to fight against chemistry?'

'Where is she now?' Ava could hear the break in her own voice as she posed the question and hated the fact that she had displayed a sign of weakness. 'Is she still alive?'

'I have no reason to think otherwise and, believe me, I would know.'

'You fell out with Bishop big time over that house in Stockwell,' Seb said, touching Ava's hand, presumably sensing her angst. 'You tried to stop Mel from meddling but failed to convince her that it would be in her own best interests to turn a blind eye. You even broke off all relations with Bishop, just to prove to Mel that you were on her side, and yet he went ahead with the house anyway. What makes you think a man like Bishop would risk letting her run wild, perhaps to the authorities, if you couldn't control her?'

'My mother is not a dog!'

'I talked Mel round, explained that she was on a hiding to nothing. That there was no way to beat men like Bishop and that even if she did, someone else would spring up to take over all the aspects of his business that she disapproved of. It would be like trying to hold back a tidal wave. That was why I took her to that meeting. So she could see for herself precisely what she would be up against, corrupt councillors and senior detectives. She eventually saw things my way, promised me that she would let it go. She had a compelling reason for making that promise, too.'

'Which was?' Ava asked.

'Bishop didn't trust her to keep her trap shut. Said she knew too much about our operation and that he'd warned me not to bring in a "do-gooder", as he described her. He needed leverage, found out about you, Ava, and said that if she breathed a word then you would be the one to suffer.'

Ava shuddered in spite of herself, conflicted by a whole raft of emotions. *Oh, Mum!* Seb placed a hand on her arm but Ava shook it off. It was important to her that Jason didn't imagine she needed Seb to support her through this ordeal of revelation, even though a big part of her would welcome a broad shoulder to lean on. Someone who understood the way the criminal fraternity worked, even if he wasn't a part of it himself. Someone who would cut through the bullshit and get to the truth, if only because he needed to find answers himself.

'Which is why she didn't come home?' Ava breathed.

'I have to assume so,' Jason replied, with a sad little shake of his head. 'She didn't confide in me. One day she was there; the next she was gone. She probably knew I would do everything in my power to talk her out of doing whatever she did. I thought she cared for me but the maternal instinct to protect you was a damned sight stronger.'

'How did she plan to support herself, do you suppose?' Seb asked.

'She helped herself to a large chunk of dosh from the club, as well as what she'd been paid for bookkeeping.' He fixed Ava with a genuine-seeming look of concern. 'She had a tidy nest egg, enough to set herself up elsewhere.'

'I see.' Ava swallowed. 'Did you try to find her?'

'Of course I did. Despite the evidence, part of me worried that Bishop might have done for her. He was never big on trust issues but he swore on his kids' lives that he hadn't laid a finger on her and I've not been able to unearth any proof to the contrary.' Jason paused. 'He wouldn't do the deed himself, of course. I spoke to everyone who worked for him at the time and none of them know anything about her, or where she went.'

'You believed them?' Ava widened her eyes.

'Darling, they would have told me they were the Boston Strangler by the time I'd done with them. Trust me, they didn't know.'

'So perhaps she's still alive after all,' Ava said in a tiny voice, breathing hard as she thought it all through. 'She went away to protect me, and Dad. But why stay away all this time?'

'Bishop still operates and has a long memory,' Seb reminded her.

Ava threw up her hands, perilously close to tears of frustration and disillusionment. 'But Mum wouldn't have any proof, not after all this time, and who would listen to her even if she had?'

'Who do you think persuaded our friend to take those pictures?' Seb asked.

Ava twitched her nose. 'Perhaps, but even so...'

'And the photographer hasn't been seen or heard of for years.'

Ava let out a long breath. 'True.'

'What did Henshaw have to do with it all?' Seb asked, directing the question to Jason as he threw the picture that included Henshaw and Bishop in front of him.

'He was a detective constable at the time, as bent as Drake.' Jason sniffed. 'A nasty piece of work, full of resentment and entitlement, simply because of what he did for a living. Took what he wanted and never expected to get caught. But he did, eventually, and resigned before he was pushed. Did the odd favour for Drake, who got him a job with the prison service. He was on Bishop's payroll.'

'You all seem cosy in that shot.'

'Trust me, there was no love lost between us but Bishop knew Henshaw would do anything for money and freebies with the girls in the club. He had no conscience so Bishop had him do a ton of his dirty work. He's a bit long in the tooth for all that malarky now but makes himself useful to Bishop in his current position. Sorry,' Jason added when Seb winced. 'I made it abundantly clear to Bishop that if anything happened to you, he'd have me to answer to.'

Seb just shrugged but Ava sensed a raft of resentment lurking beneath his urbane expression. Seb would not appreciate having had someone like Henshaw paid to watch his back, at the same time making his life difficult in all sorts of petty little ways.

'What makes you so sure that Bishop didn't set me up?' he asked.

'Not his style. Besides, he had no reason to. Blythe attacked our Lily. That made it a family affair and none of his business. He had nothing to gain by doing the world a favour and getting rid of that rapist scum.'

'Perhaps not but you two were at each other's throats at the time. Could be he saw a way to get you to take your eye off the ball. If he had no qualms about forcing women into prostitution, then sending someone to violate Lily wouldn't keep him awake at night.'

'We had our differences but odd though it might sound, there was still a bond between us. Lines that wouldn't be crossed.' Jason's hand cut through the air to emphasise his point. 'Besides, he knew that if he'd done it, I'd find out eventually and that would start a full-scale war. None of us wanted that.'

Ava sent Seb a look of bald surprise when he simply nodded, apparently accepting Jason's assurance at face value.

'What has Ruby Asquith got to do with Mum's disappearance?' she asked into the ensuing silence.

'Ruby? What makes you think...'

'My dad did some digging. I didn't know about it until I found his papers after his death. Ruby's name came up several times and was heavily underlined. That's what brought me here, in a roundabout sort of way.'

'Ruby and I were an item for a while, until your mum came along. Ruby didn't appreciate being dumped for a younger woman. She hated your mother but it annoyed the hell out of her because she could also see how useful she was as a bookkeeper. Mel picked up on it straight away *and* made improvements to our system so that if anyone did come sniffing around, they'd have a hard time proving that anything was amiss. Made herself invaluable, so she did.'

Ava bit her lip, suppressing the urge to feel vicarious pride. What her mother had done had been illegal and despite the fact that she'd done it to save Dad, she had no reason to carry on for as long as she had. Or to have an affair with Jason.

Could Lily's attack have been ordered by Ruby? she wondered. Revenge in the extreme ordered by a jealous and vindictive woman?

'Ruby made your mum's life difficult in all sorts of little ways but Mel rose above it, never let it affect her.' Jason rubbed his nose. 'I'm guessing your dad found out where Mel was working, which is how Ruby's name came into it.'

'Unless he went to see her.'

'If he did then she would have told me about it,' Jason replied with authority.

Ava frowned. 'How can you be so sure?'

'Because she's my business partner and because she is aware I want to know what happened to Mel. She wouldn't hold out on me. I have eyes and ears in that club and she knows very well that I would have found out about your dad's visit. If it happened.' Jason gave an emphatic nod. 'No, take it from me, your dad had no face-to-face contact with Ruby.'

'Would Ruby have arranged for Mel to disappear, given her feelings?' Seb asked.

'A woman scorned?' Jason rubbed his chin, then shook his head. 'Nah! She doesn't have a death wish. Besides, she knows that I never go back. Our affair had run its course. And anyway, she knew how much I valued and respected Mel. She wouldn't be stupid enough to start a war with me.' He looked away from them. 'I talked to Mel about everything. She had a sharp brain and gave me good advice. She reminded me I was doing well, very well, and didn't need to lower myself just for the sake of amassing more dosh. She also told me to choose. If I took Bishop's path then she'd walk.'

'She had scruples, I suppose.'

Ava made the concession grudgingly. What she had learned about her mother this past hour had well and truly opened her eyes to the character of the woman she had spent years placing on a pedestal.

'How did Dennis and Ray take to her?' Seb asked.

'Ah well, they hated her. They knew she influenced my thinking in a way that they never could. They were urging me to take Bishop's advice but Mel was pulling me in the opposite direction. She talked sense into me and I have never regretted that decision. She was right to ask, how much money is enough? I've got more than I can ever spend. I can live comfortably for the rest of my days and sleep at night, especially now I'm largely legit.'

'Could your brothers have done away with Mum?' Ava asked Seb.

'Nah. They ain't got the balls.' It was Jason who replied and he was emphatic.

'I was wondering about the same thing in terms of my being set up,' Seb remarked, leaning back in his chair, his expression pensive. 'I know they must have got pretty pissed off about your favouritism when nothing they ever did earned them parental praise.'

'That's because they couldn't run a piss up in a brewery.' Jason paused. 'I could see them offing Blythe in an attempt to avenge Lily but they don't have the nous to carry out such an elaborate set-up.'

'Perhaps they weren't working alone,' Ava suggested quietly.

'If they had done it, they wouldn't have been able to keep their big traps shut all this time,' Jason said. 'They would have boasted to someone sooner or later and it would have got back to me.'

Ava opened her mouth to respond but, sensing Seb's preoccupation, she turned to him, a question in her eyes.

'How come you only just found out that Ava's working here?' he asked, suspicion clouding his features. 'Presumably you tasked Dennis and Ray with keeping you informed about my employment policy.'

'Yeah, but the dozy bastards—'

'You really think they forget to keep a check?' Seb's frown intensified. 'They'd be all over anything to do with me because I'm a threat to them, especially now that I'm out.'

'Yeah, but—'

'When Ava walked into this room, you genuinely thought she was her mother. If either of my brothers had seen her, even from a distance, they'd have known who she was. And what reason would they have for keeping that information from you?'

Jason nodded slowly, his face a stony mask. 'Either they did set you up or they know where Mel is and don't want her back in their lives.'

Ava sat forward on the edge of her chair, feeling a mixture of hope and confusion swirling deep inside of her. 'You make it sound as though she's definitely alive and that you know where she is.'

Jason looked at her for a long time, clearly weighing up his options. Ava opened her mouth, searching for persuasive word, but at a warning glance from Seb, she remained silent. They both sensed that this was a defining moment. Jason had been holding something back, something important. Ava hadn't been able to shake that feeling and now, hopefully, after Seb's suggestion that his brothers had engaged in a cover-up of some sort, perhaps he would come clean. Dishing out information on a need-to-know basis was clearly Jason's *modus operandi*.

'She is alive, darling,' Jason eventually admitted.

'What the fuck!' Seb jumped from his chair. 'What the hell was all that bullshit earlier?' He shook his head. 'As usual, I can't believe a fucking word that comes out of your mouth.'

'She went away to protect me,' Ava said, her voice sounding distant, feeble.

'Not precisely.' Jason looked furtive. 'But she overheard a conversation at the Iris and knew who killed Blythe.'

'Who?' Seb and Ava asked together.

# 18

'I honestly don't know.' Seb stared at Jason, who faced up to him without flinching. 'Straight up, she wouldn't tell me where she was going. Said it would be better if she disappeared and that I moved on with my life. I'll tell you this much though; she was terrified.' Jason spread his hands. 'I couldn't talk her out of leaving, so I helped her to get away. What else could I have done?'

'Can you contact her?' Ava asked, leaning forward expectantly. 'You know how, don't you?'

Seb had a thousand questions percolating through his brain but the anger bubbling up inside of him prevented him from voicing them.

'I have a mobile number,' Jason admitted. 'But it's a pay as you go, so you can't trace her whereabouts through it.'

'She's in this country?' Seb asked in an even tone that gave nothing away about the volatile nature of his thoughts.

'Yeah.' He fixed Seb with a conciliatory look. 'I know what you're thinking, but I made Mel a promise never to speak about this and despite what you think of me, I never break my word.'

Seb conceded the point with a reluctant nod.

'If I'd known that Ava was looking for her mum, and on my life I didn't have a clue until yesterday that she was here poking around in places it's much better not to go, then I might have reconsidered. Or at the very least alerted Mel. As it is, I've made that decision on my own and if Mel doesn't like it… well, tough.'

'I don't get any of this.' Seb rubbed the back of his neck. 'Does she know that her husband died?'

'She does. Which is why she wanted to come back. She knew you were working in Switzerland at the time, Ava, and wanted to contact you again.'

'You took her to that club, where Ruby hated her?' Ava asked, her jaw dropping open. 'Why?'

'Because I needed her help with the books. Again. The daft bugger who'd taken over from her had made a cock-up. That's when she heard something she shouldn't. She never told me what but it spooked her. She said it had been a mistake to come back, that she couldn't lie to you and didn't want to earn your disapproval by telling the truth. Besides, she said something about having moved on: other commitments.' Jason held up a hand. 'And before you ask, I have no idea where she'd been living and what she meant by that. I knew she wouldn't tell me.'

Seb could see that Ava was fighting back tears and gave her arm a gentle squeeze.

'Putting aside Mel's situation for a moment,' he said, taking control, 'let's pause to assess what we do know, always assuming you've been straight with me,' he added, glaring at Jason.

Jason sat a little taller, clearly resenting Seb's implication but not calling him out on it. 'I promised Mel I wouldn't tell anyone that she was still breathing but… well, I don't want you two poking hornets' nests, attempting to find out who killed her when she ain't even dead. But I honestly don't know where she is, who she's with, or how she's making a living. She came back briefly for all of a day because I needed her and she… well, I guess she thought she could face you, Ava. But she bottled it once she got here, and I haven't seen her since.'

'You still care for her.'

Ava's comment wasn't a question and Jason nodded without hesitation. 'I'd die for her,' he said simply.

'Okay,' Seb replied, believing Jason. No one could fake that type of sincerity. 'So we know for a fact that Blythe violated Lily but don't know who set him up to do it, or why. We know someone killed Blythe and pointed the finger at me but again, we don't know who. Or why. But at least we do know why Mel went to work for you and what happened to her.' Seb turned to smile at Ava. 'We also know she's alive and that we can find her if you want to.'

'I'm no longer sure that I do,' Ava replied, her expression conflicted. 'She isn't the mother I remember, otherwise she would have found a way to let me know she was alive. She must have known how worried I would be and that I'd never stop looking for answers.'

'Okay, let's put the Mel situation to one side and concentrate on Blythe's murder,' Seb suggested. 'What do we know about him? Who would want him dead?'

'I would,' Jason replied without hesitation. 'But someone else got to him first. He was a regular at the Iris and known to all our suspects: Drake, Henshaw, Ruby, my boys, me. He was a small-time addict who'd do anything for the price of his next fix.'

'How did he know about Lily?' Ava asked. 'It's not as if she leaves this place much, and never alone, so he's unlikely to have seen her. And yet he knew she was at the park that day, without Mark guarding her for once, and attacked her.'

'We're back to Diane and her mysterious boyfriend,' Seb mused.

At a look of confusion from Jason, Seb explained about the woman who'd been in charge of Lily at the time of the attack. 'Ava tracked down a friend of hers, who told us about the boyfriend. Jessie saw him a couple of times and didn't like the look of him. Now he's in the wind and so is Diane. Diane has gone to lengths to cover her tracks, perhaps because she realised she'd been a means to an end and was scared of retaliation, as she has every reason to be.'

'My impression is that the boyfriend was recruited specifically to groom Diane, but I have absolutely no idea who did the recruiting,' Ava admitted.

Jason's expression turned dark and dangerous. 'What else?' he asked.

Seb saw no reason to hold back and so told Jason about Gordon taking the security job at the Iris, snapping the shots that Gaynor had given them, and his subsequent disappearance. 'Everyone connected to that place seems to disappear,' he said. 'Everyone except Ruby, Nancy and Bart Fleming.'

'I seem to vaguely recall the Philpott guy,' Jason replied. 'He was dead eager to please but security guys came and went all the time. He seemed efficient enough but I don't think I ever spoke to him.'

'Everything keeps coming back to the Iris,' Ava said.

Jason nodded. 'Which puts Ruby in the frame. I've thought about the possibility over the years but never considered she'd have the gall to get to me by harming Lily simply because her pride was hurt.'

'You're underestimating the determination of a strong woman,' Ava said. 'She certainly had a motive, at least in her own warped mind, and probably felt that she'd been disrespected. That would be enough to set her off in search of vengeance which perhaps went too far, especially if she had a drug addict doing her bidding.'

'Because I dumped her.' Jason raised a brow and simultaneously shook his head. 'I don't see it myself. She don't have a death wish.'

'She came on to me at about the time you hooked up with Mel and I didn't let her down too gently,' Seb admitted. 'That was probably enough to push her over the edge. She made threats that I didn't take seriously.'

'Christ!' Jason rubbed his jaw. 'Twice scorned and all that. I wish I'd known that she'd made a serious play for you. I would have...'

Seb didn't need him to finish his sentence. He knew well enough what Jason would have done, and it would have involved extreme violence. And given the circumstances, Ruby being a woman would not have let her off the hook.

'Would Ruby be able to manipulate enough people to make the set up happen?' Ava asked. 'I've never met the woman. I get that she's a force to be reckoned with, but still...'

'Well, that's a good question.' Jason appeared pensive. 'The physical evidence at the murder scene. Your cap, Seb. The witness who identified you. How would she have pulled that off?'

Seb threw back his head and closed his eyes. 'That could be down to my brothers but how the hell do we prove who did what?'

'I went to see Ruby just after you got out to discuss final clauses on the legal documents.'

'Legal documents?' Seb asked.

'Yeah, I'm selling up my share in the club to her.'

'I'd heard a rumour but didn't believe it.'

'Yeah, had enough. The first thing she said to me was that she'd heard you were out. Had her knickers in a right twist over it, pretending to be worried that you'd muck rake and that it would have an adverse effect on the club's reputation, but I sensed there was more to it than that.'

'You must be losing your edge. The club's reputation has never been stella. Didn't it occur to you that she might be afraid of what I would find once I started digging?'

Jason grunted. 'Perhaps I underestimated her. Well, no question. If she had anything to do with what happened to Lily, anything at all, then I did dismiss the possibility far too readily. You're right, Seb, I'm getting past it.' Jason sighed as he stretched his arms above his head, clearly seething. 'Definitely time to hang up me boots. This is a young man's game.'

'I think Ruby did talk to my dad,' Ava said into the ensuing silence, 'and I think she's known for a while that I work here. Your brothers will have told her because... because...'

'Because they go to the club regularly and enjoy the benefits on offer, acting the big men because I'm majority owner and so they can strut their stuff and the punters are impressed. Now that I've decided to sell out, they tried to persuade me to sign my share over to them.' Jason's grunt of laughter owed little to humour. 'I didn't come down in the last shower. They'd run it into the ground in months.'

'You undoubtedly told them so,' Seb said.

'Course I did. I believe in speaking my mind.'

'And hurting feelings along the way,' Ava said pensively. 'It seems to me that if you've constantly put those boys down, they'd eventually get pissed off and try to even the score. Show you what they're made of.' She paused. 'I know all about the futility of attempting to procure parental approval. It isn't always the children who disappoint, you know,' she added, clearly smarting from what she'd just learned about her mother's disappearance and her disinclination to let Ava know she was still alive.

'Okay,' Seb replied, reaching a decision. 'Seems to me that either Ruby or my brothers are responsible for setting me up, always supposing that you're right and Bishop had nothing to do with it, Jason.'

'I'd stake my reputation on Bishop being in the clear,' Jason replied with asperity.

'Okay, Jason. I think a visit to the Iris is overdue. And I think it should happen now, before the evening trade gets under way.' He glanced at his watch. 'If we leave now, we'll be there in less than an hour and a half.'

'I'm coming with you,' Ava said, her staunch expression making it clear that the subject wasn't up for debate.

'Sure you are,' Seb replied, smiling at her. 'Wouldn't have it any other way.'

* * *

Ruby dressed for the evening with her usual stylish precision. It was a Wednesday; always a busy night with VIP clients who needed to be kept sweet. She examined her reflection critically, just as she did daily, frowning at the development of new wrinkles. They seemed to be springing up faster than her tame Botox doctor could eliminate them nowadays. Despite her best and expensive efforts to keep her age at bay, she grudgingly conceded, it was catching up with her. Either that, or the stress of Seb's release and constantly wondering what he was going to do and when he was going to do it, was the cause of her facial deterioration.

'Fucking Carters,' she muttered, feeling her stomach lurch, just as it always did on the rare occasions when she permitted her mind to dwell upon Seb Carter's physical perfection. 'I bet his looks haven't suffered, even after being locked up for a six stretch.'

Life was so fucking unfair! She applied a little more concealer around her crows' feet, sighed and left the rooms she occupied above the club. Putting on her game face, she descended the stairs and entered her private office, stopping dead in her tracks when Jason, Seb and a woman who was the image of Mel Carter stood to greet her.

'It's been a while, Seb,' she said, recovering a modicum of poise but wincing at her unfortunate choice of words. 'Jason,' she added, tilting her head towards her partner and sending him a *what the hell* look.

Ruby almost asked him why he'd come and how he'd managed to get past Bart into her private domain but managed to hold back the question. He was still a majority owner of the club and could go where he liked on the premises. He just seldom exercised that right and she had become used to looking upon the place as her own.

Her gaze drifted towards what had to be Mel's daughter, the two Carter men standing protectively on either side of her. Talk about history repeating itself! It made her blood boil to see the way that Seb looked at her: the exact same way that Jason had looked at her mother. Ruby would have given ten years of her life to have had Jason look at her that way but had known the moment she saw the blind adoration in his gaze as it rested upon Mel that she had lost him.

She herself couldn't see what all the fuss was about. This little trollop in front of her today was wearing jeans and a sweatshirt. Her hair was tangled, as though she'd been outside and hadn't bothered to brush it. Her admittedly pretty face was virtually devoid of makeup and she had done nothing to make the best of herself. Ruby felt over dressed, over made-up, over-the-hill, over every bloody thing by comparison.

'To what do I owe the pleasure?' she asked, when neither of the men opened their mouths but instead stared at her with barely concealed contempt. Where the hell was Bart? she wondered. Why wasn't he here to support her in her hour of need? It occurred to her that Jason had probably told him to give them some privacy, but Bart worked for her. Had *her* back. He would never let even Jason stand in the way of his protective instincts. Would he?

Perhaps because they all still worked for Jason since he hadn't signed the fucking contract yet – that transferred ownership of the club to her in return for a fat wedge of cash that he didn't need. His lawyers had played hardball and Ruby had given in to their demands. The thought of sole ownership of the Iris, taking it in the direction that she thought suitable without having to obey orders from anyone, had been too tempting for her to hold out.

'We need to ask you some questions about Seb's fit-up,' Jason said without preamble.

'Me?' Ruby opened her eyes wide and pointed at her own chest for emphasis, furious when she noticed that her finger wasn't entirely steady. She hastily dropped her hand and took a chair behind her desk. 'Can I get you anything? I'll ring for Bart.'

'We ain't here to socialise,' Jason snarled. 'If you did anything to set my boy up, Ruby, you'd best come clean now or so help me I won't be responsible for my actions. And, whilst we're about it, tell me what you know about the attack on Lily.'

She glanced at Seb, unable to keep the hunger out of her gaze. He looked just like Jason once had. Being locked up had done little to alter his rugged appearance, she'd been right about that, but for the fact that he seemed harder. Little wonder, she supposed, wishing she could get over her obsession with the entire Carter clan.

Wishing the feeble Harper girl was a million miles away.

'I swear I know nothing about any of it.' Ruby shared a look between the two men. 'On my life.'

'It fucking will be if I find you've held out on me, Ruby.' Jason's voice was a threatening rumble. 'Now then, are my idiot sons involved in any of this? Think back to that time. Tell me what they were doing. And tell me about Blythe.'

Ruby closed her eyes in an effort to recall, desperate to be helpful and for Jason to believe her. She knew very well that if she wasn't convincing then her life wouldn't be worth diddly squat.

'I honestly can't think of anything that raised red flags. No offence but Dennis and Ray are interested in screwing, walking the walk and being looked up to as the big men. Oh, and complaining about stuff. They liked to mix it with some of our corrupt local worthies. Still do, come to that.'

'Did they have any particular friends?' Seb asked, speaking for the first time. 'Anyone who believed their hype and wanted to impress them?'

Ruby spread her hands. 'Honest to God, I didn't keep tabs on them. Sorry.' She paused. 'But I'll tell you one thing I've noticed recently. Every time they come in, James Bishop shows his face and they always seem to have a lot to talk about.'

'The fuck they do!' Jason groused. 'You told me yesterday that you thought James might have had something to do with the attack on my girl.'

'What the fuck...' Seb left his sentence hanging and his mouth open.

'I checked it out with Mike and he didn't. He couldn't have. James was abroad at the time and Mike was able to prove it. He just shot his mouth in front of Seb's man because he likes muck-raking.' Jason drew breath. 'You didn't tell me that my boys are so friendly with James, though.' He frowned at Ruby. 'Must have slipped your mind.'

'They're jumping ship and joining forces with your old partner,' Seb said. 'More fool him if he wants them.'

'Could they have given Bishop's son the things that got you locked up, Seb?' the Harper girl asked. No one had introduced her to Ruby but Ruby knew her name was Ava. Bloody Mel had mentioned her often enough, painting herself as Mother of the Year and then scarpering and abandoning the kid.

'James isn't involved,' Jason said, rubbing his chin. 'He hasn't got much more sense about him than my two. Besides, he had no reason and his father would have skinned him alive if he took such matters into his own hands.' He paused. 'My boys wanting to link up with Bishop, though. Now that I can believe. But why he would want them when he knows they're basically a waste of space is another matter entirely.'

'For their name and reputation,' Seb replied.

'Perhaps, but I think the time has come to ask them,' Jason said, extracting his mobile from his pocket. He dialled a number and barked an order into the phone the moment it was answered. 'They're on their way,' he added, pocketing his phone again. 'Now, did you say something about a snifter, Ruby. Might as well have one while we wait. Get Bart in here to do the honours. He might as well stay, too. He sees and hears everything in this club. He might be able to throw some light.'

Ruby felt nervous as they waited in awkward silence. She felt Seb's gaze frequently upon her, which added to her nerves, causing her to twist the stem of her wine glass repeatedly between her fingers, just so that she had something to do with her hands. Bart arrived and took up a position against the wall, just behind her desk, his solid support helping, just a little.

She felt embarrassed by the bank of screens behind her, showing early activity in the various rooms, including the private ones where a couple of the girls were already servicing punters. It was ridiculous that she didn't want the Harper girl to see but turning them off would make it seem as though she had something to apologise for, so she left them running. Ava barely glanced at them though and instead made the occasional remark in a low voice to Seb, too low for Ruby to hear what was said but significant enough to herald the onset of a fierce bout of jealousy. Knowing she could never have Seb was one thing; seeing him fucking her nemesis's daughter with his eyes was something else again. Some people had no respect.

After what seemed like forever but could only have been a comparatively short space of time, Dennis and Ray swaggered into the room.

'What is it?' Dennis asked. 'Where's the fire... whoa!' He stopped dead in his tracks and pushed his hands, palms first, towards Jason. 'What's this, a fucking reception committee?'

'Sit your arses down and shut up!' Jason told them. Both men complied, still looking cocky. 'Now then, what's this about you and James Bishop?'

Dennis set an accusatory glance Ruby's way. 'We're mates. Is that a crime?'

'Don't get lippy with me, son.' Jason slapped his hand on the top of the table beside him, oversetting his glass. Without saying a word, Bart moved from his position behind Ruby's desk, picked it up, wiped up the spill and refilled it. He then stood beside the drinks cabinet, watchful and yet silent. That was the thing about Bart. He knew when to keep his trap shut but missed little and would give Ruby the benefit of his advice when they were alone.

She couldn't manage without him but probably never told him so often enough. Still, she paid him what he was worth and that ought to be enough for him. 'Let's try again. Why are you romancing the Bishops?'

'Look, Dad, we were just watching your back,' Ray said. 'Didn't want to see you get screwed over. You lost your mojo when Mel left.'

'We thought Bishop might have offed her,' Dennis added, seemingly unaffected by Ava's presence. 'He got fed up with her getting all touchy about his business affairs. We know you cared about her,' he added, sending a lustful look Ava's way, 'and we wanted to get you some closure, like. Thought that if we fed Bishop the odd titbit, he might return the favour.'

Jason's smile as he slowly shook his head was more terrifying, Ruby thought, than when he was deliberately attempting to intimidate. 'You two don't have the sense you were born with, which ain't saying much.'

'No, straight up, that's all it is,' Dennis said. 'I swear.'

Ruby doubted Jason believed a word of it; she certainly didn't. In fact, she knew the boys were trying to earn their spurs in order to get a place in Bishop's organisation that they considered worthy of their talents. They didn't actually *have* any talents, other than using their fists, but they appeared to be the only ones who didn't realise it. They had traded on the fear created by their surname for too long. Without Jason still in the game to back them up, they would be trampled underfoot within months.

Bishop had exploited their inflated sense of self-worth. Ruby wasn't sure why and wasn't particularly interested. She, at least, knew better than to stick her nose in where it didn't belong. If Mel had done the same thing, she'd still be here today.

'Okay, we'll come back to that.' Jason drew himself up to his full height in his chair. 'What haven't you told me about the attack on Lily?'

'Whoa!' Dennis shook his head decisively. 'We know nothing about that, hand on heart.'

No one said a word, leaving Dennis's statement hanging in a tense silence. The brothers shifted in their seats, clearly uncomfortable. A look passed between them and it was Ray who eventually spoke.

'We don't know who ordered Blythe to attack Lily,' he said. 'And, believe me, we turned over every rock we could think of trying to find out. What I can tell you is that Henshaw flashed the cash not long after Blythe was offed. But he can't have done it; he don't blow his nose without permission from Drake, or you, Ruby.'

All eyes turned in Ruby's direction. 'Don't look at me.' She gave a nervous little laugh. 'What reason would I have? And why would I be that stupid, even if I did have a grievance? Besides, how would I have set Seb up, and why?'

'We both know the reason why,' Seb replied. 'But as to the how... that cap was the nail in my coffin. And it wasn't found until the area where Blythe was killed was searched for the third time.' He paused. 'There's something, a memory on the edge of my consciousness that's important and I've spent six years trying to recall but... it just won't come to me.' He let out a frustrated breath, watching Bart as he moved round the room like a lythe, oversized cat, topping up glasses, which is when it came to him in a blinding flash of clarity.

'It was you!' He pointed a finger at Bart. 'I came to the club a day or two after Blythe was found and the police had been asking questions. How could I have dismissed that as irrelevant? I was in the Aston. The roof was down and you admired the car, Bart. I left it to come in here and... and my cap was in the glovebox.'

Bart offered up a smile that didn't come close to reaching his eyes. 'Why would I?' he asked pleasantly. 'Besides, the roof was down. Anyone could have got to it.'

Seb shook his head. 'In this car park? I don't think so.'

'If you'd been driving around with the roof down all day, any opportunist could have nicked it,' Bart replied.

'And it conveniently turned up at a crime scene, incriminating me?'

'Like I asked before, why would I?'

'Because you've been in love with Ruby since the day you came here to work for her,' Seb replied.

'He is?' Ruby blinked back her shock. 'News to me.'

'Everyone knows it except her because she has her sights set above the hired help and never looks at you that way. Not that it matters, just so long as you're near her every day and she depends on you.' Seb was clearly piecing it together in his mind and as far as Ruby could tell from the shocked expression on Bart's face, he was making a damned good job of it. 'Jason dumped her and I rejected her. Ruby put a brave face on it but she lets her guard down in front of you and you knew just how hurt she actually was.' He shook his head. 'You couldn't have her disrespected in that way or her feelings trampled on and had to get revenge on her behalf. But why involve my innocent sister?'

'I don't know what you're talking about.' The colour drained from Bart's face, but he stood upright, doing his best to seem unconcerned.

'Answer the man.' Jason's voice rumbled with so much subdued menace that it made Ruby flinch.

'Sorry, Jason, but you've got it all wrong.'

Seb shook his head. 'This ain't a court of law. Convince us that we're mistaken and we'll let it go.'

Bart's glance slid from side to side, but no one spoke up in his defence. His gaze landed on Ruby, his only hope, but she looked away, making it clear that he was on his own.

'Bastards!' he muttered, making a dash for the door. Dennis and Ray blocked his way, grinning in a manner that wasn't supposed to be pleasant. It scared the shit out of Ruby and it wasn't even directed at her.

'Might as well tell us, or we'll beat it out of you,' Ray said, doing what he did best and cracking his knuckles. Dennis stood at his brother's shoulder, appearing to relish the challenge.

Bart's gaze fell on Ruby once again but she shook her head and Bart crumpled like a deflated balloon.

'Blythe was just supposed to get into your house and plant evidence of drugs. Then I was gonna have Drake do a raid on the basis of information received. You and Jason thought you were untouchable but I wanted to see you suffer the way you made Ruby suffer.' He pointed a finger at Jason and Seb, warming to his theme, clearly thinking still that his actions had been justified. 'You would have got off with a slap on the wrist, Seb, and I would have been on the side lines as always, applauding. And no one would have suspected a thing. It was sweet, or would have been, but bloody Blythe saw Lily, was high as a kite, and subsequently took matters into his own hands.'

'So, you had Henshaw silence him,' Ruby said, shaking her head. 'That's why he suddenly had a windfall.'

'Blythe was a liability and no loss to society. He would have taken us all down.'

'So why frame my boy?' Jason asked.

'Because I knew you lot would not stop looking until you got answers. I needed a diversion. I didn't think the charges would stick. That cap would have just pointed the finger in your direction long enough for the heat to die down.'

'But then a witness, a member of the public who disappeared

from view the moment I was found guilty, stepped up to identify me.' Seb let out a long breath and instinctively reached for Ava's hand. 'That, I assume, was Drake's handiwork. He needed to make sure there was enough evidence to sway a jury and he'd had it in for me ever since I stopped him from beating seven bales of shit out of Nancy.'

'Yeah, he did that.'

'And got rid of Gordon Philpott?' Ava asked.

Bart shrugged. 'Dunno. It ain't the sort of thing you talk about over a drink. I told him Philpott had been getting nosy. I caught him taking pictures where he had no right being.' Bart sniffed. 'Anyway, he was no great loss either.'

'What happens now?' Ava asked, sighing.

'Now, Bart goes to the local nick and admits to his misdeeds,' Jason said in a mordant tone.

'Ain't happening,' Bart replied, looking defiant yet scared. 'I'll take my chances on the run.'

The Carter boys had been absorbed with Bart's efforts to justify his actions and had moved away from the door. Bart saw an opportunity and made a dash for it but Ava, sitting closest, was faster. She simply picked up her glass and threw its contents in Bart's face. Momentarily blinded, he stumbled and the Carter boys pinned him down.

# 19

Seb walked with Ava in the grounds of his property two weeks later. The weather had turned cold and Lily ran ahead of them, bundled up in a coat and scarf, Wizard snapping playfully at her heels.

'You look as though you've had the weight of the world lifted from your shoulders,' Ava said, reaching for his hand and squeezing it. 'In many respects you have, and I'm glad.'

'It's not over yet, but at least my lawyer has convinced the CPS that there has likely been a miscarriage of justice and that the issue needs to be addressed.'

'Likely been?' Ava removed her hand from his and planted her fists on her hips. 'Well, of course there has been! Bart Fleming is singing like a canary.'

'He is now but only because you had the presence of mind to record what was said in Ruby's office on your phone. Without that, he would have denied it all and the word of my family would never have been taken seriously.'

She smiled. 'I wanted Ruby to be culpable but she was guilty of nothing more sinister than having a devoted slave who would go to any lengths to make her happy, despite knowing that she would never look at him romantically.'

'Ah, the power of unrequited love.'

'You never suspected him?'

'Not for a moment. Mind you, I never spent as much time at the club as Jason and my brothers. But still, Bart was always there, a fixture. A man of few words, easy to overlook despite his size.' He reclaimed her hand and they strolled on. 'All the years I had to think about that damned cap and how it came to be at the crime scene. I knew, or was pretty certain that it was in the Aston's glovebox, but it was a warm summer. I drove the car a lot and left it parked with the roof down. Anyone could have got to it. Still, there was something niggling at the back of my mind but, like I say, because Bart had made himself a part of the furniture, it never once occurred to me that it could be him. Not until he came into my line of vision in Ruby's office, filling glasses in his unobtrusive manner and moving with the stealth of a cat. Then it all clicked into place. I recalled him admiring the car, leaning into it in the same elegant way that he leans over to pour drinks. That's unusual for such a big man and stuck in my mind. He peppered me with questions about the car, the way men do when they get onto the subject and asked if he could sit in it. I gave him the keys and asked him to mind it. I had business of some sort inside and I was late, but I trusted Bart with my motor.'

'Was he responsible for that threatening email I received?'

'Apparently so. He had contacts in that casino, heard you'd been asking questions and that spooked him.'

'Well then, it's over. You got there, albeit six years too late.' Ava smiled up at him. 'What about Henshaw?'

Seb's expression closed down. 'That bastard. He spent the last year of my sentence lording it over me. At least now I know why he looked so smug. Anyway, he's in custody but Drake legged it, we think abroad. He had a nest egg accrued for that purpose, probably aware that he'd have to scarper at short notice sooner or later.'

'At least Nancy is finally free of him.'

Seb smiled. 'There is that.'

'And your brothers?'

'Jason has cut them loose. He's signed the club over to Ruby and as far as he's concerned, they're free to make their own way now. If they want to throw in with Bishop, that's up to them. I doubt if Bishop will have any use for them though.' Seb kicked at a pile of leaves, blown to the side of the path by a strong wind. They swirled in the air and settled back down on the path. 'Simple pleasures,' he remarked. 'It's funny the things you miss when banged up. You're told when to eat, when to sleep, when to use the bathroom, so the freedom to kick at leaves and not be made to clear up the mess is emancipating. Anyway, as far as my brothers are concerned, I'm glad they're guilty of nothing worse than stupidity.'

'Yes. Jason didn't cut them any slack, which must have grated.'

'True. Jason didn't do empathy.'

'You and he have mended some fences.'

Seb waggled his hand from side to side. 'Yeah. Baby steps but he's legit now and... well, blood's thicker than water.'

She squeezed his hand. 'I'm glad.'

'Right, now then, it's your turn. How did the meeting with your mother go?'

* * *

Ava thought back to the meeting in question that had taken place in a café in the centre of Chichester a few days previously. Jason had contacted Mel, insisting that she needed to know the score.

Ava wasn't sure if she agreed but knew it would be pointless to say so. The upshot was a meeting that Ava had hoped for and anticipated for years. When the time came to attend it, she found herself feeling surprisingly ambivalent, almost hostilely inclined towards a mother who had put her own interests first and left a teenage Ava to deal with a heartbroken father.

She had recognised Mel the moment she walked in the door when an elegant woman seated at a corner table raised a hand in hesitant greeting. Feeling a raft of conflicting emotions, Ava made her way between the tables.

'Hello,' she said calmly, sitting opposite Mel but refusing to address her as mother, understanding now why Seb never referred to his father by anything other than his Christian name.

'Ava.' Mel reached for Ava's hands but she kept them out of reach.

'For a dead woman, you look remarkably well,' Ava said, an edge to her voice.

'I suppose I deserved that.' Ava lifted a shoulder, thinking the comment required no other response. She asked for coffee when a waitress came to take her order, wondering if she would stay for long enough to drink it. 'You have to understand that what I did, I did it for the right reasons. To protect your father. And you.'

Ava's coffee arrived and she stirred it aggressively, despite the fact that she didn't take sugar.

'You have to understand what I couldn't explain to you as a teenager, and still find hard to talk about today. You adored your father but I'm afraid he had feet of clay.'

'People in glass houses.'

'Ouch! Anyway, he got into trouble with the business but instead of asking me to help, he took equity out of the house and ploughed it into a failing business. He forged my signature on the papers because he was too ashamed to tell me. Thought he could dig himself out of a deepening hole. Then he turned gem smuggler when the opportunity arose, insisting that he thought it was just a case of tax evasion.' Mel rolled her eyes. 'Anyway, I took on extra bookkeeping and the job at the casino in a desperate attempt to resolve matters and… well, you know the rest.'

Ava fixed her mother with a contemptuous look. She was dressed expensively and her almost unlined face implied that she'd had work done to retain a youthful look. Clearly, wherever she had gone to, she'd fallen on her feet. 'Where did you run to? Why didn't you try to contact me? Why did you let me think you were dead? Didn't you even care about my feelings?' Ava threw up her hands. 'The questions are endless.'

'I did come back but… well, I was ashamed. Then I overheard something Bart said. He caught me eavesdropping and even though I didn't know what I'd heard, I also knew my card had been marked. He scared me. I had to get away.'

'Looking out for yourself again,' Ava replied scathingly.

'I fell for Jason, I won't deny it, and I tried to straighten him out. But when his partner threatened you, and more to the point, when I overheard Bart and Henshaw talking about a murder, I knew I had to get out and stay out.'

'Where did you go?'

'Newcastle. I reverted to my maiden name and took a bookkeeping position with a firm of lawyers. One of them had young children.' She addressed the next sentence to the surface of her coffee. 'His wife died in an accident and… well, we married five years ago and I raised his children.'

'Forgetting all about the one you'd made earlier.'

'I never forgot you, but I didn't know if it was safe.' She twisted her fingers together on the surface on the table. 'Besides, Robert, my husband, doesn't know about my past and I would prefer it if it stayed that way. You were settled and I'd reinvented myself so it seemed better to let things be.'

'Better for whom?' Ava shook her head in disgust. 'Talk about a hypocrite,' she said softly, standing. 'Don't worry. He won't hear about it from me. In fact, you'll never hear from me again.'

She ignored Mel's plaintive cries to be reasonable and left the café dry-eyed, head held high, determined not to look back.

Not ever.

She gave Seb an abbreviated account, finding it surprisingly easy to talk about the episode.

'I think she finds her life dull and uninteresting, to be honest,' she concluded by saying. 'Her husband sounds like a bit of a stuffed shirt, albeit a safe, wealthy pair of hands. A far cry from the exciting times with Jason. But Robert would never countenance any connection to a criminal and Mel lives in fear of him finding out. He doesn't sound like the forgiving type.'

'Which is no excuse for leaving you wondering if she was still alive,' Seb replied. 'A postcard, a letter with no return address, an email... anything to put your mind at rest.' He slipped an arm around her shoulders. 'If you ask me, you're better off without her and now that you know the truth, you can forget all about her. Or at least, put her to the back of your mind.' He nodded towards Lily and Wizard, playing in the leaves ahead of them. 'You have a new family now.'

Ava rested the side of her cheek on his broad shoulder and smiled. It was true; she did. The agony of discovery had been a means to an end and she didn't regret a single moment of it.

# ACKNOWLEDGMENTS

My grateful thanks to the wonderful Boldwood team and especially my eagle-eyed editor, Emily Ruston.

# MORE FROM EVIE HUNTER

We hope you enjoyed reading ***The Kill***. If you did, please leave a review.

If you'd like to gift a copy, this book is also available as an ebook, hardback, large print, digital audio download and audiobook CD.

Sign up to Evie Hunter's mailing list for news, competitions and updates on future books.

https://bit.ly/EvieHunterNewsletter

Explore more gritty revenge thrillers from Evie Hunter...

# ABOUT THE AUTHOR

**Evie Hunter** has written a great many successful regency romances as Wendy Soliman and is now redirecting her talents to produce dark gritty thrillers for Boldwood. For the past twenty years she has lived the life of a nomad, roaming the world on interesting forms of transport, but has now settled back in the UK.

Follow Evie on social media:

twitter.com/wendyswriter
facebook.com/wendy.soliman.author
bookbub.com/authors/wendy-soliman

Printed in Great Britain
by Amazon

27039273R00145